STARLITE PULP REVIEW #3

Pulp done right.

FEATURING:

Craig Clevenger ✦ Jean-Paul L. Garnier ✦ Trevor Holliday ✦ Sean Jacques ✦ Nolan Knight ✦ Terrance Layhew ✦ Brodie Lowe ✦ Patrick R. McDonough ✦ Jim Ruland ✦ Aaron Paul Schaut ✦ Alex Slusar ✦ C. W. Stevenson ✦ Phillip Thompson ✦ Manny Torres ✦ Brian Townsley

Starlite Pulp

These stories were chosen by the editors at Starlite Pulp through submissions sent to our Submittable page.

For information, contact : editor@starlitepulp.com
Site : www.starlitepulp.com   Instagram : @starlite_pulp
Youtube channel : youtube.com/@starlitepulp

Executive Editor : Brian Townsley
Associate Editor : Jake Naturman

Book and Cover design by Tristan and BT

ISBN: 979-8-218-32656-2

first edition: December 2023

"I was born lost and take no pleasure in being found."

John Steinbeck

"There was an enormous revival of pulp fiction that started in the '60s and continued into the '70s, which in large part gave rise to things like 'Star Wars' and 'Indiana Jones,' among others. But I developed an appetite for the original stuff at the time, and that appetite has never really abated."

Chris Roberson

"My lifestyle determines my deathstyle."

Frantic, Metallica

STARLITE PULP REVIEW #3

LINER NOTES

Issue 3 is in the books—each of these collections has a unique shape and tenor, and this one feels a bit darker in tone than some of the others. As the issues begin to take shape, the editors here talk about not just the types of submissions we're getting, but why the ones we're choosing are being selected. We never have an agenda going into any issue, nor do we have a quota as to what sub-genre of pulp is chosen (though we certainly do hope to have one of each of the majors included), but the tone of the pieces, regardless of genre, carried a similarity this time around. Perhaps that's a reflection of the times— things have pretty fucked up recently, if you've been in a bunker for the last decade—or, of course, it could just be coincidence (although we all know what any fictional detective would say about that). But while some of the pieces in this are a bit on the darker side, even the pieces that are not at all 'noir,' we are ecstatic with the quality of this collection.

'Locust Eater' and 'The Depression of John Stonebrook' both feel like they should have Rod Serling introducing them, while 'Disophonia' and 'The Coldest Trade' are probably the most 'straight up' Sci Fi stories we've published thus far. The bounty hunter Rye Lonehand returns to print in 'Lullaby for the

Damned' in here, which manages to turn a western story on its head by the end, while 'Devils in the Sunrise' has a twist all its own. 'Zombie Wasps' and 'Fairy Tale Mission' are reminiscent of classic pulp tales from the glory days of the 'zines.

For crime, we've got a murderer's row in this issue: 'Rats,' 'Dead Gangsters,' 'Vultures,' 'Pit!,' '1974 Monte Carlo,' and 'Bet' are probably the strongest group we've had in any issue thus far. And 'Snowbirds,' well, that's a first for us at Starlite. It feels like a modern military tale with a western bent, and while we sat around and debated the 'pulpiness' of it, we didn't debate the fact that it's a damn good story.

What haven't I mentioned yet? The authors. And boy, what a group. Just head to the author bio's if you want proof, but really, many of the names here speak for themselves.

Big props to Jake Naturman, who helped to edit this issue, and added a knowledgeable and nuanced voice to the chorus here. Hope you all dig the issue—it was a blast to put together. Until next time, here's to the blank page.

~BT, Starlite Pulp, Winter 2023

LOCUST EATER
BY BRODIE LOWE

The wood-paneled van toiled over jutted rutile, its shockless suspension whining as it wended down forgotten switchbacks of mica-flecked gravel. The vehicle's roof had been torn away. A curious assault by some beast, perhaps. No man could've peeled away steel in like manner. The tops of the frames appeared as if they had been melted and then left splayed and cool-stiffened into jagged flower petals. But the van labored onward—this rust-blotted machine—appearing and reappearing in the weak moonlight, shingling past reflective eyes of the nocturnal peering from sumac.

Levi turned the wheel, the white ruffle trim of his shirt flapping against his sternum. He had left his blazer back at the church, had forgotten where he left it. In a pew, maybe. Or behind the pulpit where they kept the copper offering plates. It was one of those wild Sunday night services. One with visitors who stood and ambled jointless down the aisles for the altar call. Somehow, he felt as if the service had been guided by an unseen hand, keeping him on his toes, preparing him for something else that would come up against him later, harder, faster. He raised a hand and patted the peeling paper tape that bordered the square of gauze over his jugular. "Awful humid tonight," he said.

His mother spoke from the front passenger seat beside him. "Tell you one thing." She swatted away a lightning bug that had found itself unaware in the drift of wind somewhere along the dashboard. "God wasn't lying when he said he was a maker of peculiar people. Just never dreamed I'd have a hand in it."

"What you mean?" He turned side-eyed toward her to make sure she wasn't grinning.

"You and that crazy thing you had inked on that neck of yours. Two years of taking over the church and you're still telling everyone that the cyst ain't healed up. You ain't regret that yet? You don't think you're paving the road for them to start doubting if you're their healer when you can't even heal yourself?" She reached over and jammed a finger in the center of the gauze. "And look at what you had to go and do when the big man upstairs called you out to be different than all the rest."

"I've done told you that I ain't never heard a voice calling to me like that."

"Remember when your daddy got baptized by Pastor Clayton over at Nottely River?"

"Yeah." The road continued on before him, but it took on a hypnotic quality as if it were a re-run of a show he'd seen too many times to count, and he could now see, in his mind's eye, the thrashing of creek water and the yelling for mercy and Pastor Clayton high-stepping through the muddy water and over to Levi's father and swinging the buckle-end of his belt at the water moccasin that had already bitten his father and was now a blurred flourish of scales diving back into the murky depths, its home.

He had been ten years old when it happened. Twenty-five years ago. Could still see his father grabbing at his own neck and saying, "I think something bit me." Some strongman competitor who had, just weeks prior, slammed into the little church's altar and asked for forgiveness, picked Levi's father up and carried him over to dry land and tried giving him chest compressions.

Levi had to close his eyes to wipe away the memory of how his father's chest turned to mush while the strongman kept performing out-of-sync compressions with elbow-locked arms as big around as any man's thigh, saying, "Lord God Almighty, let him live. Let him live."

His mother coughed and spat phlegm into a patch of poison ivy on the side of the road. "Night before that happened, he couldn't sleep," she said. "Woke up telling me that all he could see every time he closed his eyes were those little leather moccasin shoes choking the life out of his feet. Said he didn't know what it meant. Said he never even wore the things before."

"Think that was a sign?" Levi asked.

There had been times when his father would drink bourbon like water. Times when he would tear off his clothes and run out into the woods, baying at the moon, telling God to bring him back to his glory days, the days where he could lay hands on people and watch them fall out before him. And in those nights of madness, Levi couldn't focus as he watched a black-and-white movie of a man named Larry Talbot who walked around in a suit and a cane with a handle made of silver and a concerned gypsy woman looking at his palm. Levi found himself wondering if there had been some mark on his own body to which he wasn't privy. And in those moments, he wished he had his own little gypsy woman beside him, telling him to beware. So that he would not turn out like his father. But all he could do in those childhood moments of despair was unzip the little King James Bible with the red-edged pages and open it somewhere near the middle and slam his face into the gutter where he would pray for sleep to come over him.

"That man wasn't right in the head," she spoke. "Who am I to say any different?"

"But I felt deep down somewhere that, as crazy as he was, he knew something we still don't know."

The glove compartment popped open when the van hit a divot in the road, and she slapped it shut with open palms. "You ought to date more," she said. "I want some grandbabies. I don't have much longer here on this earth, and you know it."

"Not much to choose from around here, Mom. Not much at all."

"There's that lady that's twice divorced. Lives over there near the farm where they caught that thief hiding out last month."

"I know. She comes down every service to get prayed over."

"And what do you do? Keep your distance and place one little finger on her forehead. If I was a betting woman, I'd suspect she wants you to get a little closer. Pray a little harder over her."

He never liked it when she got to talking about him marrying and forming a family. Never did appreciate it when she brought up his shyness. Truth be told, he didn't want to have a family. Felt that he'd end up losing one of them like he had his father. "She might make me crazy like you did Dad."

She spoke no further.

By and by, the van climbed one last hill, its flickering headlights finding a tin-roofed cabin with the crumbling rock chimney the caller had told them to look for. "Got struck by lightning," he'd breathlessly told Levi over the phone. "And if you look close enough, you might can still see the weathervane stuck up there beside the chimney. That's how you know it's our house."

Levi leaned forward over the steering wheel, peering up and searching until he saw an iron rooster propped between the tin and the brick. He drove a little further. Heard something crunch beneath the tires. And when he rolled through, the spoked tire of a pink tricycle popped out from behind them.

"Boy, look where you drive," she told him. "This thing's about give out."

He looked at his watch. Ten o'clock. They were arriving an hour later than what he told the man over the phone, and he half-wondered if he and his mother shouldn't just turn around and head back and call the man on the morrow to tell him that they couldn't find the place in all that dark. But his mother had already opened the door with the van easing forward, and she stepped out onto the chert drive, saying, "Let's get this show on the road. Don't want to miss my episodes."

"They say you could miss a whole month of those soap operas and still know who's dating who by the time you came back to it," he said.

She gave him a look.

"Should've driven you on home and then come out here by myself." He put the van in Park and turned off the engine. Black smoke drifted from the lips of the crumpled hood.

"You've done screwed up and made a decision that's permanent right there on your neck. Lord's only going to give me so much longer to watch after you and see that you don't get yourself kilt. People don't live as long as Methuselee anymore. World's too rough for that to ever happen again. And I ought to be here so that you don't screw anything else up."

He opened the door and stepped out of the van. Stood on his toes. Stretched his calves. Heard something crack deep in his ankles. "This boy's daddy sounded nervous over the phone," he spoke at last.

Levi remembered hearing something banging in the background and having to ask the man if something else was in the house. Then a roar that might've come from a human had followed. Or might not have. He wasn't for certain, and so he looked around the property to make sure there were no rabid Dobermans lurking with chains around their necks. He'd seen plenty of those when he would visit the sick. But nothing moved in the night.

"What'd he say he needed praying over?" she asked him.

He tucked his chin and closed his eyes and tried remembering something that he had only tried memorizing a week ago. "Then he said to me. Prophesy to the breath. And tell the breath. Tell the breath. Tell," he whispered to himself. But he could not remember the rest.

"What? What'd he say his boy needed healed?"

He opened his eyes but would not look at her. "Not so sure it's a boy. Stay behind me," he said. And he walked through the front yard, stepping over discarded house appliances as they came into view. His eyes seemed to be ever adjusting. He worked his way to the top step. A porch light came on over him.

"Only because you say so," she said.

He could hear her shivering and scratching her hairless forearm with her paint-chipped nails.

The screen door opened, and an old woman stood at the entrance, her free hand covered in a yellow rubber glove and dripping with what looked to be soapy dishwater. She looked at Levi's neck and the ruffles on his pressed dress shirt. Something moved superficially under the loosened skin below her eye as she looked into his eyes and waited for her vision to adjust. "You caught us in the middle of bath time," she said. Then her face livened up a bit, and she looked over his shoulder at his mother standing on the bottom step who was straightening the hem of her garment.

"Should've had a mind to tell you to pick up some soap down at the gas station," a man spoke from behind her. He stepped forward and reached out his own dripping wet hand and kept it there near Levi's navel. "Mark," he spoke.

Levi hesitated at first, but when he saw Mark's glass eye looking somewhere near the top of the screen door's spring, he had pity on him and shook the calloused hand. "How's your boy holding up?"

"Just sitting there. Like a knot on a log." Mark nodded his head backward toward the darkened center of the house.

"This here's Beth. I blame her for letting him run wild out there in the world."

"Who's that there behind you?" Beth asked.

"My momma," Levi said. "We had us a late church service, and I couldn't stop at the house first. Figured I'd come out here with her."

"We ain't planned for anybody else to see our boy like this." Beth looked back at her husband. "Did we?"

Mark considered her comment for a moment. "We just ain't let little Johnny out in the public's all. Been a long time. We tend to keep to ourselves."

"Come in," Beth ordered. "Just you."

Levi looked over his shoulder at his mother and said, "Won't take but a minute." He stepped inside, and they closed the door behind him.

In the living room, a broad back of muscle sat in a kid-sized swimming pool made of plastic, sky-blue and cracked. The little hair-matted head atop swiveled ever so slightly. But no words came from the man's mouth. Soapy water had risen around his lower back to where he was wrapped in a nimbus of popping bubbles. He appeared to be nearly eight hundred pounds.

"How old's your little boy there?" Levi asked.

"I'd say he's in his forties," Beth said. "He went out there in the world and partied to his little heart's content. Drank that Liquid G stuff, that Drain-O stuff, and took a bunch of ecstasy. That's what his friends told us when they dropped him off and left him here. Never saw them again. Brain's done been fried. Never been the same. Hardly ever speaks. I think something's really wrong with him."

"But he came back," Mark said. "We don't love him any less for it."

"Sure enough," Beth agreed.

"They don't carry his kind of soap anymore down at the gas station," Mark said, drying his hands on the tail of his shirt. He had disappeared down a narrow hall with waist-high cedar panels. "Might be some leftover detergent back this way."

"Reckon that might be his problem?" Levi asked. "Washing him a little too much?"

"All he wants is to be clean, preacher." She moved her fingers through her hair. A bobby pin fell out and onto the floor. "Hair just keeps getting too thin to hold those little things anymore." She shook her head in disappointment. "It ain't such a good idea to waltz in here and kick a man when he's down like my son is. I don't reckon it makes little Johnny too happy hearing that."

She walked over to her son and whispered something in his tiny cauliflower ear.

Levi walked to the side to see some part of Johnny's face. But something approached in his peripherals. Mark was walking back down the hallway with a beach towel and a pair of pants. He stopped.

Levi turned and looked at his dimensionless silhouette. "Something wrong?"

"We got us a peeping tom," Mark said. "Right here in our midst. What say you have yourself a sit, preacher. Let little buddy here get himself some drawers on and then you can start to lay those hands of yours on him."

Levi sat in a wooden spindled chair and waited.

Mark and Beth stood on either side of their son, grabbing him by his elbows and grunting, doing most of the work, as they helped him stand from the dirty bathwater. He stood lock-kneed. Mark handed the pair of pants to his wife and walked behind Johnny and grabbed the towel by the corners and spread it out tight behind his son as if he were some matador. He peeked over his shoulder and said, "Boy, I know you ain't looking."

Levi turned his head. Noticed the wall-mounted horse collar with mirror inlay. Watched their reflection in the distorted image.

"We ain't much different, preacher," Beth spoke. "Back before all this mess with my son, I could think clearly." She grabbed a dish towel from the table and was wiping down Johnny's limbs. Then she helped him step into an old pair of jeans. "Might could write a whole novel. The focus I had back then. It was something. They called me a scribe. Said I'd be somebody like old what's-his-face on the TV. That pastor who took all that money from the church's tithes. You know he's got himself a big old jet plane now. Don't hear much about him anymore. That's a shame."

She looked down at her toe and wiggled it around. Stood there staring at it. And Levi was hard pressed to tell if she was waiting for it to speak back to her in a way he could not. She shook her head, dizzy-like. One might've assumed she'd just taken a shot of whiskey that could double as paint thinner. "It's true. Matter of fact, we got us this old shoebox of Johnny's up under the bed somewhere. Think I have a few cassette tapes of me singing from way back when."

"He didn't come here to listen to that," Mark said.

She waved her hand. "I faltered," she looked at Levi. "Missed my calling. If little Johnny here hadn't slipped right on out of me, I'd've had me a life behind the pulpit. Would've had myself all dolled up like that woman on that one network with pink hair and them big old eyelashes."

"If you don't mind me saying, Beth, I don't think your life's over just yet," Levi said. "God used Abraham and Sarah when they were about as pruned as raisins."

She helped her hulking offspring step one foot after another into the torn pair of pants and then helped him over to the center of the room where he stood in front of Levi.

"Here, son," Beth said. She dragged over another chair and said, "Pop a squat."

Johnny collapsed in the chair, and Levi half-expected it to break into pieces beneath his weight. The big man bent at the waist and picked up a television's remote control and started digging its end in his navel.

Mark walked over to the kitchen sink area and opened a cabinet. He took down a jar full of dark bodies. Unscrewed the lid and handed the glass container to his son. Up close, Levi could see that they were dried-up locusts. Johnny reached in, grabbing them by the handful, shoveling them in his mouth. Some dropped on the floor, skidding against Levi's shoe.

"He likes him some locusts. Don't know why," Mark said.

"Oh, I know why," Beth said. "Because that's the only tale you ever told him from the time he was in the crib to the time he was yay high. The story about the wild and crazy man living out there in the desert eating locusts and drinking up the honey."

"Well, it's my favorite story to tell," Mark said.

Beth looked back at Levi. "You don't think you can just take little Johnny on out of this world? Just let him pass on through that giant pearly gate up there? I'm sure the good Lord's got a plan for him up there. Because they sure as hell ain't no plan for him down here."

"I've prayed over men who thought they were too short. Seen them grow a couple inches in height. I've prayed over somebody who wasn't satisfied with six abs. He wanted two more. And by the time I got done with them, he about looked like one of them jacked up kangaroos." Levi couldn't look neither of them in the eye.

She stared blankly at him for a series of long seconds. He opened his mouth to clear the silence, to cause her to blink, but she beat him to it, nodding as if in agreement with her thoughts. "If it don't work," she said, "it's okay with me and Mark for you to take him on back behind the shed and do the Lord's work on him. Help him transition on out of here." She smacked the heels of her open palms against one another, slipstreaming one off the other and shooting in a crooked arch through the air. "Maybe then I can have my remote control back."

"I respect your wishes," Levi said. "But that's no part of who I am. When I arrive, the dead come alive."

"Now, wait a minute," Mark spoke. Suddenly, he seemed to have a mind of his own. He worked a cupped hand under his stubbled chin. "Say you've brought people back from the long home?"

"Just one time. He'd been laid up in a claw-footed tub up in the attic the family never used. Couldn't bring themselves to put him six feet under yet. Had him stiff as a board, his arms and legs all shot out and rigid like plastered cardboard. Smelled like the dead. Longer feller than what walked around the streets on any given day. Was a basketball player. Used to play church league over in those gravel parking lots in Lincolnton. Took up with the big boys in the city churches with those air-conditioned gyms. Beat them every time. Ran circles around them."

"Well, I'll be," Mark admitted.

"Where's he at now?" Beth asked.

"Shooting hoops with the Harlem Globetrotters, matter of fact," Levi said.

"I doubt all that," Mark said.

"It's about as real as that drool dripping down your boy's chin."

Johnny stared blankly ahead, shifting warily in his seat. The jar of dead locusts was already half-empty. Levi watched him as he picked away tiny limbs and parts of wings from between his teeth and popped them to the back of his tongue.

"We waiting on you, preacher," Beth said.

Levi didn't want to touch the dome of the man's bald head. Didn't want to make him feel uneasy. So, he leaned forward and gently grabbed the big man's wrists. He closed his eyes and tried to remember the words. "So, I prophesied as I was commanded. And as I was. As I was prophesying, there was a noise. A rattling sound."

The wooden floor rumbled beneath them, nails squeaking on joists, vibrating Levi's feet so much that he felt as if he were tap-dancing while seated. The mirror fell to the floor and shattered.

Johnny raised his face from the ground and his brown eyes shifted to a milky-white as if he had suddenly aged into a state with cataracts.

Levi could feel the man's strength now, and he held onto the wrists for as long as he could until he felt a strange prickling along the equator of his skull, from his forehead to the back of his scalp. Felt as if some sharp-brimmed hat had been jammed on top of his head. And his grip loosened as he felt tiny stabbings in the centers of his hands and the tops of his feet. He finally let go when Johnny threw back his head and opened his mouth, and a soft gossamer material sprung from the man's mouth. Ectoplasmic discard, striated with flourishes of aortic valves, hovered above his face, tiny lightning storms working through the wormy core's smoky foundry.

Somewhere in the storms, Levi could see his ten-year-old self, immobilized by the creek bed, watching in horror as his father fought for his life. Some crystal ball, he thought.

The tape on Levi's neck lost the last of its stickiness and the gauze drifted to his pants leg. He reached for it, but it slid off and fell, covering one of the dead locusts on the ground.

"What you got there on your neck, preacher?" Mark asked.

The strange material changed from crystalline to a creamy-white and shot back down Johnny's throat in a sped-up rewinding fashion. His eyes were no longer cataracted, and he stared at the winged creature inked on the side of his healer's neck. Levi could tell that Johnny recognized it as the same insect as he had eaten.

"He looks hungry," Mark spoke.

"No telling what he might eat now," Beth said.

"Go ahead on, little Johnny. Have yourself a meal."

Levi leapt backward off his chair, clearing the top of it in a bowlegged stance he didn't think his body could maneuver.

He turned for the front of the house. Standing frozen there in the doorway was his mother, her hand to her mouth. He ran for what little light the stars shared outside and grabbed her by the arm.

Mother and son ran down the steps, Mark and Beth calling for them to stay for a meal.

While running for the van, Levi could hear the big man bounding down the steps behind them, the wood breaking beneath his naked, clubbed feet.

Levi started up the engine and slammed the van in reverse back down the beginning of the curved road.

Johnny ran and grunted for more. He reached his hands out for the hood, and when he was somehow close enough, he threw his body on the metal, denting it and already working his way to his knees.

"Oh, my God!" his mother yelled, and she leapt from the van as the behemoth stepped over the roofless front windshield and grabbed her son by the neck. She ran off into the woods.

Levi let go of the wheel and the van took on a life of its own as he pressed the pedal to the metal and grabbed Johnny by the forearms. He heard a wheel pop, and the axles scraped over the ground, the back of the van slamming to a stop against a tree.

He worked his way out of Johnny's grasp and scrambled out of the van onto the road. He looked up and saw Mark and Beth waving at him from their front porch. Mark slung an arm around his wife's shoulders and pointed at Levi as if enjoying this spectacle.

He heard Johnny coming up from behind him and he turned around on his knees, bowed before him. Some monkish figure suddenly devoted. He reached out and pulled at Johnny's trousers. Tried to gain some sort of control, some sort of stability. His frayed fingernail caught on a torn hole at Johnny's knee. He heard the thread give way and there was a concerning rumbling in the brute's rib-caged bowels.

Johnny placed both palms on either side of Levi's head and bent at his knees, picking the healer up off the gravel until Levi's toes scraped and etched packed chert.

Deep inside, Levi felt like some pariah flung aside, into the wilderness, cut off from churchgoers who had spoken of journeying into such regions where the fasted and the tempted dwelled, covered in sackcloth and ash. Untamed places the preachers had spoken about, but never dared enter. And he developed an envious anger toward those who had only spoken of situations like this.

A dizzying moment hit him somewhere in the center of his brain, and in the far-off ringing of his ears, he could barely make out his mother's feet scampering back to the road and out of the woods, tripping and falling face first, as if some lesser form of hallowed spirit had hit her there. She posted up on her elbows and screamed for her son's life to be spared.

But Johnny picked Levi up and pressed his visitor to him, chest to chest. At first, Levi kicked and beat on the man's shoulders, but as Johnny squeezed, the less energy Levi had to burn.

As Johnny's glazed-over eyes focused on the inked locust, his mouth opened. Levi was filled with a regret of wishing he had never laid hands on the sick and the infirmed. He knew that the one who disapproved of him the most would rise from the leaves for a gulp of the same mountain air that he now felt cooling the blood that trickled down the side of his throat, giving him the selfsame goosebumps that he had felt on the backs of necks and arms of those approaching him at the foot of the pulpit for answers.

He boxed Johnny's ears with open hands, saying, "And the bones came together, bone to bone. Tendons and flesh appeared on them." It was all coming back to him. "And skin covered them. But there was no breath in them. Come. From the four winds and breathe into these slain. That they may..."

"Levi!" His mother floundered to her feet and began running toward them with her hands outstretched before her face.

But he could not finish the last word. It only came out muddled, his lips canted and one-cornered, words and phrases jumbled and punctuated with question marks, his tongue knocking against the roof of his mouth as if he had found some other tongue whose origin was not of angels but of the disapproved and the forsaken.

As he collapsed wholly into the brute's arms, their converged silhouettes settled into a fully formed and grotesquely knuckled fist raised against the star-pricked sky, no longer resembling fleshly forms, but some great boulder that might roll away.

DEVILS IN THE SUNRISE
BY NOLAN KNIGHT

Mallory Burkhalter baked in desert heat, freckled flesh afire, soles of her jelly sandals melting atop cracked asphalt as she gazed up at the largest, greenest cactus she had ever seen. Thing was cartoonish, so much so she contemplated giving it a hug, wrapping her arms around it as if it were her late mother—just a nice tight squeeze to pierce the organs and send her down to Hades. Or Heaven (Who knows, right?). Shit, it was hot here. Mother wasn't joking over the years, cursing her to never venture to Wonder Valley. Mallory had to tip her Padres cap to the woman. She was still a few miles outside Twentynine Palms. Hours up from San Diego and trapped inside a whole new world rife with Joshua Trees and tie-dye shorts and pro-life picketers and black-socked tourists waiting in lines for ice cream or coffee or bibles or polished stones to take back to lovely homes. She contemplated the cactus squeeze for ten more seconds, longer than any rational human. Not like poor decisions hadn't already stained her life. She took a photo of the cactus that resembled a rising demon and rambled back to her vehicle; had to pull over once the engine started to smolder up the high desert pass: a 2009 Nissan Cube. Poor decisions, man.

She was meeting the real estate broker at The Palms Restaurant, a local haunt in the middle of the desert that Bourdain partied at once. After a few pops, she would accompany the broker to a house—the one she drove up for, a home she'd imagined the contents of since childhood, now going on thirty-eight years. She gassed up at a Circle-K before entering the Valley, having been told of its emptiness for miles without any pumps.

The Cube snaked across worn asphalt, careening past dilapidated shacks and rusted vehicle skeletons. Every so often, a lonesome windmill would appear, electrical poles here and there, nothing else but dirt, shrub and an endless blue sky. She gazed up at cloudless heavens, curious of the types of folks who chose to live out here, hermits and retirees probably—or druggies sucked to the end of the line, ready to party their exploding hearts. There was at least one person she knew of out here who'd ran away from life's responsibilities, tragedies and misdeeds. And he had a house for sale with her name on it.

Her cell had lost service a while ago, but the building up ahead looked like the spot, an adobe structure with a smattering of palm trees. She pulled into its dirt lot, past a sign with a buffalo proclaiming The Palms and parked beside an old Suburban with a scrotum dangling off its tow hitch. The Cube coughed to a halt, heat sizzling off its hood. From her purse she took out the broker's business card: Chip Reynolds. She studied his android-smooth face to recognize him in case he was already in the cups, slurping margaritas. His waxy grin made her cringe, a smile that stared back at her in the mirror sometimes. She wiped both armpits with a Kleenex, then straightened out her blood red tank top. Before exiting, she opened her purse and removed a large obsidian egg, sleek and acrylic—carefully placing it in the center console. She strolled toward the entrance, knock kneed and pigeon-toed, the Cube's alarm chirping its sad silly song.

***

Five months earlier – Legoland, Carlsbad

Mallory was working the aquarium, guiding tourists through Lego accentuated wonders of the deep. This was her favorite part of the job, a thirty-minute commute from mom's apartment in San Diego's Mission Valley. Over the years, long days spent helping cram folks on coasters or grilling lousy burgers had become soul crushing; she'd planned on accomplishing more in life, once upon a time. At least she wasn't stuck in the water park, leering at flabby tattooed flesh and snot-nosed kids, selling booze to parents second guessing their decisions. Hell, after the face painting incident yesterday, she was glad to be indoors. The smell was best in the cold aquarium too, all salt and brine. A tiger shark swam through her peripheral, forcing her to stop, trapped in its menacing glide: a predator. She was startled by a hand on the shoulder.

A co-worker whispered, "Georgie needs to see you. Like, right now."

She cringed and deflated, knowing exactly the issue at hand.

\#

It wasn't bad enough she was seated at the head of human relations' desk, the life-size Lego Darth Vader lasering down at Mallory had her throat parched, as if its telepathic Lego grip was crushing her larynx. The desk was large and had no chair, the whole room built up to ADA Compliance. Georgie Baker was one of those babies born with Brittle Bones Syndrome, a tiny man forever turtled into a mechanical wheelchair. Reminded her of that dancing guy on *Twin Peaks*. They'd began working Legoland the same week, years back. Both assigned as farewell wishers at the park's exit gate. How Georgie charmed his way into an executive suite was beyond her, as mysterious as why he needed a desk. The pitch of his wheeled apparatus could be heard storming the hall. Mallory stood to greet him, to which his nubby fingers swiped her back down as he parked beyond the desk.

"Tell me about the face paint," he said.

"It's not what it seems, for starters. The boy asked to be painted like a gorilla—"

"The boy's mother says you painted him in blackface and left him, unsupervised mind you, for all to see. We've had over thirty complaints from visitors—videos of it are spreading across social media. Local news has been calling me all day. This has become a *major* issue."

"Georgie, I ran out of paint to complete it—I needed a tan and a grey—the sun must've dried 'em all up. I rushed to grab them fast as I could."

"That's what your walkie talkie is for."

"Look, I called Frank for backup but some lady had a seizure by the churro stand, okay?"

"Still—"

"Still nothing, man. I was doing my damn job, regardless of how it looks!"

"Family of the boy is threatening to go to CNN, along with a lawsuit being filed. Apparently, the father is one of those billboard attorneys. You really stepped in it this time, Mallory."

She sunk into the chair. "Don't I always? Fuck me."

"Not anymore you don't."

She perked. "What are you saying?"

"You know what I mean. Don't make me say it."

"Fucking say it!"

"You're fired, effective immediately."

Mallory rose and went to the door, numb as a drilled tooth. "You know, Georgie. I only ever wanted to work here to make people happy. Thought that might make me happy too."

"You tried, Mall. Gave it your best, but this isn't the first incident for you, by a lot."

She nodded, shoulders deflating. "Won't be my last, I bet."

"That's up to you."

"Is it though?"

"The Devil's in the sunrise."

"Devils?"

"Satan. Something my mom used to say. For me it meant a person has the *choice* to do good, every single day." Georgie spun his chair to gaze out the window at giant marauding dinosaurs.

Mallory held in her own thought: That Georgie's mother must've felt her life with this special-needs child, day in, day out, was hell on earth. How could she conjure such a wicked thought? She tossed her nametag in his trash bin and left.

***

Mallory walked through The Palms' front door and was met by a dank wood bar with a marlin on the wall; light from outside turned every liquor bottle into exquisite stained glass. Once her eyes adjusted to the darkness, she noticed three patrons and a lone barkeep in a porkpie—his face like Buster Keaton. Of the three stoolies, none were Chip Reynolds. The two gentlemen at the far nook had just enough teeth to chew their burgers, donning hats for the Outback. The third was a woman, older yet refined, her hair with wisps of grey, party sunglasses on; she was cutting a deck of cards before a clear pint of something.

The barkeep pointed to a stool at the center and said, "What'll it be, miss?"

"Cold beer sounds nice."

He poured a glass of ice water and set it before her. "Miller Lite?"

"Sure."

He reached into an icebox, its chill steaming, twisted off the cap and slid it over.

"How much I owe you?"

"Three dollars cash, or you can start a tab."

"Tab's fine."

"In here we ask you to keep track, then we'll total it out at the end. Easier for us behind the bar. Stick around long enough, and you'll see."

The cold beer to her lips was like a dip in a river. She swiped the bottle to her neck, noticing the older woman staring back.

"Hot enough for you, miss?"

Mallory smiled. "Do you ever get used to it?"

"Never. Where you from?"

"San Diego." She stuck out a hand. "I'm Mallory."

"*Mallory*, that's your real name?" The woman scoffed.

"You find that funny? What's yours?"

"Sparrow."

Before Mallory could laugh herself, the woman splayed her deck of cards atop the bar and said, "Pick one."

"You a magician? The Great Sparrow?"

"We're all magic, miss. These here are my tarot cards."

Mallory looked at the white index sheets with ink scribbled messages. "I've never seen a set like this before."

"Been crafting them over forty years. The concept is similar, but like I said, they're *my* cards. Come on. Pick one. I'll tell you your future."

Mallory smirked and caught a glance of the barkeep shaking his head. She grabbed one in the middle.

"What does it say?"

Mallory cleared her throat. "Trouble thy seek on this day of wrath which you keep…" She stammered, eyes skipping ahead through the oddity.

"Keep reading."

"And enter this endless void for your mother to weep."

"Ah, yes. I dreamed that line in 1984. Couldn't tell you what it means, but it surely deals with a death."

"I was born in eighty-four."

"No shit?"

Mallory took another sip, re-reading the card. "My mother recently passed too."

"Oh, my gawd. These fucking cards never disappoint!"

The barkeep grabbed Sparrow's pint, to which she protested. "Can't keep scaring away the new customers."

"I'm not!" She turned to Mallory. "Am I frightening you?"

"No, you're fine." She readjusted her ballcap. "I'd like to buy her another round, please."

The barkeep grumbled, filling the pint with ice and gin.

Sparrow guzzled the hooch as if it would evaporate.

Mallory checked her phone for the time: Chip Reynolds was officially late.

***

Four Months Earlier – Presidio Apartments, Mission Valley

Mallory glided through the pool, imagining her feet as one giant fin, a blood-thirsty tiger shark like the one she'd marvel at in the amusement park. The new job search was a non-issue since she really hadn't begun one. Her savings dwindled, but she embraced being a nobody once more, an invisible agent to the human race—an unabashed afterthought. She slapped the pool's side, launching up for breath, arms resting on cracked brown tiles; she could hear mother cackling with fellow sunbathers, their daily routine as far back as Mallory could remember. Cigarettes, chardonnay and sunshine: a feast of the gods. Chlorine stained her sinus cavity. She blew her nose in the water, thumping a clogged ear just in time to catch the tail end of mom's latest monologue:

"I mean, *really*...who gets fired from fucking Legoland? My daughter, that's who!"

The sunbathers gut-busted, blue-haired skulls to the sky, sunglasses refracting death rays across the peach patio; their bathing suits were meant for women thirty years younger. *Talking lizards*, Mallory thought as she pretended not to hear a word, avoiding a fight with mother today, just like yesterday and every day the woman had left. She held her breath and dunked for another lap, one to the far side of the pool where she could exit without anyone watching to drip quietly back toward the apartment. There she could shower and nap and brood—maybe even watch a soap or an old episode of her favorite show, *Black Magick America*. Mostly brood though.

What was her purpose in this cesspool called life...?

#

A pretzel clung to Mallory's lip as she zombied on the TV, watching one of the best soap episodes she'd seen in years. A young man had poisoned his mother with her own pain killers and was now seated in the woman's favorite chair, watching her claw herself across shag carpet, face writhing, foaming out the mouth. The extreme dramatic pauses were painfully laughable. In his hand was a copy of her life insurance; he re-read his name on the document out loud, entitled to the entire estate, his face contorting to sinister status. The woman grasped his leg with her dying strength, but the young man didn't pause from his glee to notice, eyes glazed with mania at the fortune coming his way. A tear fell from Mallory's chin.

The apartment door unlatched.

She composed herself, wiping her face, changing the channel to a police show. By the lack of greeting, she knew mom was drunk again, the heat not an ally to boxed chardonnay. Mallory heard the fridge pop and a beer crack; then the pantry door.

"What happened to my pretzels?"

"There in here, mother."

The woman slithered into the living room, can in hand—left nipple exposed for all to see.

"Oh, mom." Mallory launched from the sofa to adjust the bikini top.

The woman grabbed the pretzels from Mallory's grip, swatting away her helpful hand. Mallory froze, eyes to the floor as mother retreated to her bedroom, most likely for the night. The bedroom door unlatched. Mallory got brave for the first time in forever.

"Tell me about my father, again."

The door's creaking rivaled a coffin. Mallory slowly turned to see her mother leaning against the hallway, eyes swimming, ready to spew vitriol on the person who'd ruined both their lives.

#

"He was an evil fuck, no doubt. The things he would call me—the mother of his child!"

Mallory leaned over the kitchen table to crack another beer for mom, pretending she'd never heard these horrid tales before, like she hadn't re-lived them whenever the old lady got stewed. "But he had a job, didn't he? I mean, he was employable, right?"

Mother swilled. "He did. A fine job with an appraisal firm in downtown. Had a corner office on a top floor and everything—not far from the Gaslamp. But that dried up when they realized he wasn't who he said he was. Hell, I wanted to fire him myself, the con man. I was duped too, you know? He never had any license to comply with the state to perform real estate appraisal, and when word came down, oh, it must've been when you were barely five months old—"

"They fired him."

"Yes, and unfortunately, you've inherited that gene from *him*, but I wouldn't worry too much 'bout it—you have my demented cunning and inexhaustible character."

A chuckle escaped from Mallory.

"Yes, laugh away, dear. Your father's evil vices are what you should be most afraid of. He used to watch all those black magick T.V. shows you seem to adore."

"I don't *adore* the occult."

"No one does dear, they're all spellbound by dark powers from beyond. Your eyes light up whenever you watch those things, believe me, I can tell. Satan will have his way with anyone who's willing to do his—"

"Satan's in the sunrise."

"What's that?"

"A dumb saying I heard. Don't ask me what it means."

"Ugh. I've lost my train of thought. What was I saying? Oh, yes. I told you all about your father's pet skull, right? A real-life human skull—he'd parade the thing around the house like some morbid trophy. Christ, maybe it was. You two are birds of a feather."

"Mother, don't kid."

"I'm not kidding! The man was an enigma, and so are you. His love of the occult was too much for me. On and on about Crowley and Parsons and Cameron and Anger... Dark arts superstars from what I could surmise. I'm sure you could tell me all about them, right? He wanted to be like them, but couldn't because your father was a *fucking* loser. He destroyed my life. The taking of an actual human life by him wouldn't surprise me at all. Death preys on the weak, and others' lives meant nothing to him, obviously. I surely hope you don't have the same morbid desires..."

"*Please.*" Mallory frowned, longing for a stiff drink but would never clink cups with mother. "And he's up near Wonder Valley now?"

"Last I heard. And don't you ever go up there!"

Mallory reflected on all of mother's poor decisions with other men over the years that also helped dig this grave, men who gawked at her at thirteen, fifteen and so on—ages where mother yelled at her for enticing their stares. Men she'd placed curses on with library books on witchcraft, spells that never took. "Why don't you ever say his name?"

Beer dribbled from the woman's lips to her wrinkled bronze chest. "What did you say?"

"You've always just called him the bastard—"

"Because that's what he is!"

"Of course, but—"

"Listen, when the time comes, and I part this wicked world, you'll find your birth certificate among my papers and financial documents. On that day, you can speak his name all you want. But, until I croak, he'll be the *fucking* bastard in this house."

Mallory smiled, watching mother's eyes dance in circles, as if they were to pop from her cold leathered face. "I think I'll take another swim, mom. You'll be okay without me, right?"

"Of course. I was always fine before you came along." The woman caught her tongue. "Have a nice swim, dear. I saw a clean Navy boy walking through the courtyard earlier. A wall of muscles, my God. Wear that two piece I bought you—the red one. Your father never shut the fuck up about some *Scarlet Woman*—maybe all men are fools for a woman in red. But, what the hell do I know? I'm going to lay down. This conversation—this life—has taken its damn toll."

***

One beer led to three, and Chip Reynolds was still a no show. Mallory wanted to call or text him but service was non-existent, as if she were on the moon. The barkeep delivered deep fried mushrooms and a cheeseburger to soak up the suds. The burger was expertly crafted, beyond Legoland standards. She ate with gusto, not having a full meal all day. The tarot woman had been replaced by a younger girl whose hair was too short for style, yet too long for a shaved head. Mallory figured her to be newly released from a padded cell, her ice blue eyes hardly blinking. They spoke of warm desert sunsets, how this time of year was the best two weeks to be out here, blah, blah. Mallory waved off a complimentary beer, then rescinded, the frost on its neck too enticing. As she sipped, a sign across the bar proclaimed *No Sling Blades, No Kung Fu, Violators*

Will Be Spanked. A few folks walked in, then suddenly vanished. She turned to the young girl.

"Where'd everyone go?"

"Out back. The experimental music fest is set to begin."

Mallory excused herself and headed around the bar's elbow to catch the festivities, hoping her broker was outside.

#

A full-scale guillotine (chained-up for safety) greeted Mallory at the rear exit. She took in the rusted blade before the expansive desert which could be seen in every direction; the enormity of this music event was larger than anticipated. Roughly a hundred desert folk were gathered around a concert stage among lawn chairs, huddled in the dirt, swilling bottles or passing joints. The eclectic onslaught of wardrobes and twisted faces had Mallory in awe. Among jumbled conversations, a low humming sound began to resonate, hushing the crowd. A person donning a balaclava and gingham skirt emerged onstage. The hum grew louder, peppered by pulsing *beeps* and *bops.* The crowd suckled their nectars, silent in repose to the sound bath washing over them. The spectacle, at first, made Mallory want to laugh, but after five long minutes of soundwaves coursing her nervous system, she relinquished all judgement and surrendered to the hum.

The song evaporated as quickly as it began. Over an albino gentleman's shoulder, she caught a familiar grin: Chip Reynolds, clad in all black attire. He was chatting with a musclebound bald man in a crimson poncho. Chip's smile was a beacon in the dipping sun, a grin for a twenty-year-old, not someone in his late sixties. Mallory brushed her way through the crowd toward him. Another sound bath built its lifeforce, quelling the crowd to gasps.

"There you are," said Mallory.

Chip slowly panned, his conversation coming to an end. "Hey— Melody, right?"

"Mallory."

Church bells clanged louder than God. Chip pointed to his ear.

"Mallory!"

He pointed to the bar and walked toward the back door.

Inside, the noise was less deafening as Chip guided her to a corner booth. "I'm sorry about that. Let's start over. Chip Reynolds."

She took his grip. "Mallory."

"Ah, that's right. Why did I think Melody?"

"Prolly 'cause the music out there couldn't hold one."

He laughed, plastic teeth twinkle-twinkling.

Out a rear window, she saw the man in the poncho slowly walking far off into the desert. "What's your friend doing?"

Chip followed her stare. "I don't know that guy. He asked for a cigarette."

"Big boy, isn't he?"

"Linebacker, I bet."

"Is he safe out there, you think? Don't the animals come out at night?"

Chip thumbed his chest. "Most of us party in the daytime."

She broke her gaze on the poncho, a red blip on the horizon. "Almost gave up on you, Chip."

He signaled to a new barkeep and checked Mallory's beer. "You good?"

"Yeah."

"Give up on me...why? I've been here for some time."

"So have I."

"In the bar? Ah, no cell reception, huh? Man, I should've known to tell you."

The bartender delivered a tequila-rocks, placing it on a napkin before him.

"Put that on my tab."

"Oh, please."

Mallory leered at the frosted tips of his thinning hair. "I insist."

"Twist my arm, young lady."

Those teeth again.

He took a hearty slug. "Have you considered any other homes in or around Wonder Valley? I have two more about to go up—they're in rough shape, but you'd have a bid in early. This market is hot, let me tell you."

"Tell me."

"After the pandemic, every stooge in Los Angeles wants a house out here. A safe zone, or so they think. You're not from there, right?"

She fingered her ballcap. "San Diego."

"Yeah, well—I've sold just under four million this year—lots and remodels mostly. Been in this business long enough to surf the oncoming waves. Own a few rentals myself."

"That's nice, but this is the home I want."

"May I ask why?"

"Couldn't tell you. My mother just passed—"

"I'm so sorry. Covid?"

"No."

"I only ask because this friend a mine—"

"Death preys on the weak."

Chip gulped, taken aback.

"To answer your question, I saw this house online and immediately thought, That's what mother always wanted. The tranquility. The peace. It's exactly what she deserved, but never found in life. Call it dumb luck. I have to have this house, Chip. And I've inherited enough to pay cash."

"Alrighty then. Let me finish this drink, and we can be on our way."

Mallory floated a vacant smile, adding up her tab in the brain before pulling out bills for the bar.

"That's an excellent tank top, by the way. I love the color red."

"It's scarlet, actually. But thank you."

#

Chip insisted on driving with the dirt roads being so unpredictable. Mallory knew he was buzzed, but it was only a short cruise. She excused herself before getting into his Lexus SUV and ran back to the Cube, knees knocking to retrieve the black egg from out the console—placing it snug in her purse.

The interior of his car smelled like cinnamon, but there was no air freshener. Most likely Fireball whisky. He regaled her on land parcels he'd sold at every turn, the car sliding atop loose sand, onward toward a turquoise box in the distance. His tales were long and meandering, always insisting he was making a long story short. Mallory smiled out the window, searching for desert predators gearing up for night—and that man in the poncho, stalking among them.

***

One Month Earlier – Presidio Apartments, Mission Valley

Mother was taken in her sleep at the hands of her own doing. Mallory found her that morning, the woman crumpled on carpet, her bottle of "sleeping pills" and "happy pills" both empty, bedside. Beside the body, there was no note. An accident, perhaps? The party had to come to an end eventually. Mallory hid the empty bottles after calling the paramedics. She thought of that soap opera episode a few months back as EMTs pumped mother's chest, pretending she wasn't already a footnote in life.

The cremation took a week longer than custom, the funeral home overbooked with pandemic casualties. To think mother lived through one of the worst medical catastrophes the world had ever seen, only to lose her own life by her own detriment was disturbing. But the woman birthed her after all; not like Mallory hated her—she loved her and would do anything for the woman.

Mallory's problem stemmed from never quite feeling any love in return. That's why she'd ask about father when mom got stewed; Mallory wished to find the bastard and make him pay for his sins—return home to tell mother, quelling the distance between them, mending their lives into one beating heart. But that wish never came true. Then again, wishes were for fools with pennies at fountains, not for Mallory, destined for doom like her poor dead mother. She was done with all the wishing; from here on out, she'd *will* everything she wanted into existence.

#

Gliding through the pool, a tiger shark at bay, Mallory rose from the depths, met by three of her mother's old chums. She blew snot and wiped both eyes. The sunbathers had lip filler frowns, blue-haired skulls pristine, sunglasses refracting death rays down at her; their scent of suntan lotions packed a punch. The short, plump one spoke for the trio, donning a Polynesian print one-piece that pegged her for a pineapple.

"We'd like to know where you'll be spreading your mother's ashes?"

Mallory spat. "I haven't decided yet."

"Your mother always told us she wanted her final resting place to be somewhere peaceful. Can you please let us know when you finalize your plans?"

"When the day comes, you lumps will be the first to know."

"Excuse me?"

"You loves will be the first to know."

A huge, bald gentleman with monster biceps approached the pool, beach towel in his fists. The ladies moved back to let him pass.

Mallory climbed from the pool and received the man's towel. "This' Kenny. Kenny, the girls—my dead mother's dear friends. Mother's the reason Kenneth and I met in the first place—isn't that right, dear? She saw him in the courtyard, told me to pounce. I was in this killer red bikini... I couldn't have conjured a better man. Can you believe he was a Navy Seal?" Mallory refrained from mentioning Kenny's head trauma from years of battle. "Rides a Harley too."

The women put on their best excited faces. The pineapple extended a, "Thank you for your service."

Kenny gave a simple nod and grunt before wrapping the towel around Mallory.

The women leered at the odd couple exiting the peach patio before sauntering to familiar poolside chairs, sun-dried automatons, Sauvignon Blancs in hand.

#

Considering the chaos in mother's closet, her desk was in order. Files from every aspect of life were color coated, stretching back to the seventies. Mallory handled mother's diploma from some Central Valley hell, then an award for photography from the Fresno County Fair. She scoped through years of tax filings and medical documents—a pink slip to a car she didn't recall. At the tail end of the final drawer, she stumbled upon her birth certificate, careful not to crease its magical existence. She read through the document slowly, saving that name of a lifetime to savor like a rich dessert. And there it was, besides mother's (Mercedes). Her eyes bounced on the syllables. She knew the last name wouldn't be Burkhalter, her mother's maiden name. She said the name out loud, tears beginning to sprout, maniacal. She lunged for her cell phone to see what this scoundrel—this *bastard* was up to nowadays, a daughter possessed.

#

Three Weeks Later – Modern Times Brewery, San Diego

Kenny carried two tall pints of pale ale from a long bar top, its undersides made from stacks of vintage hardbound books. Mallory loved this place, its inventive façade an escape from the industrial district and strip clubs surrounding it. She was seated at a table with her own book in hand, a bible for the occult—a book she'd read her father referencing on social media. After weeks of research, the bastard's online footprint was tremendous with an alias of the Mojave Beast. Most of his posts and videos were ridiculous, but it was clear her mother was correct in his dabbling in the black arts. She thanked Kenny for her pint as he crammed into a chair. His silence was what she loved more than his muscles: her own Frankenstein monster. That and the man's life had been spent taking orders. She turned to a page that featured a painting of the Scarlet Woman holding a large black egg.

"Kenny, you love me, don't you?"

Kenny nodded.

"And you'll do anything for me, right?"

Kenny grunted.

"I've finally found my purpose in life, dear. I was born for one purpose and one purpose alone: to right a wrong...for mother and myself. But I'll need your help in doing this." She pointed to the painting. "Remember all I was telling you earlier about this woman? Babalon."

He nodded.

"She's been summoned to the desert. And I've been summoned—*we've* been summoned to accompany her. To procure a house. And at this home, we shall unleash mother's ashes as Babalon restores the universe..."

Kenny's brow furrowed.

***

The turquoise home sat atop twenty-eight acres of sand. In every direction, Wonder Valley stretched its snug arms; the dipping sun sent a rosy kiss to sand. Mallory exited the SUV and removed her ballcap; freshly dyed auburn hair fell to her shoulders. She turned and squinted to see The Palms not far in the distance, its rear stage pulsing in spectral hues like a glistening gem.

"Alright, here's your future abode." The sight of his client's appearance had Chip halt in his tracks.

Mallory approached, sultrily. "What is it? You look like you've seen a ghost."

Chip approached the front door. "You just remind me of someone...with that hair. Can't place it."

"You will, I'm sure."

The front door opened. Chip extended an ushering hand, and Mallory walked in.

The décor was a bachelor's dream, everything down to the wet bar inside a globe and living room fish tank—its interior light bathing the home with watery walls. Inside the tank, tropical creatures glided through a neon reef surrounding a human skull.

Mallory smirked and asked, "It's a two bedroom, correct?"

"Technically it's only one, but I made the pantry into a small office."

"You *made* a small office? How so?"

"This is my house. One of them."

"Ah, I see. Well, it's lovely, and I'll take it."

"Don't you want to see the backyard?"

"Of course."

Chip walked to rear blackout curtains, gliding them open to expose sliding glass doors. His twinkle-twinkle grin dropped like a domino, the view outside bringing instant alarm.

Kenny towered beside his chromed motorcycle, clad in a red poncho; as he approached the home, winds ruffled his garment into the that of a hangman's mask.

Kenny backpedaled toward Mallory. "The hell's the meaning of this?"

Mallory took the obsidian egg from her purse and held it with both hands, mirroring the painting of Babalon. "Hell *is* the meaning of everything for you, Chip Reynolds. Or have you forgotten? You conjured me. Over years and years—through centuries past, I've heard your call—elaborate rituals helmed by the great Mojave Beast."

Chip fell to his knees. "No! It can't be... I—I don't believe you."

The sliding door crashed under Kenny's boot, glass shards raining, snipping at Chip's face, blooming freckles of blood.

Mallory leaned down and wiped bloody tears from Chip's cheeks, smearing them across the egg. "Oh, but surely you *do* believe now, Chip. I'll prove my earthly presence to you."

Kenny grabbed the broker's arms and cranked him to his feet; Chip writhed in this monster's grip, quickly succumbing to the bind.

"Last time we met, I had just been conjured in San Diego. A baby whom you abandoned—my demon mother too—Mercedes Burkhalter."

The man's leaky face sank.

"You remember her, don't you? The birth certificate you signed together that named me Cameron—mother had it changed to Mallory when you left us, father." She unclasped the tip of the egg, its contents containing mother's ashes. She approached the Mojave Beast, splashed the egg's contents atop his head and chest like holy water, besmirching his all-black ensemble. Kenny opened the man's mouth for ash to drain. When the egg was empty, Mallory tossed it to the floor and went to the fish tank; she washed her sanguine hands of father's blood and mother's remains, turning the tank gory, the home's walls awash in crimson. She reached for the skull inside the tank and rolled it before father.

"Please," Chip cried, coughing through chalky lips. "I'm sorry. *Please* let me go!"

Mallory nodded to Kenny who released the man.

Chip fell to the floor, writhing in pain, crestfallen. "I don't want to die."

"You want to live forever, I know." Mallory crushed the skull under foot. "But death preys on the weak, Mr. Reynolds."

Kenny's hulking hands grabbed the man's skull and jolted a simple twist, forcing a *crack* heard like no other.

Mallory gazed upon her lifeless father, baptized in mother's remains, and waited for Kenny to go outside and retrieve the gas tank at the rear of his Harley.

#

The home's inferno raged with the sun's final dip, sending plumes to block a galaxy of stars peppering the night sky. Mallory turned one last time to admire her calling—a life fulfilled—her purpose accomplished, one forged by blood. The flames sent a warmth she could feel from mother for the first time; only then, she embraced abandoning all her history up to this moment. Mallory was reborn, recalculated: a phoenix lifting in flight. The motorcycle roared to life. She squeezed her man's barrel chest as they launched across desert, gunning north through blackened Joshua trees to destinations unknown, one day at a time, kiss-by-kiss until devils in the sunrise extinguished their flame.

LULLABY FOR THE DAMNED
BY BRIAN TOWNSLEY

Oklahoma territory, 1869

The man rode to the top of the gully and stepped down from the carriage and cart, the wood framework sighing audibly under his weight. He made his way down the hill slowly, feathering the near waist high weeds with his fingers, the thin reeds bending in riotous play. The late afternoon sun was warm on his shoulders and back, which stretched near an axhandle across, and he hummed to himself a ballad softly. Fall was fast approaching, and with it some semblance of hurry that seemed unconnected entire from the extended summer days. He removed his hat and swung about his long black hair like a beast shrugging loose some unwanted burden and rehatted himself. He lay one palm on the handle of his Bowie knife in its scabbard, more sword than dagger. At the base of the hill lay two men, twins in more ways than not—both prostrate in the mud, both with arrows protruding more than a foot from their flesh at incongruous angles, and both alike in the sum of appearance. They looked, in fact, like brothers, because they were.

They were mostly silent given their grievous wounds, the stillness interrupted with a hitched breath or desperate wheeze. Each of them had their hands on the wooden shafts, as if to pull them out, though neither attempted that futile exercise. Rye saw that he had missed badly on the second, name of Declan. Had shot him through the chest. That one certainly wasn't going to make the trip to Cherry Hill breathing. Rye looked skyward in silence and sighed. There's a $50 loss, he thought and shook his head at his own incompetence.

The other brother, Seamus, had been shot in the thigh, and he was holding his leg and making a growling noise under his breath, spittle flying onto his speckled beard, and pinwheeling in the mud as he kicked with his uninjured leg. Seamus looked up at Rye with eyes both desperate and hurt, a cornered animal, Rye thought, but said nothing. For the formality of the thing, Rye removed from his vest pocket a folded document, and read aloud: "As a licensed hunter of criminals in the state of Oklahoma and the Indian lands thereabouts, I, Rye Lonehand, am facilitating said license to apprehend and relocate both Mr. Declan McMath and Mr. Seamus McMath from and through these tribal lands to deliver said individuals unto Marshall Wright in the town of Cherry Hills. This decree comes from the bench of the honorable Judge Ezekial Stephens. You two men," he said, speaking directly to Seamus, "are worth $100 individually, dead or alive, or $250 together, alive." He looked at Declan then, and continued:

"Unfortunately, as my rifle needs a recalibration of sorts, a bow was necessary, and I don't think your brother there takes much to arrowheads, so I reckon I'm out $50 on said possibles." He spat a wad of tobacco juice at that, not at either man writhing but instead into the earthen mud and it was a gesture not without worth. A brown tributary of it ran from his mouth and found purchase in the untended thicket of beard. "And what that means, Seamus McMath, is I get $100 for you, alive, dead, or just your head. I'd ask ye to ruminate on that."

He leaned over and picked up the two pistols that had been tossed into the mud, then walked to the nearest tree, where he collected a beat-up Henry Rifle that leaned against the trunk, as well as the two nags tethered there, and began leading the horses up the hill to his own horse and cart. After a handful of steps, he stopped and turned to look at the men and said: "I need ye to get the both of yall boys into the back of that cart."

Seamus looked at his brother Declan, whose eyes were untenably wide and whose lips wore a large blood bubble, and then at Rye and said, "How the fuck am'I sposed to do that?"

Rye shook his head once at the question and said, "If I have to do it, you're both going in still." He adjusted his hat, a dusty black flatbrim model with a pinchfront, and walked the steeds up the short hill. There was a hint of lavender on the breeze that rode west.

*

"Goddamn injun," Seamus said, with nothing to accompany it. As if the expression alone were both meaning and explanation.

Rye smirked at the man then. The two sat next to each other in the cart led by a single horse, whose name was Finley. Seamus wore irons about his wrists, put on shortly after hoisting his brother into the cart.

"My father was Pawnee," Rye said, by way of explanation. "My mother, well, she was of your tribe."

Seamus spit wildly into the passing terrain and exclaimed, "like hell you say!"

"Yes," Rye nodded, "she was Irish. As far as America is concerned, two bastard heathen races," he said, and nodded.

Declan groaned loudly in the back of the cart, a long, mournful dirge that spoke of sadness and loss and held in it no meanness or threat of any kind. A return to innocence before the arms of eternity, Rye reasoned.

"Ye should kill him," Rye said.

Seamus looked at Rye's profile for a time, then said, "I ain't killing my own kin."

"He's already dying," Rye said. "You're just putting him through unnecessary pain. Doing him a disservice." Both men briefly looked back at the young man, struggling for breath, one hand still clutching the arrow shaft gently.

"Why don't you do it," Seamus asked, sheepishly.

Rye focused on the road ahead and said nothing. The terrain was a mix of highcountry brush and the beginnings of forest, and bore with it any combination of juniper and elm saplings as well prickly pear cacti, whose yellow blossoms had folded back in on themselves after a summer bloom. "Because I'm not his brother," he said in answer, finally.

"Yeah, well. He's tough," Seamus said, though his face betrayed the idea.

"You're an idiot," Rye said. They rode on.

*

The three men sat on the cabin porch, and were, by any estimation, an odd assemblage. Seamus lay on a bench, the shaft of an arrow askew and shunting perhaps eighteen inches upward from his bloody thigh. He was out cold. Or dead. No, his chest heaved. Not dead.

Rye sat in a rocking chair working on his Sharps rifle, one known for its marksmanship but whose calibration was off and so for him was lately an exercise in humility. The third man was a slight, gingery sort, all milky skin and freckles and reddish wiry hair. He wore spectacles and an apron over his shirt and vest, and leaned down to take a closer look at the arrow wound.

"How much fixing does this gentleman require," he asked in a lilting voice that still carried with it the hint of the old country, his fingers playing about the puncture area, just short of touching it.

Rye looked up from the rifle and spit a large wad of tobacco juice in the direction of the pan in the corner. "Just keep him alive until we get to Cherry Hill, I reckon" he said, and shrugged.

"Why keep him alive at all?" the man asked.

Rye did not answer this query for some time. Long enough that the pale man set to other duties. Finally, Rye said: "I didn't intend to kill either man. So what we have here is a small failure, and I'd like to avoid extending it further."

The thin man nodded, then looked at Rye again. "Why arrows?" he asked, the hint of a smirk at the corner of his mouth.

"I overcorrected the sight, missed a still deer yesterday by three feet," Rye said. "Couldn't chance that with these boys—killers of women and children as they are." He nodded with his head towards the cart, stationed some fifteen feet away from the porch. "Killed his brother though. Or damn close enough."

The thin man, whose name was John, and was in actuality Rye's first cousin, as well as a questionably competent doctor, stood then and walked down the porch and peered into the carriage. He touched the arrow there, protruding from the cart without the man attached in view, and from that place came a wincing bellow of pain. "Yeah," he said. "You put this one through his lung. Through and through the sternum, broken ribs, you name it. He's a mess." John walked back onto the porch.

"Yeah," Rye said, and focused his attentions back to his rifle, turning the knob of tobacco in his mouth.

"You said Cherry Hill?" John asked.

"That's where the marshal wants 'em."

"Been hearing some strangeness about those parts," John said. He wiped his hands on his already soiled apron. "Too close to them cave savages, ask me. Spiritual this, and sacred that, nonsense."

The two looked at each other then, whole conversations unsaid, two men who shared blood only.

Seamus groaned then as he moved his leg slightly, a high-pitched endeavor that ended in a shuttering breath. Then he farted loudly. It occurred to both men that the fart only came because of the groan first but neither knew if that made any sense and what was the point.

"Treated a fella right here last week, had the top half of his ear shot off, bleeding like he had extra, and he told me his whole outfit was told to keep away from Cherry Hill because of the curse put on by the savages on account of the sacred mountain or somesuch," John said. He stopped then, looked at Rye, and, seemingly aware his words could be taken as offensive, set to adjust them: "not your kind of savages, I reckon, but cave savages still."

Rye took a sip of clear whiskey from the bottle and rubbed the remainder of what ran down his chin into his beard as if a tincture of sorts.

*

They left early the next morning, Seamus with the arrow removed and a fresh bandage wound tightly about the thigh with a healing salve about the puncture. They both assumed Declan was dead but before the sun had fully risen they heard still a moan from the cart and Rye stopped the carriage and hopped deftly in back and placed his hand over the man's mouth. Seamus did not attempt to stop him nor utter a cry of protest. With little resistance at all, the man passed from this world into whatever others await. Seamus made the sign of the cross, the chain links from the cuffs clinking, as teardrops hung pendant in the rims of his eyes. Rye took the man's boots off then and replaced his.

As the afternoon settled in, Seamus spoke: "My leg hurts something fierce, fella." He waited for a response and got none. Then he added, in a low voice: "We ain't did what they said we did, y'know, to that injun family."

Rye nodded, and looked at Seamus. Looked him up and down, as if they had not spent the last day together. "Ain't for me to say," Rye said, finally. "My job is to pick up who the warrant says."

Seamus shook his head as if some injustice had been done. As if he were bound to some private darkness alone.

"Although," Rye added, "if you did, you'd be among the godless. Ain't an easy thing, killing a whole family in their home. Rumor says it looked like a couple of the kids tried to set afoot, and y'all shot 'em in the back." Rye looked at the man then, his eyes without judgment or contempt. "Must feel like a real hunter, a real outlaw, shooting unarmed young'uns running away." He spit a wad of tobacco into the weeds, its arc the shape of a rainbow. "That man was Osage. He was educated back East and worked as a translator for the Cavalry and the government. He was working for peace, in his own way." Rye paused here and pinched his face towards the dying sun. "And I don't reckon the wife and daughter got off so easy, did they?" The question sat there uneasily like all things the shamed wish dead and buried and then they drove past it as Rye

shook the reins and Finley picked up his pace.

*

"Daaaaaaagghhh!" Seamus screamed and sat bolt upright from sleep. He was

sweating and shaking some and it was unclear if its roots stemmed from wound

or dream but either possibility left in its wake some semblance of suffering.

"Jeee-zus," he exclaimed, looking wildly about, his lank hair matted to his beaded

forehead.

Rye was up already, tending to Finley and the cart. He looked at the

man without expression and sipped from his scalding tin can of coffee.

On the road to Cherry Hill, the two men rode in silence like that were some

currency in itself, their thoughts guarded and separate. The road was a

hardpack and the cart bounced along and the sun shone. One thing that did not

go unnoticed was the silence, and not between the men but instead the earth

itself. It had begun a bit earlier in the day but by this point had become

impossible to ignore. Though the sun shone on their hats and a breeze rose

intermittently through the juniper and cypress trees, the world otherwise was

silent. Rye did not hear the clatter of squirrels on bark or birdsong in the

branches. The silence was unnatural, and with it some change unannounced,

and a fog had begun to cling in the margins and to occupy space where space was

found. A chill had set about, no doubt due to the fog, each man allowed.

"Oh, Lord almighty," Seamus said, breaking some seal about the place. He touched his cuffed hands to Rye's arms, his eyes focused on the road ahead.

Rye looked down at the pair of cuffed hands like something alien and then at Seamus, curious. He halted the horse, who snuffed his disapproval for reasons to his own mind.

"That tree," the Irishman said, and pointed to a gnarled Elm, blackened by fire, its naked appendages twisted and misshapen against the mist. It gave Rye a thought of a living corpse.

"That was from my dream," Seamus said, and shuddered. "It had...shit, man...it had bodies all up in it. Dead ones, they were beset upon it. A part of it. Hanging from it, skewered by it." He looked at Rye, the whites of his eyes large and childlike. "One branch went right through the mouth of one and out the back, and it was moving its mouth like it was trying to talk. Some had no heads." Seamus moved his lips as if there were more to say, but nothing came out. Rye said nothing in return. When Seamus spoke again, his voice quavered and he sounded like a child. "And the babies were stacked at the base of it. So many tiny bodies, and there was this...squirming, you know. Like everything was dead but wouldn't stay still." He looked back at the tree, and sobbed, once, and it seemed as loud and obscene as a clap in the quiet. Tears ran down his filthy cheeks, mining tributaries through the dirt as they fell.

Rye wanted to bludgeon the man. Wanted to tell him to grow up. Wanted to remind him of what he was accused—but his body was racked with a shiver instead. Worse was the realization that he did not know if it was a reaction to the cold, which seemed to have settled bonedeep, or that he himself had recognized the tree, and the scene as described, as he had bore witness the same dream in the night.

*

Cherry Hill was less than an hour's ride at that point but it took the cart more than twice that to navigate the fog. Rye had set foot in Cherry Hill a few times in the past, and had both delivered men to a marshal there, most recently Marshal Wright, and stocked provisions as was his wont. He didn't like it much, but there was nothing unique to that, as he didn't like towns much, period. It was a small town built to a small scale—comprised of a single avenue, with perhaps upwards of fifty properties, ranches, and bungalows on its outskirts that called it 'town.' The main road consisted of the standard working definition of civilization, complete with a sheriff's office, a saloon, a general dry goods and feed store, a church, a barber, a telegraph office and the like. Rye was trying to remember the geographic details as he passed a wooden sign, the likes of which had been altered since his last visit. He may need them, those details, he reckoned. He sat the cart not ten feet from the wooden sign and both men struggled to read it so thick was the mist.

"What does that say?" Seamus asked, leaning forward and squinting towards the sign. He held his arms to his chest closely in an attempt at warmth.

Rye looked at the writing there and did not answer, making sense of it. Over the town name, which had been rendered in careful scripture, was a crude collection of letters in crimson, the ends of which dabbed and dripped below their given shapes. 'Cahriksuupiíru' was written.

"That ain't no word," Seamus said, more question than statement.

Rye looked at the man and nodded. "It means 'enemy' in Pawnee," he said

"*Pawnee*," Seamus exclaimed, surprised. "They're up on the banks of the Mississippi, up Nebrasky way. What the hell," he said, and rubbed at his shoulders.

"It makes no sense," Rye said, under his breath, more to himself than to the man beside him. *Unless someone knew I was coming*, he thought, but did not say.

"You an enemy to someone here?" the man asked.

"I don't reckon it's referring to me," Rye said, and did not elaborate. He turned his head and grinned knowingly at Seamus. He lightly slapped the reins to Finley's back and the horse stepped forward reluctantly.

The silence and the mist about and the cold seemed to sharpen as they entered the town. If it was silent before, now there was a complete absence of sound; if it was hard to see before, it was now foggy to blindness; and where it had been chilly, now both men chattered their teeth uncontrollably, although Rye had wrapped himself in a buffalo robe from the cart and was much better off than the Irishman.

"Mister, my leg is hurtin' something fierce," Seamus said, his words making billows of smoke in the air. "Ever since we got into town it's...worse," he said. They began to pass the first businesses on the street, though they could only see in vague concepts—the shapes of signs without the words to accompany them, such was the geography of oblivion.

"What if there ain't nobody here, mister," Seamus asked. "You cain't just leave me," he said, though it was not a statement. His words had been whispered, but seemed somehow indecent in the deafening silence.

"I leave ye, I don't get paid. Now, is it possible to close that aperture," Rye queried, whispering.

"What?" the man asked.

"Be silent," Rye said, and the tone of it did not leave space for argument.

He halted Finley, who snorted in disapproval at the particulars, and they sat there in the elements: the fog, the silence, the mist. And with it, some small disturbance, barely discernible. Then both men heard it, and looked at one another. There was a tapping, or clicking, that could just be made out over the absence of sound and the horse's exhalations, a patter like tuneless and muted piano notes riding the mist.

Rye walked the horse in the direction of the tappings, the path taking them through town. They reached the far end of the single block, and here Rye sat the horse and tethered him and then clicked the cuffs on the Irishman to an iron ring at the front of the carriage, to which the man did not complain. Rye dismounted and pulled the rifle, straight shooter or not, from the cart. He knew now from where the noise was originating, and with it recognized the particular source of the clatter: it was a telegraph machine.

He walked towards the small clapboard building and cinched the buffalo robe about him such was the cold, his breath billowing before him like things tangible and given weight. His bootsteps in the dirt were loud in the absence of sound, like he were yet the first man and as such brought with him the chaos of life. He reached the wooden steps and saw the door to the building ajar and jumped into the doorway, rifle raised. The room was a small one and contained in it a large desk with the tapping machine, two chairs, a hatrack, and a divan that clearly doubled as a bed when needed. A woman in a blue flecked dress with her brown hair in a bun sat in one of the chairs, but did not face Rye, even after entering the room with all the subtlety of a water buffalo. Rye pointed the barrel of the rifle towards the floor and said, "Sorry ma'am, I'm looking for Marshal Wright."

The woman continued the tapping on the small machine and did not look his way. Rye looked again about the room, then out the door. Nothing moved; The town was as still and silent as a crypt. And still, the tapping. Rye walked to the woman in the chair and bent down to her level and set to speak but instead caught his breath in choked confusion.

The woman *looked* dead. Her skin had shrunk to her skull and her eyes had been sewn shut and her mouth the same although only in the corners, two X's in thick black thread—he recognized it as sinew, most likely from dyed buffalo tendon—and from the center of her mouth a small piece of parchment protruded. Rye looked then at the woman's hand, tapping in some dissonant rhythm on the telegraph machine. He had an urge to move the hand, to smash it, perhaps. Instead, he simply stared.

"What's happening," Seamus asked from the cart out on the street. His voice was threaded with fear and was obscenely loud given the situation.

Rye thought of words to say and found none and said none in return. *What, exactly, was happening?* Good question, Seamus, he thought.

"You okay in there?"

Rye took the parchment from the seam of lips and pulled it carefully from the aperture. It was a small piece of thick paper, folded over. "Fine," he replied. "I'll be out soon."

"Who's doing that tapping in there?" Seamus asked.

Rye unfolded the paper and looked upon its content. It held two words in a careful, looped script: *LEAVE HIM.* Rye made a face at this and looked down again at the woman, if woman she was at one time. Now a lifeless husk, stitched about the mouth and eyes, and the hand and finger tap-tapping away, staccato and chaotic. Rye had only a rudimentary knowledge of the code being used, but whatever was being transmitted over the machine held no sense in any language he knew.

Finley whinnied in the street and it brought Rye out of whatever reverie in which he found himself and he knew he should leave this town, and do it now. But he had expected to meet Marshal Wright here, and owed him at least the respect of checking on his whereabouts. Wright was a good man, and he would bear him deference in that. He would bear witness the saloon, and sheriff's office. If they were empty, well. Then he would leave.

He took one more look at the tapping corpse and wondered again at the message being broadcast along the telegraph lines, and hurried out the door. He untethered Finley and rode three storefronts down to the sheriff's office, which was conveniently located directly next to the saloon, which Rye knew also served as hotel and bath house, as well as containing women of domestic repute.

"What're you doin'?" Seamus asked. "And unlock me. *Something's wrong here, man.* What was that tapping from?" His questions were panicked and came one atop the next.

Rye brought his finger to his lips in a universal gesture of silence. "I need to check on Marshal Wright. If he's not here, we go," he whispered.

The young Irishman wore an expression of panic and fear and stress that belied his years. "It was Declan did it," he said, finally. "It was all his idea." He looked down at this admission, but his gaze went someplace that was only his, some black compartment of his own making.

Rye rode the block south and dismounted the cart, rifle in hand and entered the sheriff's office at a run, despite the chill. It was an office he was familiar with, but had never seen it quite so empty. There were three desks, all unmanned. Papers were strewn about the floor. There was a Winchester rifle leaned against a desk and a shotgun on another, and Rye discarded his old Sharps there and grabbed both weapons. He heard a sound from the cells. He had looked there momentarily when he entered, but had seen nothing. Now, upon second glance he saw what he would never again unsee. There was a white man in each cell, pinned to the back wall. That didn't cover it though; they weren't *pinned* to the wall so much as *a part of it.* They had become one with the brick and stone, their hands and face and feet seeming stuck to it and laced with some organic material at their ends, and what he had heard was a muffled cry from one of the men. There were parts of them moving, but not in a natural sense. As if there were things inside the men shifting.

The man on the left made a guttural noise and both men, in unison, raised their heads to look at Rye, but neither man had eyes to speak of anymore. They had been removed, and over the sunken sockets were the same sewn X's as he had seen on the telegraph woman.

Rye held each gun in a firing position and began backing up. Sweat was dripping into his eyes though he never recalled being so cold, even with the buffalo robe cinched at his neck. The two men seemed to be watching him, their heads turning in unison with his movement, and when Rye was two steps from the door he turned and ran through it and out into the street. He heard a cry and ran into the back of the cart, breathing heavily from shock and fear, his breath cloudlike in the fog. He could feel his heart at a hummingbird pace. He heard another cry, this one he placed from inside the saloon, and he jumped onto the bench seat of the carriage and grabbed the reins. It was only then that he realized that both Irishmen were gone. No trace of them. Finley, however, seemed quite ready to go and pawed at the ground with his front hooves and whinnied and carried in his eyes something near panic.

"*Fuck*," Rye whispered, and got down from the cart and with willpower alone made himself walk, stiff-legged, to the saloon.

He placed his back against the front façade of the saloon and leaned his head in the double doors to get a glimpse inside. He held the rifle in one hand and the shotgun in the other, and they seemed weightless, such was his adrenaline. What he saw made no sense and so he squared himself and stepped through the swinging doors.

There was a lot to take in. *Someone has been busy*, Rye found himself thinking. The floor was littered with the bodies of white men and women, settlers and citizens. All were posed in various directions, their arms stiffly at their sides and legs straight out. In the middle of the room lay a matted stack of hair nearly as high as he stood. He recognized it immediately as scalps, an enormous pile of bloody, reeking scalps. His eyes went quickly to the bodies, some of which seemed to move internally but were clearly all dead, and glanced then at their heads. Each had a narrow bloody swath above the forehead. He noticed then that there were also drawn designs on the wood floor, and that the bodies had been placed in some sort of celestial organization, with the unmistakable rays of the sun coming from the circle in the middle upon which sat the pile of scalps. The design was crude and resembled the cave paintings of the

Anasazi tribe, which, of course, made no sense, as The Ancient Ones had been gone for many a year, but there were other tribes who kept only their own counsel and mountain landscapes, cultures mired in an antiquity without modern equivalence.

Rye heard a grunt then, and looked up from the floor and its antediluvian markings, and peered upon the back wall, whereupon the staircase split and led both left and right. On the wall between the split, Marshal Wright had been hung in a Christ-like pose, his scalped head bloody and slick. He had been shot through with arrows in each hand, and four more protruding from his chest, while his booted feet dangled limply. He hung only by the shafts that held him up, arrowheads embedded deeply into the wall behind him. He raised his head and made a short, high-pitched groaning noise. Rye quickly raised the rifle and shot the man twice in the chest. The marshal's head slumped forward in silence.

As he lowered the Winchester, he noticed something move on the floor. Then he saw it: the face of each body, heads caked with blood and eyes sewn shut, had turned towards him. Watching him. Or perhaps something else was watching him through each of them. He took a step back and heard a scream upstairs. He thought it was probably Seamus. He also didn't care.

He backed slowly away from the bodies in the direction of the front doors. He heard a voice, more like a hum than actual words, but the message was clear enough: *leave him.* The bodies on the floor all seemed to be imploring him, *leave him,* some undead chorus in repetition.

Rye turned and did just that, ran without feeling in his legs to the cart and threw the guns on the bench and slapped the reins on Finley's back and then the horse was running in the fog and although he had a wagon trailing him and the horse was encumbered and Rye was whipping the reins and Finley was frenzied and despite every action he and his horse took they could not possibly flee fast enough from the town of Cherry Hills.

*

That night he sat by a small fire, and tried desperately to think of anything besides to what he had witnessed in the saloon. He had an open mind about the spirit world, and felt the universe was much larger than his white brethren did, but understanding would not come. He went into a saddle bag he kept in the storage section underneath the bench on his rig and pulled a bottle of whiskey from it. He was not much of a drinking man, but this night that held no sway. He sucked deeply from the neck of the bottle and in time its warmth led him somewhere approximating sleep.

Rye Lonehand woke in the morning to a head that felt too small and a mouth that felt as if it had never known water and a burning at his right elbow. He sat up, and the world swayed a bit, and he vomited into the coals of the fire. He scratched at the inside of his elbow but that did nothing to extinguish the burn there, and when he pulled his shirtsleeve up, he saw there a crude design that had been etched into his skin. It looked like a cave painting, and resembled an eyeball, surrounded by an eyelid with four lashes coming from it. Or perhaps

they were rays. He would vacillate on drunken evenings and late-night

explorations as to whether it more resembled an eyeball or a sun, and debated

himself on its meaning over time, as he bore the mark of it for the rest of his

days.

PIT!

BY SEAN JACQUES

The scrappy red was laying waste to the blood-soaked blonde while a wave of whooping and hollering spurned him on: "Finish it, red! Finish it!!"

The buzzcut referee rushed in and stomped his boot between the bloody birds and called it. Then more rowdy eruptions launched as crumped tens and twenties passed from one dirtied hand to another.

The winning handler, Juney Kruger, let out a victorious "Whooeeee, goddamn!" He leaned over and clutched his winning red and then strutted around the boarded pit, hoisting his champion cock up-and-down like a post-hole digger. "That's six in row, mother fuckers! Six in a mother fuckin' row!"

Meanwhile, the handler of the losing bird, a scrawny kid named Boone, bent down and gently picked up his dead blonde. He was barely in his twenties, with a pimply face and long greasy hair, and he looked like he was ready to bawl.

"Don't let your nutsack shrivel, kid," Kruger chuckled. "You run up against a stud cocker is all. You gotta get a little more training skill under your belt. Let your roosters let loose on some hens once a while, and you'll get yourself a winner. Hell, you might even get lucky enough to get yourself some backseat tail feathers while you're at it."

Kruger cackled, figuring the young blood would take kindly to the humorous joshing. But the pimply face loser didn't react at all and scooted off with his bloody cock in his hand.

"Well fuck you too," Kruger yelled out before he went back to laughing.

The promoter of the day's events, Dubb Boetticher, threw his arms into the air to grab the mob's attention. "All right, everybody, all right, I think it's time to take us a little break! Go get yourself a beer, or three, and a hotdog or two, and hellchrist, I might need to bust out some watermelons to cool us down from this godawful heat!"

The drunk and sweaty horde idled down from its enthusiastic blood-buzz and ambled out of the open-air barn, headed for the grub and a piss behind the trees. A few of them were out-of-state breeders and handlers and hardcore cock enthusiasts, but most were local Ozarkians who'd come to the fighting pit out of curiosity and the chance to win a buck or two. Nearly all were husky and bearded and red-eyed men, wearing sweat-stained trucker caps, some shirtless, others in cutoffs. There was also a smaller congregation of subdued Mexicans costumed with straw cowboy hats, snap-button shirts and Wranglers, and their stone faces told that they were deadly serious about the action taking place in the pit.

Since the August afternoon was sweltering, most of the drunken spectators headed straight for the cans of beer iced down in wash tubs where Boetticher's wife and daughters were manning distribution. Naturally, the price was sky high. Although Boetticher was no cockfight connoisseur, he was a slick businessman. Last fall, his cousin, Lyndell Johnson, had told him there'd been a severe lack of cock derbies in the Mid-South ever since a big raid went down in Arkansas a couple years back, and it only took Boetticher a half breath to realize that he held a prime location to set up a new enterprise. Over this past winter he went to work clearing five acres of timber on his private property near the Arkansas-Missouri border then he directed his sawmill workers to build the barn and a couple of pits. Then by June, he and Lyndell sent whispers around the Ozarks and beyond that they were open for business. Besides a mandatory $200 entry fee, contending handlers had to pay an additional $50 service charge for each cock that entered the pit. There was also a $25 entrance fee for every spectator, plus another $15 to park a vehicle. Boetticher left the betting itself up to individuals to sort out the particulars amongst themselves, although he tabbed Lyndell to referee the contests, and placed his three sons on security with holstered .45s and slinged AR-15s in case anybody got out of line.

Five minutes into the break, a faction of Mexicans had parted from the herd of hungry and drunk *gringos* and had massed together under a canopy of trees. All of them were immigrant workers at the sawmill, brought to Missouri by Boetticher because they were more dependable than the shifty locals who chose monthly government checks over lawful employment. As they were shooting-the-shit in Spanish and sipping on homemade *micheladas*, they spotted a fellow countryman sauntering by, and yelled out if he cared to cool off with a drink. The stranger gladly accepted their invitation, said his name was Curro, and that he'd driven up from Princeville, Arkansas. He and his Princeville *amigos* had brought six of their best fighting birds, were an even 2-2 so far today, and he claimed the best of the bunch, a Radio Rooster, named *Venganza* was up next. When one of the Mexican sawmillers replied that it might be tough going against the loudmouth arrogant asshole with his slew of winning cocks, Curro chuckled and said, "Maybe today is the day that fucker's luck runs out."

After Curro drained his spicy tomato beer, he thanked the sawmillers for their hospitality, and then he strutted off toward his parked Ford pickup where he found the half-dozen others in his party from Princeville. They were all huddled together, watching the trainer, Thiago Macias, meticulously tape padded moleskin and razor sharp short-heel gaffs to *Venganza* legs, while another man, nicknamed Manos ("Hands) firmly held the cock upside down.

"How's he looking, Thiago?" Curro asked.

Thiago was too preoccupied to speak.

"How about you, Manos? You ready?"

"Of course."

Curro nodded to Manos's confidence then wheeled his dark eyes about his circle of friends. Their silence and their stone faces said that they had more riding on the next match than a just a winning rooster.

#

The lives of the Princeville Mexicans hadn't been the same since the big raid had gone down in Sutton County, Arkansas. The cockfighting derby that day had barely even started when the Arkansas State Police, the County Sheriff deputies, the Princeville cops, the Arkansas Game and Fish Commission, the U.S. Forestry Agency, the U.S. Wildlife Service, and ICE officials crashed the party. A helicopter descended from the sky and hovered over the pavilion like a starving buzzard, bellowing, "Do not run! Do not run! Drop down on your knees!" while a convoy of forty law enforcement cars and trucks came barreling down the dirt road. The coppers swooped in and encircled the fighting grounds and broke out of their vehicles with rifles and pistols drawn. Some aimed at heads. No one escaped. The local married couple who had sponsored the event, and twenty-four handlers listed on a hand-written roster, were booked on felony charges. The eighty-odd spectators were slapped with a misdemeanor and fine.

No doubt, the big raid made a dent within the Mid-South cockfighting circles, or at least for a time, it had. But the more serious and long-term ramifications had been dealt to the Mexicans that were there that day. Ten out of the twenty-four arrested handlers were either green-card workers or undocumented. And all ten were deported by ICE within six months. Curro's older brother, Ramon, was one of those sent packing, along with the promise that he'd never be allowed to set foot in the states again. It was a similar story for all the Mexicans who'd come up today from Princeville, each man had lost a relative or friend. And Thiago, a legal U.S. resident for over twenty years, had paid an even heavier price: a three-month rap at the Texarkana Correctional

Facility, a $10,000 fine, and his entire flock of 400 fighters had been confiscated—roosters, hens, chicks, and all.

Before that big raid, there hadn't been much discord between the Mexican contingent living in Princeville and the native Arkansans, other than the usual name-calling and the snarky remarks about an invasion of Spanish-speakers at school. But when ICE started knocking on doors, the Mexicans fell into perpetual mistrust of their neighbors, and they still didn't understand why a gamecock contest had raised such a fuss. Many of them had migrated to Sutton County to work as chicken ranch hands or wholesale slaughterers for the local poultry plants, and now here they were being called felons for raising and killing chickens. None of it made any damn sense in Spanish or English. And for Curro, Thiago, and the other Princeville Mexicans in their party, that big raid had always felt a bit sketchy, so much that they still believed that someone was behind a sinister plot to run them out of town.

#

A cowbell rang out. The twenty-minute intermission was over, and the next set of fights were set to begin. The now drunker and sweatier crowd of white men began to mosey back toward the barn and pit. Meanwhile, the Princeville Mexicans fell into a walking parade behind Thiago and Manos, and as they passed by Boetticher's pickup, piled full with dead cocks in its bed, Curro hawked a loogy and spit at the back tire.

As the Princeville Mexicans entered the barn, the sawmill workers gave them a round of whistles and hand claps and "Viva Mexico!" salutations, while the Ozarkers and the hardcore cock enthusiasts kept on jabbering bets and odds.

Boetticher set the cowbell down on a table and yelled out, "All right, everybody, the next round has a Hatch breed from Juney Kruger going against a Radio Rooster that's come up from some Mex boys out of Arkansas. Weigh them up, gentleman."

Usually, the birds would be weighed earlier in the day, before the spurs were put on, but Boetticher was more concerned with the pace of the fights. More fights, more money, so he revised a few common rules and practices. He only allowed birds to go at it for ten minutes, and if there was no clear winner, the birds were sent to a smaller pit outside the barn to finish, and the next match took over in the main pit. Fast fights, fast money, get in, get out.

Thiago and Manos stepped up to the table and placed *Venganza* onto the scale. As the rooster flapped and ran its legs, cousin Lyndell squinted at the measurement and announced, "Four pounds, two ounces."

Boetticher repeated, "Four pounds, two ounces. And from what I can decipher, this Radio Rooster has a record of two wins." He raised two fingers, and Thiago nodded. "Yes, two wins."

The crowd huffed, shaking heads, waving off bets. Juney Kruger then strode up with his Hatch breed and sat it on the scale. It too flapped and squawked to get away.

"Four pounds, three ounces," Lyndell reported.

"All right, that's four pounds and three for Juney's Hatch," Boetticher repeated to the crowd. "How many wins for this bird, Juney?"

"Not a one. Yet. He's breaking his cherry with this fight, and I'm betting he'll win at least ten more after we're done here." Juney eyed Thiago and cracked a smartass grin. "Sorry your little cock there is going to be laying limp in a minute."

"A cocksucker would know," Thiago replied in English, smiling.

"Ohhhhh... That's a right smart one there, Mex. You got me." Kruger laughed. "How long's it been since we pitted against each other? Two, three years now? I figured you'd retired."

"Not yet."

"Who's this you got with you?"

"My handler."

"What? You not up to handling your own bird against me anymore?"

"I'm training the man, too."

"Well, you outta know it ain't the handler that'll get you a winner." Kruger winked at Manos. "Hopefully, my champ here won't bloody up your cock too bad. That way, you won't get your panties messy."

Manos nodded, as if agreeing to whatever Kruger was saying to him.

"Let's get to the pits!" Lyndell barked.

A few in the crowd cried out their final bets. The odds had settled 5-1 in favor of Kruger's Hatch. It wasn't that anyone particularly wished to root for the arrogant son of bitch, especially since he hailed from some Podunk shithole near Little Rock, but no one could deny that he'd managed to breed a line of cold-blooded assassins.

Kruger stepped into the pit first, lifting his rooster up high and setting it down on top of his head like a crown. "It's another win for King Cocker, boys! You already know how this is gonna turn out!"

Thiago handed *Venganza* to Manos then whispered in Spanish, "You know what to do. If the moment comes...take it." Manos nodded back and made his way into the pit with *Venganza.*

"You want to bill them first?" Lyndell asked the two handlers.

"Not unless the Mex cares to," Kruger replied with his shit-eating smile. "My Hatch here is rarin' to go without it."

Manos looked over to Thiago, who yelled out on his behalf, "Yes! Bill them, yes!"

"Okay, get ready then," Lyndell commanded. "Bill your cocks!"

Kruger and Manos cradled their roosters and stepped toward the center of the pit. They stationed themselves about two feet apart and let the birds go pecking at each other. Kruger's Hatch quickly proved to be the more aggressive of the two, but *Venganza* still laid a couple of powerful beaks onto the Hatch's combed dome.

While watching from the edge of the pit, Thiago cussed a few words in Spanish, guessing that the Hatch belonged to the same bloodline that he himself had bred a few years ago. After that big raid had settled, over two hundred confiscated roosters had been kept in solitary cages in the prison yard of the

Sutton County Jail, including ten of Thiago's best fighters that he'd raised from chicks. No one had come forward to claim any of the birds, for fear of being arrested, until Juney Kruger stepped up and offered to take some cocks off the county's hands. Juney told the sheriff that he was simply needing some strong roosters for his egg-laying farm hens, and the sheriff was tickled to death to unload as many shit-smelling fowl as possible. Plus, since Juney had not been at the derby the day of the big raid, no one could point the finger at him for any illegal shenanigans. Still, anybody on the cockfighting circuit with a half-lick of sense could mhe'd thieved a brand-new brood of winners. It's just that no one had been able to do anything about it.

"Pull them apart, pull them apart!" Lyndell ordered. "Move back behind your line!"

Kruger grinned at Manos. Manos nodded and flashed his gold-tooth smile back him. Then the two handlers stepped back behind their assigned lines, about eight feet apart, and squatted down.

Some in the crowd barked and hollered in anticipation. Lyndell stood erect with his hand raised in the air, then he glanced at both handlers. "Cockers ready?!" Kruger and Manos were knelt and holding their own cock's tail feathers, waiting for the moment of truth to arrive.

"Pit!"

Venganza and the Hatch wasted no time in getting after one another. They met in mid-air, slashing their leg spurs, bumping chests, and when they fell to the ground, they both bounced straight back up and started savagely slashing again.

The chatter amongst the crowd picked up as the birds continued to air battle but then both cocks got their gaffs stuck in the other's bleeding breast and halted the action.

"Handle!" Lyndell shouted.

As the handlers moved to disentangle their birds, Kruger spoke out, "Keep your goddamn hands off my bird, let me do it!"

Thiago stood up in protest and stared at Lyndell to perform his referee duty. Lyndell rushed over to the tangled birds and warned Kruger, "You can pull them apart, just make it fair."

"When have I not made it fair, Lyndell?"

"Give me no shit, Juney!"

Thiago nodded at Lyndell, thankful for the fair play. He didn't trust Juney Kruger enough to step on. It wasn't only that Kruger had stolen his bloodline, but the sneaky bastard had still never paid his former losses to any of the Mexicans.

Before his recent streak of tremendous luck, Kruger had a real bad run of losing every time he went into the pit, and he'd stacked up a steep bill in lost bets over the years. That was all before the big raid. Then when he started rebounding, winning most of his fights, gaining cash on his bets, he began paying off debts. Except he never paid squat to any Mexican he owed money, which added to the hate they carried for him.

"Cockers ready!" Lyndell went. "Pit!"

Manos and Kruger let go of their birds and they quickly went back to knifing each other in the air again. Feathers floated around their deadly dance and blood drops dotted the dirt of the pit. *Venganza* was beginning to show its Radio Rooster strength of an air fighter and kept above its opponent, pecking its beak downward, and aiming his gaffs at the Hatch's tiny brain. But the Hatch was no slouch at fighting and held its own, coaxing the Red Rooster into a ground match.

"Handle!"

The birds had hung up a second time, so Kruger and Manos moved in to pull them apart.

"Looks like your cock's coming up a little limp there, *amigo*," Kruger joked.

Manos smiled, said nothing. He looked over this shoulder to glimpse his Princeville buddies sitting and standing together at the edge of the pit. Curro raised and pumped his fist.

Only six months ago, Curro and the others hadn't known much about Manos. He was simply a new arrival at the poultry plant, and everyone had started calling him Manos after noticing how fast he could yank live chickens out of crates with his hands. Then one day during lunch break, Curro was bitching about a sideways fucker who'd snitched to the cops and that's what had led to the big cockfighting raid. The others then added their own threats and promises to stomp the rat fucker into the ground and slit the mother fucker's throat.

Manos was sitting in the corner of the room, slurping homemade stew, minding his own business, then he stood up and asked to know more about it.

"Cockers ready!" Lyndell yelled out. "Pit!"

A third time Kruger and Manos released their roosters, and a third time the roosters attacked to kill. *Venganza* was winded and his right wing wasn't flapping, so the battle was turning in favor toward the Hatch and its superior ground tactics.

The crowd was getting more raucous as the birds kept wheeling around each other, pecking at the other's eyes, shuffling, mushing together, hopping up and sticking a gaff into legs and thighs. The gory effects were showing on both birds.

Believing the fight was now his to win, Kruger grinned his stupid grin and shouted, "Come on, pick that bird's fucking eye out!" All the while, Manos never said a word, never showed his thoughts, never took his eyes off the two fighting cocks, other than to glance at Thiago for a signal.

It was Thiago who'd first learned from a cock breeder from Tulsa that Juney Kruger was the sneaky devil fucker that had ignited the big raid in Sutton County. According to this Okie, who'd heard it straight from Juney's running mouth, Juney admitted that he was the one who had whispered to the Chief of Police at Princeville about when and where cockfighting events were taking place. Reason was, Juney had found himself so far in debt, and had been losing fights so bad, that his only hope of digging out of his hole was to wipe out some of his competition. He figured if the local fuzz made a surprise appearance at the next scheduled illegal derby, and put a little scare into his rivals, then the top handlers might lay low from the fighting circuit and give him better odds. But what Juney hadn't figured on was that right after he'd tattled to that local copper, the chief called up and squealed the information to the state police, who then whispered to the feds, the memo then hit the desk of Immigration and Customs Enforcement, and all the dominos fell from there. Still, Juney had never regretted what he'd done. He told the Okie that the Good Lord works in mysterious ways, and if that way just so happened to play into Juney's hands, then the Good Lord must've wanted it that way too.

"Handle!" Lyndell barked to halt the action. The birds' long spurs were stuck inside their diced-up breasts again. After wiggling out the Hatch's gaff from *Venganza's* wing bone, Kruger spun away from Manos and went to nursing his wounded cock, spitting on its beak and rubbing its back. Manos performed similar massaging moves on *Venganza,* trying to stroke him back to life, though the Red Rooster showed little sign that it could be revived.

"It's over!" bettors in the crowd barked.

"Give them another pit!" others chanted.

Lyndell peeped at Boetticher who checked his watch then nodded to let the fight go on.

"Thirty seconds!" Lyndell gave the handlers.

Manos squatted down behind the line and waited. He peeped over to see Thiago tugging at his goatee. Curro jutted his chin and spit. The rest of the

Princeville Mexicans remained stone-faced, their confidence in Manos written in their stiff stances.

Manos had told them that he could handle their problem. He'd encountered similar dilemmas back at his village in Durango, except in Mexico, the stakes were either do whatever it takes to stay alive or face a brutal death. He also said he had undertaken extreme measures when he worked as a town cop and had to deal with members of the Zeta and Sinaloa cartels. He didn't reveal what these extreme measures had been, other than to say that his actions had forced him to leave Mexico, but the Princeville Mexicans believed what he said. And they all agreed to pay him five grand if he succeeded in taking care of Juney Kruger.

"Cockers ready!" Lyndell yelled. "Pit!"

This time, *Venganza* slow-walked and took a turn toward the wall instead of meeting the Hatch head-on for another violent burst of gashing. The Hatch on the other hand sprinted with its neck bobbing and its wings pulled back like Lucifer coming for a damned soul. It cut-off *Venganza*'s escape and the two began savagely carving each other up. *Venganza* managed to stab the Hatch a couple times in the leg, but then the Hatch lifted into the air and began cutting wildly at *Venganza's* ruffled neck. The frothing crowd went into a peaked frenzy. "Get him! Gaff the fucker!! Gaff him!" Then one of the Hatch's sharp spurs pierced straight into *Venganza's* square-shaped head, and when *Venganza* slumped over and stopped moving, the Hatch took to pecking its beak at its lifeless opponent.

The chorus of cusses and cheers boomed over the pit and barn as Lyndell hurried in and called it official. "Juney Kruger wins!"

Crumbled bills traded between winners and losers. The sawmillers grumbled and tossed their sorrowful frowns over to Curro and the others, who were dully staring at their prized dead rooster lying motionless in the pit.

Kruger threw arms straight up over his head and turned in a circle like a prophetic rainmaker. "Seven up, seven down, mother fuckers!" He then craned his head toward Thiago and winked. "You got any more cocks I can chop up for you? Maybe Boetticher can slide you a little bacon grease and ya'll can fry up a mess of chicken livers for your supper."

Thiago tipped his cowboy hat in a gesture of sportsmanship. The other Princeville Mexicans glanced at one another, shook their heads, then curled smiles onto their stone faces and chuckled at the winning clown inside the circle.

Kruger then began performing his signature move, yelling, "Whoooeee! Whoooeee!" while hoisting the Hatch up and down from his waist like he was stroking a giant pecker.

As the rambunctious crowd glanced away, slapping backs, caught up in a blood fever, Manos stayed squatted, not twitching a muscle. Then like a gliding ghost, he picked up *Venganza's* carcass and went to exit the pit, and when he whisked by Kruger, his fast free hand grabbed hold of the Hatch's feet and stuck its gaffs straight into Kruger's groin.

One by one, folks spun their drunken attention toward the ear-piercing howls, and saw Juney Kruger hopping up and down on his feet and trying to wrestle the squawking Hatch off his crotch. Some of them figured he was just showing off as usual. But once he managed to yank out the three-inch gaffs from his privates, he kept screeching like a batshit banshee, and fell backwards on his ass, with his hands cupping his family jewels.

Boetticher rushed into the pit, noticed Kruger pissing his pants in blood, and looked at Lyndell for an explanation. "What happened?! What happened?!"

"Hell, if I know!" Lyndell shot back.

Boetticher pried Juney's gripping fingers off his soaking crotch and saw the nasty gashes and blood pumping out from the ruptured femoral artery. "Holy fucking shit...! Hey! Listen up, listen up . . .!! His goddamn rooster cut him! He's bleeding something awful!"

A hush washed over the crowd. Boetticher peeled his eyes over them, falling into a stunned state of shock over what to do. "Well, somebody get a goddamn rag or somethin'!"

Thiago and Curro and the Princeville Mexicans watched on with their stone faces. Manos stood amongst them, holding dead *Venganza* down by his side.

Nothing pleased them more than to witness the sorry son of bitch screaming misery, clutching his cock, bleeding out to death in the pit.

DISOPHONIA
BY JEAN-PAUL L. GARNIER

The noise almost never stopped. Constant distraction. No matter where Frank went, it followed. And then there was silence. It replaced the sound of the engines, finally something to interfere. For a moment a blissful rising inside of him, a rush of beauty that was so unlike the cacophony that generally sounded him that it almost went unnoticed. In fact, he didn't notice the sound of the engines die off, it was the silence in his mind that struck first. Pleasant at first, a rare beauty, foreign.

Words. Words had filled his mind for the entire trip. Now, nothing. The absence crept up before he knew that the words were gone from him. He spoke several out loud to see if they had gone entirely, they came out as mush. If there was someone else to speak to he would have tested the mush to see if it was understandable, but alone, alone, alone. It was probably why the words had stopped. He rarely spoke aloud, there was no reason to, unless he felt the need to keep himself company in the loneliness of the trip. He figured it was why his mind was always reeling, always speaking to himself internally. But now the silence.

So what if the words were gone, the silence was welcome. But where was the sound of the engines? Whenever he stopped his internal mumbling, theirs would take over, like the gentle lull of a cat's purr, always there to accompany him whether welcome or not. The music of the ship he had called it. And he wasn't a fan of music. Something he had had to convince himself was not true, frequently reminding himself that everything had its rhythm, its tone, frequencies, phase cancellations, and all that. A mess, really. But where had they gone? Welcome change or not, the ship should be noisy.

He sniffed. An electrical problem? Fire? He smelled nothing. The ship was as vacant of scent as it was sound. Was the lack of stimuli emanating from him? How could nothing emanate at all? Pinching himself, he found that his sense of the tactile remained. He could feel. Everything looked to be in order. For a moment he feared that the oxygen had somehow been vented, but he had no trouble breathing. It had not grown cold either. But that silence. It was as if the void had entered the ship and accompanied him in the cabin.

Again he spoke, but no sound reached his ears, nor did the internal mumble reach him from within. The sensation was not unlike being underwater, cut off from the visible world around him. It was tempting to test the silence with music from the speakers, but he had brought none. The silence of space was one of the appealing parts of the trip, but that was before sound had stopped altogether. The absence would have brought panic but there were no words inside to express the feeling. Nothing.

Was there a hull breach bringing on the early effects of hypoxia? His cognitive ability didn't seem impaired. At least he didn't think so. On to system checks then. While the problem might not be an easy fix, identifying if there was a problem at all should be standard procedure. He went about it. Nothing. As deep a nothing as that which kept his mind silent through what should have been horror.

I'm losing my mind? the words were mouthed, but again, nothing but the movement of his face.

He froze. The system checks had revealed nothing. He strained to listen. Nothing. Not even the sound of his own heartbeat. The silence was total. It was thick and unnerving. Taking a different approach, he drummed on the console. Nothing. He fingered his ear. Nothing. He roared against the silence. Nothing. No way to express the feelings that accompanied his predicament.

Internal dialog has ceased. Akin to some forms of enlightenment he had heard of, but the terror that this silence brought did not speak to any form of wellbeing, or peace. He checked the lavatory mirror to make sure that he was still there. It revealed nothing new, merely the same image he saw every time he visited the john. He thought to make a call to mission control, but the time lag would stifle any possible comfort it might bring. He did it anyway, to see if the playback might bring his voice back to life. The FFT flatlined in front of him. He could see the silence like an EEG announcing the death of a loved one.

The void had entered him. More nothingness than imaginable. He had to know why. Had to know why even amidst his non-terror that terror spoke so softly as to be silent. The void knew. It must. And if the void had entered him, did it still permeate the outside? Was the empty loneliness of space still omnipresent on the other side of the ship's thin walls? There was only one way to know for sure. Floating past his unoccupied space suit he moved to the airlock, punched in the command to vent the cabin, and entered the void, straining to hear the music of the cosmos.

A WAKE OF VULTURES

(FROM A WORK IN PROGRESS)

BY CRAIG CLEVENGER

The Starview Drive-In had screened its last feature back when aliens were still called *Martians* and came calling in hubcaps strung from fishing line. Its shuttering had been unforeseen and instant, one blustery Saturday night when teenagers had gathered to see the Earth besieged by invaders from outer space, giant grasshoppers or some such mutant horde and maybe try their luck with each other.

The wind lulled, the stars came out and the screen lit up. Two reels later, a single gale swept across the surrounding desert, its white noise roar lost to the shrill music and the screaming of thousands as the world ended. It snapped the forty-foot screen from its footing and sent it crashing downward as the moviegoers crouched behind dashboards or ran for their lives. The wreckage lay in the dirt for months until a crew patched the fence and hauled away the remains, but the Starview never re-opened.

Deputy Maya Cruz arrived code 2—lights, no siren—and pulled through the Starview's open gate to find Chief Deputy Sturgis propped against his vehicle, contemplating a dark mound before him.

"Chief."

"Deputy Cruz."

"What do we got?"

"Got us a hit-and-run with a bulldozer, looks to me like."

Dead center in the lot as though reckoned with chalklines lay their John Doe. Dungarees, denim jacket, flannel shirt, and boots all splattermarked white. Hair black as crow feathers, the color drained from his skin to a blood sheet beneath him that had thickened in the cold. The mixed splay and furl of his limbs suggested an articulated mannequin half-stuffed into a suitcase. The cooling blood held the impressions from vultures like tracks through roofing tar, but the dead man's eyes were still in tact. Not even the flies had gathered.

"You beat the scavengers."

Sturgis raked a thumbnail over his chin. "Rolled up on a wake of turkey vultures compromising the crime scene."

"Mighty decent of the vultures," said Maya, "paying their respects."

"The plural." Sturgis hadn't taken his eyes off the body. "*Flocks* are for Christians and geese. Word for vultures in the plural is *wake*."

"Well, good on you Chief, sending that wake packing."

Sturgis nodded. He never wore sunglasses—almost unheard of in the desert—but his expressions were no easier to read. "Protecting and serving," he said.

The scrappers had long ago stripped out the miles of wiring and decapitated the cast aluminum speaker boxes. Maya and Chief Sturgis presently stood over the victim amidst an orchard of barren metal posts.

"Don't see anyone getting up the speed to do this kind of damage," Maya said. "Not with this kind of obstacle course."

"Guess my bulldozer comment was not apparent as sarcasm."

"No, Chief. I got it."

"Any kind of hit and run," Sturgis said, "there ought to be tracks. Not top speed but fast enough to do him in. Something like that's liable to leave drag marks and bloody treads leading out of here."

Maya said, "Hair's clean."

"If you don't count the brain matter."

"Thinking there's a hat someplace."

"There been a hat, it's someone's trophy," said Sturgis. "Reckon a small group with tire irons and baseball bats and what have you."

"Or he just fell from the sky." Maya surveyed the lot, the asphalt pocked and pitted like a warzone airstrip, arrow-weeds sprouting from the cracked footing around the playground.

"Already checked it." Sturgis caught her eyeballing the concession stand. "Place is boarded-up to withstand a wrecking ball."

Taggers had covered the Snak-Shak's cinderblock face with a likeness of the burned-out Starview neon that read, *Starve, You.*

"Main entrance was wide open," Maya said.

"Gate was propped shut with a couple-three bricks when I got here. Found this." Sturgis held up a twist of dark metal and lobbed it to Maya. A severed link of heavy-duty chain caked with rust. "Used bolt cutters, I guess, but it ain't recent."

Maya tossed it back and brushed the oxide dust from her fingers then looked overhead. "Thrown out of a plane I'd say, except his hands aren't bound."

"My guess, man was a laborer." Sturgis eyed the deceased. "No jewelry. Boots worn to Hell and back. Don't look like cartel material."

"Suppose a wallet with a current driver's license would be too easy."

"You suppose right. And that shit all over him, it's all white. No color, so I doubt it's paint. Might ought to ask around, see about any drywall crews. Visit the usual labor pickup spots."

"Not a lot of talkers in those places."

"Nope." Sturgis showed no urgency, no hint of any action beyond contemplating the dead man and relaying his cursory observations to Maya.

"ETA?" she said.

"On what?"

"A van. The M.E. Techs on scene."

"This your first, Deputy Cruz?"

"No, sir."

"How many of them you work, had teams in moon suits, picking over the site with tweezers?"

"We searched for evidence, Chief, with more than two people. Like a crime scene." Maya took a breath and said, "Sorry. I was out of line, sir."

"Crime scene, then." Sturgis scratched his chin again. "Reckon we might out to radio for the coroner's transport, but we'll have to make due with just the two of us with the tweezers."

Chief Deputy Sturgis radioed for the Deputy-Coroner's van while Maya rifled her gear bag for a camera. She checked the date and time were set then circled the ragdoll John doe twice before divining her first shot. She photographed the deceased while Sturgis diagrammed the scene on a pad of graph paper.

"Last time we had any real wind?" Maya said.

"Been a couple-three weeks. Ball-shrinking cold, maybe a breeze, about all."

"Should be a hat here, somewhere. Whatever stained our man's clothes here, it's everywhere but his head."

They canvassed the Snak-Shak exterior and the crumbling, front entry ticket booth. Maya shined her light through the open door, onto a fog of cobwebs and bales of faded one-sheet programs. The metal stairs outside the projection booth had nothing securing them to the building and no concrete footings. Sturgis tugged at the railing and the whole fixture shifted. They climbed slowly. Up top, Maya tested the handle and the door collapsed inward, dust clouds billowing about a solitary folding chair inside. They canvassed the lot to the fences, searched the playground that had devolved to rubble and rust. They found bobcat prints, coyote scat and a sidewinder's drag marks but no blood, no tire tracks or footprints to cast, nothing to bag and no hat.

"Don't suppose the DEA will snatch this one up," Maya said.

"Ain't a drug murder."

"Ain't a bar fight."

"Reckon not," said Sturgis.

"We'll see what the M.E. says. Still got to run prints and check Missing Persons."

"You understand, he might be illegal. Won't be in the databases."

"I understand," said Maya. "But we shouldn't assume he's undocumented before that."

"Undocumented," Sturgis echoed. "'Course not."

Maya stood fixated on the tracks in the dead man's blood.

"What's on your mind, Cruz?"

"Vultures hadn't touched the body."

"They took off when I got here."

"They had an hour. And the crows would have taken the eyes before either of us got here."

"Offer you some advice, Deputy?"

"Okay."

"People die out here, lots out-of-towners who don't know any better in these parts. Don't overthink it."

"That what happens? No ID, no next of kin, we *don't overthink it*, just file it away?"

"Not much else we can do. Sometimes they just fall out of a clear blue sky."

Twin Sisters Highway peaked at thirty-eight hundred feet, two miles of twisting road glazed with black ice during the deep cold of winter. The straightaway was posted for forty and the bend for twenty, but the front-wheel coupe took them both at fifty and the driver woke spit-coughing airbag cornstarch, squinting through the sting of blood and powder at the road he'd left behind. A Highway Patrol officer determined the spin-out had caused no lane obstruction, property damage or serious injury, so she'd issued a citation and went on her way.

Forty-five minutes later, Slim's flatbed idled on the shoulder while he crouched in the the thin layer of snow for a view of the stranded coupe's undercarriage. His four bull terriers waited impatiently inside the cab. They were the cast and sheen of raw hematite and left muzzle smears on the window as they jockeyed for an eyeline on their owner. After he spied the snapped rear axel, Slim figured then he might ought to let the rabble loose to do their business. Maybe they'd simmer down and let him better assess things.

He opened the passenger door and John, Paul, George and Ringo burst forth like joyous and drooling canon fire to root about for a spot to relieve themselves.

Soon all four had their snouts pointed to the same patch of snow, Ringo sniffing and his brothers howling. Slim set the winch cable down to see what the fuss was about. The dogs had circled what was maybe a large knuckle of root wood, looked almost like a dark-skinned elbow. He stepped closer and something shifted beneath his boot, the ground not quite giving to his weight. When Slim reached for the apparent chunk of wood breaking through and spooking his dogs, he wished right then he'd been wearing gloves.

Jane Doe lay spread in the snow and dirt as though her bones had spontaneously uncoupled before she was thrown from a speeding truck. A wizened black woman in her late sixties, she'd been ill-dressed for the cold. Lowtop basketball shoes and a feeble housedress the color of dandelions. The snow had fallen between four and seven that morning, enough to conceal the tiny figure. But for the spun-out rental car, Slim and his dogs, there were no tire tracks or footprints. The Twin Sisters, a pair of massive boulders shadowing the bend, stood a full twenty yards from the Jane Doe who'd been long past fit for rock climbing when she was alive.

"Driver is one Douglass Bower," said Chief Sturgis. "Sober, no record. Doing some kind of coffee table book, out here taking photos of abandoned shacks or something. He said, quote, *I saw the reflection, I think, but thought it was a mirage*, unquote. Guy takes pictures for a living, doesn't know how light works."

"Our friend?" Maya said.

"Slim's rattled pretty bad. He'll need some time."

Maya photographed. Chief Sturgis sketched. The medics loaded Jane Doe into the Coroner's van and Slim hoisted Douglass Bower's car onto his flatbed, tipping an imaginary hat to Maya as he drove off.

Tobacco-stain light of late afternoon winter. *STARVIEW* splashed across a monster jet wing arrowhead, the letters trimmed in dead neon the color of cataracts. Crows perched above the entrance sounded a warning of Maya's intrusion and the others within the drive-in's fence called back.

John Doe had cratered the asphalt a good two inches, most of his blood draining into the cracks. Fresh bobcat prints had gummed about the edges and faded toward the dirt, the remaining pool still viscous from the cold. Insects struggled against the surface, here and there a thrumming wing or twitching leg. A prehistoric tar pit in miniature.

The few day laborers who hadn't gone frozen and mute at the sight of her in uniform told her nothing. They shook their heads and crossed themselves when shown the photograph but nobody had recognized John Doe.

Binoculars in hand, Maya left the blood and bobcat prints and crossed the lot, back through the main gate. She glassed the pale flatlands to the north in a slow arch. A pair of jackrabbits like miniature donkeys standing frozen and alert, then bounding away. A tarantula crawling underwater-slow among the rattleweed shrubs and screwcap oil cans gone red-black with rust. More of the same when she searched east. The sun was too low to stare into the west so she walked to the south side of the drive-in while she still had light.

She stepped through remnants of the collapsed projection screen, scraps of old footing and the hastily built fence. Across the two-lane highway, Maya hiked out beyond the utility lines where she scanned another wide arc over the landscape to the south. Empty shotgun shells, green and red plastic paled by the sun. A small half-ribcage stripped of flesh and color.

A hazy shock of blood-orange.

She scrolled with her middle finger, adjusted focus. Something like a scrap of safety vest, too bright to have been exposed to the elements for long. The sun sank further. Maya walked into the desert.

The orange billcap had snagged on a flap of beavertail cactus, the surrounding dirt undisturbed but for the ground squirrel scratch marks. The sun was sinking into the horizon, the sky still the color of a dying fire but everything on the ground thrown into shadow. Maya pried the cap free from the cactus spines then held it beneath her flashlight. No blood or teeth marks. It held shape without the stiffness of prolonged rain and sun, its color still bright and uniform but for the hardened white splatters on the outside. Same as those on John Doe's clothing. She hastily carved a stake from a shoot of greasewood and drove it into the ground with her boot heel.

Back at the drive-in, Maya dropped the orange cap onto her front seat. All evidence indicated John Doe had either walked a full day or more to throw himself against the pavement hard enough to shatter his own skeleton and rupture his every internal organ, or had materialized in the clouds out of nowhere before plummeting to his death.

The remaining band of blue to the west had darkened to a cloudless new moon, and there was no telling the sky from the earth but for the stars abruptly stopping. Darkness swallowed the marker where the bright orange billcap had touched down, almost a mile outside the Starview's eleven-foot fence. Maya pondered how far a skydiver drifts when falling, how long a meteor drops before catching fire and bursting apart midair.

1974 MONTE CARLO
BY TREVOR HOLLIDAY

Tawny was given the name Ellen when she was born. She took the name Tawny when she left Apache Junction, Arizona. After learning the palm reading trade in Tucson from a full-blooded gypsy woman named Dolores, Tawny never looked back. Tawny, of course, had read a few books about palm reading and astrology before coming to Tucson, but working for Dolores felt like a graduate level course.

Dolores told Tawny she personally was pessimistic about the future. Dolores said the fortune telling industry faced too much competition from 900-line psychics who were ruining what used to be a fairly dependable business back when Dolores started out.

Before she taught her any of her secrets, Dolores made Tawny promise she would not go the psychic hot-line route, no matter what financial incentives she might be offered. The secret to palmistry, Dolores said, once you've learned as much as you could about the lines on the left and right hands, was return business. Dolores said above all else, you had to build rapport with your customer.

"Build rapport and your customers eat out of the palm of your hand, honey, and the pun *is* intended," Dolores said. "Build up their trust. They'll keep coming back. You don't need to make up nothing after that."

"Rapport," Tawny said.

"That and get yourself some business cards. You'll be surprised how handy they are for repeat business."

Dolores's place was near the highway and she had a big hand-painted sign out front offering live psychic advice. Tawny walked in asking for a job, but not really expecting much. Dolores said she must have caught her on the right day.

Dolores had Tawny sit down in the chair across from her. Staring at Tawny's high cheekbones, Dolores recognized raw potential in Tawny combined with exotic good looks.

"You look like a very young Cher, even before she met Sonny Bono," Dolores said. This was after Dolores had hired Tawny, and they were just talking. Dolores was a big Cher fan and knew all about the singer's rise to fame. "I mean, we're talking about back when she was just plain-old Cherilyn Sarkisian from El Centro, California."

***

Tawny met Earl by accident in early fall soon after she arrived in Tucson and after she started working with Dolores. Tawny was supposed to meet a guy named Ray at a U-tote-M on Speedway. She'd met Ray out at a club on Miracle Mile the night before, but Ray never made it to the U-tote-M store. Tawny didn't tell Dolores about either of the men because what Tawny did on her own time was her own business and none of Dolores's affair.

Tawny was hitchhiking back home from the U-tote-M when Earl picked her up and gave her a ride back to her place in his yellow Cordoba. She had been bummed about Ray not showing up and even though she'd gotten the job with Dolores and she was learning a lot, before Earl picked her up Tawny was considering leaving town. If anybody had asked her, Tawny would have said both Dolores and Earl restored some of her faith in humanity.

Earl was a little older than Tawny, but neither of them minded. He dressed nice, wearing a lime green sport coat that day with the sleeves pushed up. She gave Earl one of her new cards and the next day Earl came and met her at work.

Dolores liked Earl and said she would steal Earl away if Tawny wasn't careful.

Earl let Tawny drive his car. Tawny really did know how to drive. She wouldn't have made it a day in Apache Junction if she hadn't had *something* to do and what she'd done up there was drive her uncle's El Camino out into the desert. Her uncle didn't mind until she'd blown out the engine by not paying attention to the oil level and even then he didn't mind very much because he was out of town for a few weeks. By the time he got back, Tawny had left Apache Junction.

***

Earl met a man named Troy at the Crazy Horse and they started talking. Troy had not been in town long. He came from Indiana and he wasn't sure how he felt about the desert heat yet.

"This is nothing," Earl said. "You missed the summer."

The two men talked for a long time. It turned out they had common interests and they agreed they would probably run into one another again.

Earl brought Tawny with him to the Crazy Horse the next night. She got on the *Pinball Wizard* pinball machine and was racking up replays so she didn't see Troy when he first scootched down next to Earl.

Earl had been thinking. He liked Troy's company but he wasn't sure how much time he wanted to spend with Troy. Earl had a feeling Troy could cause problems on account of his youthfulness and his habit of jabbering. Still, Earl more or less enjoyed talking with Troy.

Troy had gotten the idea Earl had a vast criminal past. Flattered, Earl did not disabuse him of the notion.

While Tawny played pinball, Troy and Earl continued their conversation.

Troy asked Earl what kind of businesses were the best targets for a stick up.

Just hypothetically, and not out of the clear blue like that. The two of them had been talking for a while, gradually increasing their familiarity with one another.

Earl answered seriously.

He said bowling alleys and some dry cleaners. He emphasized *some*. Not all, of course. As long as you were careful about what you were doing and followed an established script. If you did such a thing, and he was still a long way from recommending it, you had to follow a script.

Troy nodded seriously. Treating every one of Earl's words with respect.

By this time, Tawny had grown sick of the pinball. There was only so much of the game she could take. She'd heard the last part of the conversation. Earl hadn't meant for her to hear any of it.

Tawny said she could do the driving.

"Just like Bonnie and Clyde, right?"

Earl shook his head.

"No," he said. "Bonnie and Clyde let themselves get too greedy. Sprees aren't good. You do a job here and there maybe you end up all right. But then again, there's never any guarantee. And no banks, for crying out loud."

Earl was now speaking with authority. As if he knew what he was talking about.

"Jeez," Tawny said. "Nobody would've heard of Bonnie and Clyde except for the banks, would they?"

"They would've been a lot better off if nobody had ever heard of them," Earl said. "You pay attention to the last part of that movie? You don't get to live long with a legendary status."

***

The next night they were back at the Crazy Horse Saloon. Earl didn't really want to go there this night as much as Tawny.

Troy came in excited. He told Earl and Tawny about the car. This was the second evening the three of them were together and now Earl was caught up in the enthusiasm. Earl was having a good time and even he had to admit it.

Troy's big news was he had lifted a particular car which would be perfect for what they had in mind.

Earl shook his head. He reminded Troy that everything they had talked about so far had been in a hypothetical sense. They were only playing a game of make-believe.

Troy said sure, but the car he got was real. There was nothing hypothetical about the car.

They finished up at the Crazy Horse. Tawny wanted to see the car.

"Why not, Earl?" Tawny said. "You've been talking about all this with Troy and me like you're the big expert."

"Yeah, Earl," Troy said. "Why not? Let's go look at the car, anyway."

"Whoa, Nelly," Earl said. "Hold the phone. We're not at that stage of the game yet. We're still in the talking-about-it stage. We're not nearly close to the two-to-get-ready part. You two both need to hold your horses."

"It's three-to-get-ready, Earl," Troy said. "Just so you know. Then it's four to go."

"Well," Earl said, "we're not there yet either."

***

The car was a 1974 Monte Carlo 400 Turbo Fire V8.

Troy had stashed it behind a Dunkin' Donuts on North First Avenue.

Tawny wanted to take the car up Mount Lemmon. Why not?

"I threw a tarp over it," Troy said. "One of those blue tarps that got the grommets on the corners? I got it held down with six cinder blocks I found down the alley. Well, technically five cinder blocks. I looked for a sixth but I couldn't find one. But even like that, nobody's gonna mess with it. I'll bring it up you can see for yourself."

Earl was reluctant.

"I bet nobody figured that car was gonna get messed with before, right?"

Troy shook his head.

"That's not the same thing," he said.

"Is this car red by any chance?" Earl said. "I used to have a red Monte Carlo, matter of fact."

"Unh-uh," Troy said. "Who do you think I am? I wouldn't touch one of those if it was red. Too high profile. Red's a cop magnet. This one was up on Limberlost Road. You know where that's at? It's over near Campbell. There's a trailer park with a sign showing a cactus and some kinda wagon wheel. The car itself is tan with a brown landau roof."

"Next you're gonna tell me tan's a good color for the desert," Earl said. "And then I'll bet you're gonna tell me it's got wire rims."

Troy nodded. Grinned.

"I lived near the Limberlost Swamp when I lived back in Indiana," Troy said. "Lotta people aren't aware how swampy Indiana is. Two hundred years ago, mosta the whole Hoosier State was swamp. That's why I was surprised to see a street called Limberlost when I got down here in the desert. Honest, I didn't expect to see that."

Earl looked at Tawny.

"Wire wheels no less."

Earl said the car was probably too flashy but he would keep an open mind.

Before they went to see the car, Tawny made Earl stop at Walgreens for a bottle of red wine. They all got out of Earl's car and Troy and Earl smoked cigarettes while Tawny went in.

Earl looked at Troy.

"I don't have to worry about you and Tawny, do I?"

Troy was tapping his foot and looking at the Walgreens.

"Unh-uh, Earl," he said. "I got a girl coming down next month from Indiana. Soon as she finishes up all her coursework she's coming down."

"Good," Earl said. "That's good."

Tawny was signaling from the door of Walgreens.

"Hey," Troy said, "She wants us to go in there."

Tawny steered the three of them into a photo booth. A few minutes later the machine spit out two strips of black and white pictures. All the pictures of Tawny and Troy looked different, but in each shot, Earl was on the side, glowering.

When Troy showed Earl and Tawny the car, Tawny got behind the wheel like she owned it.

"Oh, this is nice, Troy," she said. "Earl, isn't this a nice car?"

***

With Tawny behind the wheel, Earl and Troy robbed two bowling alleys. Not on the same day. Five days apart. Earl did the talking behind his mask and Troy held a sawed-off shotgun he bought south of Broadway. Troy bought a Raven MP-25 for Earl, but Earl waved it off.

"Keep it," Earl said. "That shotgun you got is intimidating enough for what we're doing."

Troy shrugged and put the Raven in the glove compartment of the Monte Carlo.

Earl had said bowling alleys were good and reliable.

Making every word up as he went along.

He said none of the bowlers pay attention to what goes on back at the counter. Nine out of ten times you got teenagers working and for the most part casual bowlers weren't paying attention once they rented their goofy shoes and started drinking beer.

Different story on league night, Earl said. You don't want to ever do a job on league night. Those people were paying attention, jack. And most of them carried concealed weapons. That was just a fact.

Troy was impressed how well the bowling alleys went.

He followed Earl's dictum. No talking during the job. Let Earl do the talking. Troy kept quiet and kept his mask on. It was tempting to speak up, just to emphasize what Earl was saying. Amplify. But Earl knew what he was doing and Troy kept his mouth shut, even though it pained him to do so.

"Just follow the script," Earl said. Like a broken record he said it.

Troy wanted to do a third bowling lane. Maybe up in Marana. He figured Marana was far enough out of town so they wouldn't be establishing a pattern.

Earl said no.

"*Whatever* you do establishes a pattern," he said. "Don't try to get too smart. Don't get greedy. Word gets around and people figure out your pattern before you even know you got one."

Earl looked at Troy.

They were back at the Crazy Horse.

Tawny was looking at Troy's palm. Troy was trying to at least pretend he was paying attention to what Earl was saying.

"You don't think bowling people talk to each other?" Earl said. "They talk a hell of a lot among themselves if you want to know the truth. I'm not saying it's like some kind of formalized thing. I'm not saying that at all."

Neither Troy nor Tawny was listening to Earl.

"You have an interesting left hand, Troy," Tawny said. "Have you ever had your palm read?"

Earl looked at Tawny holding Troy's palm.

"All right listen up, you two," he said.

Troy pulled his hand away from Tawny, shook his head, and straightened in the vinyl seat in the back of the Crazy Horse.

Bad Company was on the jukebox.

Rock 'n' Roll Fantasy.

Here come the jesters.

"What about the dry cleaners," Troy said. "You said some of them were good."

"Dry cleaners are good for cash," Earl said, "you just gotta be careful a nut-job didn't come out of the back with a gun."

"How you gonna know something like that ahead of time?" Troy said.

"Yeah," Tawny said. "How are you gonna know something like that?"

Earl knew this one particular dry-cleaning business and he happened to know there was just one nice old lady in the place and a drawer full of cash.

"What about washaterias?" Troy said. "What about them?"

Earl looked at him.

"What is it you want? You wanna hold up a laundromat and then lug around a buncha bags of quarters? Think about it," Earl said.

"You call 'em *washaterias* up in Indiana? Laundromats?" Tawny said. "That is so cute. I swear."

"Okay fine," Troy said. "I hear you, loud and clear. But I gotta at least ask, what about banks? I mean, it's higher risk maybe, but you might get more. I mean we haven't exactly gotten rich here, have we?"

Troy was right. They had not gotten rich. They had made a grand total of seven hundred and forty-eight dollars. Earl was keeping the money for now, but they were going to split it three ways with Earl throwing in the extra two bucks to make the math easy.

"No banks," Earl said. "Ever. No banks."

"What the hell," Troy said. A pink plastic basket filled with salted peanuts in front of him. "I don't see why not. We got everything we need, Earl. Take another look at the car, wouldja. You kidding me? Why *not* do a bank?"

Troy was feeling bold on account of the success they'd had and the fact that Tawny had her hand on his leg under the table where Earl couldn't see.

Earl looked at Troy and the peanuts. Shook his head. They should never have used that car in the first place. Too flashy.

As for banks, Earl wouldn't even consider it.

"To do a bank you need another party. Can't do a bank otherwise. You wanna split the take with another party? Is that what you're telling me?"

Troy shook his head no.

"Unh-uh," Troy said.

Earl looked over at Tawny.

"What about you?"

She tightened her lips and shook her head. Rubbed Troy's leg.

"All right then," Earl said. "I guess that's it then."

"We gonna do a washateria?" Troy said.

Tawny laughed.

" *Washateria*," she said. "That is so *cute*."

***

Troy didn't like it when Earl told him they were done.

Earl had thought it over and they were done. He had been holding onto the money, but he was going to give Troy his share tonight. Tawny too, for that matter. The sooner he was done with this business, the better.

No dry cleaners, no more bowling alleys. Nothing.

Earl didn't want to come out and say it, but he knew with these two, he was pushing any luck he had. He'd come to his senses and now he was done.

***

Troy *really* didn't like it when Earl said Troy was going to have to dispose of the car. There was no sense getting sentimentally attached to an inanimate object.

"Like in this case, the car," Earl said.

"I know what an inanimate object is," Troy said. "You think I don't know that?"

"I just wanted to be clear," Earl said. "You're gonna have to ditch the car."

"What if I wanna do some more jobs myself? I can get another license plate, no problem. Same as I did the first. You go over to the university, back of those old fraternity houses? They got plates from all over. You want me to, I can switch one out any day you like."

Earl shook his head and asked Troy what the hell he was thinking.

"There's only so much luck you get in a particular vehicle and you don't want to use up your luck. You know how to wipe a car down? Get all the prints out of it?"

"Course I do," Troy said. "Maybe you'd rather have us just take it out to the desert and put the match to it. It'll burn good."

"You just wanna get out of cleaning the prints, don't you?" Earl said. "The truth is, a burned car still shows prints if anybody wants to find them. You're just gonna have to clean that car out. Wear some gloves and park it down at the airport long-term lot. Leave whatever plates you got on the car."

***

Troy was willing to accept Earl's plan, except for the airport part.

He talked it over with Tawny at the Crazy Horse Saloon.

The two of them were getting along now pretty well. As a matter of fact, he wondered what she'd been doing with Earl in the first place. Troy had Tawny's business card and he had used a pay phone to call her at her job. Troy asked Dolores if Tawny was there and after Dolores said yes, he'd waited for what seemed like twenty minutes before she came to the phone. She'd agreed to meet him at the Crazy Horse.

Earl didn't have to know anything about all this.

They each had a Schlitz and listened to *Feel Like Making Love* on the jukebox before going outside. It was still hot on Speedway, even though it was nearly the middle of the night.

Troy explained what he wanted to do about the car.

"I'm fine with ditching it," Troy said. "I just don't wanna ditch it at the airport like Earl says. I'm thinking of taking it down to Nogie. Leaving it in the Safeway parking lot down there. Take the bus back. What the hell, you know?"

"Do you believe in karma, Troy," Tawny said. "It's a real thing."

Troy shrugged.

"I dunno. I guess I never thought about it," he said. "Is that where somebody says something and you think it's happened before?"

"Unh-uh," Tawny said. "That's *déjà vu*. Kinda different."

Tawny explained the concept of karma to Troy. She rubbed his arm while she was talking to him.

"Oh yeah, yeah," he said. "What goes around comes around. I heard of that. I believe in that."

"You're what, twenty-four now?" Tawny said.

"Twenty-five in September," Troy said.

"It's time you started making decisions for yourself," she said. "You want to take that car down to Nogales, go ahead. Why not?"

"You think so?" Troy said.

"I know so," Tawny said.

"What about the money? Earl's still got it."

"Is that what you think, Troy? You haven't looked in the trunk of that car, have you? Under the spare tire?"

"He put it there?"

Tawny smiled.

"What makes you think *Earl* put it there?"

Troy looked at Tawny. She was tapping her chest.

"You serious?"

"Sure I am," she said. "You go ahead on down to Nogales. In fact, you might even be able to convince me to go down there with you."

***

By late spring, Earl was selling tickets over the phone for a hole-in-one contest sponsored by a men's club in Tucson. He was sitting at a desk in a dark room in the back of the club with four other men and two women. Earl used a script, but he wasn't sticking to it religiously.

"All you gotta do to help out? That's the easy part," Earl said. "Buy a ticket for ten dollars. Simple as that."

Receiver propped between ear and shoulder, Pall Mall going in Earl's right hand. Air conditioner going full blast in back of the club otherwise Earl would be sweating Tucson's spring heat.

Instead, Earl kept his lime green jacket on, the one Tawny used to say made him look like a praying mantis.

Earl hadn't seen Tawny for a long time and the truth was he hadn't thought about her or Troy very much.

"Better yet," Earl said, "why not pull out the long green? Buy yourself five tickets for forty bucks? Increase your odds. You got a slugger's chance of making a hole-in-one."

Earl wasn't unwilling to disclose the location of the contest or the date the contest would be held. But he didn't dwell on the details.

"Sure," he would say. "It's hole number seven. One hundred and forty-seven yards. Didn't I tell you that already? I apologize. Roadrunner Golf Course. It's near Arizona City. Listen, I play there all the time. It's what we like to call a hidden gem."

Why get into all that, though? This gig was like the Policeman's Ball. Nobody really went to the ball. Well, maybe a few couples, but they only went once. Earl wasn't selling the event. He was selling the tickets.

For the golf event, like the Policeman's Ball, everything was above board. The hole-in-one contest was part of a scramble held a good fifty minutes north of Tucson. The temperature would be hotter than hell in July, but Earl emphasized the contest was for charity.

"What we're trying to do is raise money to get some kids a trip up to Splash-a-Rama in the summer. Kids who normally might not get a chance to go."

Earl liked this part of the script. It was designed to tug at the heartstrings of the man he was pitching.

"You're a man with a big heart, I've heard," Earl would say. "They say you've got a big heart and a pocketbook to match."

And the funny thing was, it worked for Earl.

"No sir," he would say. "No reason in the world you have to field a team for the scramble. Not at all. All you gotta do is put the ball in the hole from the tee and you win twenty-two grand or a brand-new Corvette Stingray. I'm not kidding. That's all you gotta do. Hell, some holes a hundred and twenty yards is a long putt, right? Just hit her low and let her roll. No shame in that. You drive away in that Vette, you're the one laughing, right?"

Earl was calling businesses. Asking for the boss. Ask for the man who was in charge of the checkbook. Be direct.

"Stick to the script," Earl always said.

***

A guy walked into the room and tapped on Earl's desk. Discreetly. When Earl looked at up, the man held up his hand like he was telling Earl to take his time. Finish the call.

The call was a bust anyway and Earl hung up.

Phone sales is a numbers game. You gotta keep dialing.

Dial and smile.

The man held a card in one hand. He smiled. Big guy with a nice suit. White shirt and striped tie. Cop could have been written on the inside of his suit as easily as a Dillard's tag.

"You're Earl Blevins?"

Earl nodded. Reached for his pack of smokes on the corner of the table. Shook one out and lit it with a paper match.

"Gene Hanratty," the man said. "Cochise County Sheriff Department. You doing okay today, Mr. Blevins?"

"Sure," Earl said. "What can I do for you?"

"Just following up on an incident," Hanratty said. "Troy Fielder, age twenty-five. That name mean anything to you?"

"Unh-uh," Earl said. "I don't think so." Casually. "Should it?"

"Depends," Hanratty said. He flipped his badge out. Nobody else in the boiler room saw it. "How about Ellen Julie Sutton? AKA Tawny Sutton."

Earl started to say something and then stopped.

Hanratty made a motion with his head toward the front door.

"Maybe you might want to take a short break. Come on outside with me."

Earl stood up. With his cigarette dangling he took the green jacket off and hung it on the back of his chair. Walked out of the building and onto the sun-drenched sidewalk outside the men's club.

"Those names don't mean anything to me," Earl said.

Hanratty looked at Earl and shrugged.

"That may well be," he said. "Fielder's body was found a few days ago out near Dragoon. You know where that is? We found him behind the driver's wheel of a Chevy. This was in one of those canyons outside town. Hardly anyone goes out there, but sure enough, a couple of old timers were doing some prospecting. Looking for gold, I guess, but they found Fielder. We can only speculate about the time of death because there was a pretty advanced state of decomposition in place. Cause was simple. Couple gunshots to the head with a low-caliber firearm. Coulda been months since the event, though. Ugly scene."

Earl raised his eyebrows.

"Sounds bad," he said. "What's this got to do with me?"

"Maybe nothing," Hanratty said. "Maybe nothing, maybe something. I don't know."

He reached into his shirt pocket. Pulled out a strip of pictures.

"Found this in Fielder's wallet. Not much else in it other than an out-of-date Indiana driver's license. I keep thinking about that song, you know? *Indiana Wants Me.* Just that and a card for a fortune teller. Oh, and some money in the trunk."

He held the strip of black and white pictures in front of Earl. Troy, Tawny, and Earl, stuffed in the photo booth.

"I took a long shot and visited the fortune teller. Woman way out on Speedway by the name of Dolores. Interesting gal. She identified the girl and said you two were friends. Gave me your name and I tracked you down here. Had to do some detective work for that."

"Well yeah, I guess you did," Earl said. "Matter of fact, me and the girl *were* acquainted, but it was just one of those things. The name you said doesn't ring a bell with me. I guess I never knew the man's name. He said it was something else when I met him. Butch or Buck, or something like that. I forget. That night the picture got taken? That was the only time we met."

Hanratty nodded. Pointed at Earl's scowling face almost out of the frame.

"Looks like you weren't having the best time of your life, that night."

"Guess not," Earl said. "She took off with him and tell you the truth, I'm probably better off for it."

"Okay," Hanratty said. "I just wanted to let you know. In case you and the man were personal relatives or anything. You never know, right? I'm following up on everything. That's what I do."

"Right," Earl said. "You never know."

Hanratty looked at Earl. Giving away nothing.

"I just wondered," he said. "You know anything about any criminal activity these two might have been involved in? The reason I ask is we believe Mr. Fielder and Miss Sutton perpetrated a string of bank robberies south of here. Douglas, Benson, Willcox. Took over twenty grand. There was a shotgun in the back of the car that matches the bank's descriptions. The money we found in the car was a little over seven hundred dollars. Down under the spare tire. Tell you the truth, it looks to me like a case of love gone wrong. Twenty thousand dollars is a lot of money."

Earl shook his head. He felt his breath grow small in his chest.

"I don't know anything about that," he said.

Hanratty nodded and handed Earl a card.

"Well, I didn't expect you would," he said. "But if you have more to say, just give me a jingle.

Earl watched Hanratty leave.

Everything had turned white on the sidewalk from the blazing sun.

He needed to get back inside the dark room with the phones.

ZOMBIE WASPS FROM HELL!
BY PATRICK R. MCDONOUGH

Ken Valentine adored bugs. When asked what he wanted to be when he grew up, he'd say an entomologist. Adults always acted like that was an inconceivable word for an eight-year-old. As if they were too old to remember when they were his age. He wasn't some dumb little baby that didn't know words bigger than "dog", "bug", or "fart".

He knew naughty three- and four-letter words, too. Like "ass," "taint," "shit," and "clit."

Those he learned from the latest issue of *Bug Horror!* His most favorite magazine at Roach's Groceries, where it always waited patiently, snug between copies of *Fangoria, Playboy,* and some dumb sports rags. When Ken and his mother did their weekly shopping, he'd race to the magazine aisle, pull up the latest *Playboy,* wonder what exactly a bunny woman was—he wondered if it was some kind of beautiful were-rabbit—then grab the latest issue of *Bug Horror!*

Every issue was full of bug facts (sometimes new discoveries on plant and insect life), horror and Sci-Fi short stories, and articles covering old creature features from when his parents were his age. But the thing he loved the most, the reason his heart raced like a jack rabbit escaping the mighty jaws of a predator, was to get to the mail order section.

"So cool!" Ken shouted, as he jumped up and down in excitement, magazine in both hands. He didn't care about the group of stupid kids walking by snickering, or the fat, bald grocery clerk watching him in curiosity. What the magazine offered was what got him through the tough times.

"Kenneth," said Mom. Her voice crawled through his ear canal like an earwig. She had that effect on him. Any time she spoke, he felt the drag of an invisible earwig's claw-like forceps rake and tickle, tickle and prick, until it reached his brain. That grating voice had a way of ratcheting up his nerves and twisting his anxiety into a tight thorny ball that anchored in the pit of his stomach.

He looked up from his magazine and said, "Yeah, Mom?"

She looked at him with her usual narrowed eyes of disappointment, encased in angry wrinkles she called crow's feet. "If you want that weird magazine, then put it in the cart and let's go. Now." Talking to him like a helpless puppy only tightened that thorny-gut ball, and the grip on the one good thing he had in this world.

***

Ken stared at his magazine for the entire drive back home, as he did every week from Roach's. The van's air freshener was an overbearing scent of an unidentifiable flower, and the windows in the rear only moved sideways (not up and down) by a few inches, making it impossible to properly vent. To make things worse, Mom's music stunk. He'd rather listen to a turd dribble out the backside of a turtle shell, than his parents "classic rock." They listened to that sound-garbage when they worked on their art. Mom is an illustrator for children's books and Dad is a novelist, which meant they were always off in other worlds, trapped in their own heads, never paying attention to Ken or spending time together as a family. On the flip side, it also meant they didn't care *that much* what Ken watched, read, or played, so long as he explored his creative side.

When they got together, usually it was over a meal. Talk was always challenging for all involved. Ken didn't enjoy talking to them, because they wanted him to be an artist. A little reflection of them. Ken wouldn't budge for a single second from his ardent interest in bugs, though.

That all said, Mom was fine with him reading *Bug Horror!* so long as he read the fictional stories in it. Dad, on the other hand, protested. At first. Dad didn't write that type of "senseless crap"—his words, not Ken's. Dad wished he would read a science fiction or adventure paperback like he did at Ken's age.

Mom said it was better than nothing and the conversation ended there. Ken didn't care all that much about the fictional stuff. The fiction writers could never seem to capture the insanely fascinating details like the articles on real bugs could, or excite him like the descriptions for the mail order items.

Ken waited until dinnertime to look at the mail-in items. Something to look forward to. Scrolled across the top of the page was the most exciting thing he had ever seen: *Zombie Wasps From Hell!* Radioactive green dripped from the tar-black font. It reminded Ken of bug guts. Beneath that, the price and a description wrapped around a white oval—a wasp egg. For the low-low price of $19.99 *plus* shipping and handling Ken could make his new obsession a reality.

A bag full of undead zombie wasp eggs! Can you bring them back to life? Can you create your own undead zombie wasp army? We can show you how! Instructions sent along with eggs upon receipt of purchase.

His eyes raced over the lines again, and again, and again, thinking about how cool it would be to watch them hatch. How they'd look up at him with their faceted eyes and know he was their Daddy.

Their commander.

What excited him the most though, was having his zombie wasps eliminate the two people that made him feel like he didn't belong.

***

Two weeks after placing the order by phone, an inconspicuous manilla envelope showed up on his doorstep. Ken grabbed the package and locked himself in his bedroom. Posters of his favorite bugs, an award he won in a science fair, and a row of *Bug Horror!* covers lined his walls. His parents decorated every other room in zany and colorful patterns and schemes. Even Ken's room was a misfit. His time of being outnumbered was coming to an end.

Secured in three plastic vials were a few dozen wasp eggs, not even the size of a pinky nail. The vial covers were bound with a piece of black electrical tape for extra security.

The instructions were on a single-sided sheet of paper.

One Simple Step To Grow Your Zombie Wasps From Hell!

1 – Plant the eggs in a warm place. Give plenty of water.

Enjoy your ZOMBIE WASPS FROM HELL!

A warm place. Hmmm. It didn't take more than a few seconds for him to come to the obvious conclusion.

***

When they weren't creating art, Mom was usually flipping through some art magazine, while Dad had his nose in a Don Winslow or Robert B. Parker paperback. What type of artist Ken would be when he's older, which agencies could help get his foot in certain big publishing houses, and how he'd end up with a beautiful art beauty, just like Dad, it all looped in his mind, which usually just built up his anxiety. Not today. Today, all those feelings and disregard for who he was as a person was being pressed tightly behind a forced smile and a fluttering heart.

Ken got permission to make his parents breakfast, and the laugh begging to break out almost felt orgasmic. The bacon wasn't hard to cook until the grease sizzled and popped, burning his flesh with hot shrapnel. He imagined that's what the acid from a bombardier beetle felt like. The burning sensation made him smile. Made his balls tingle. Next came the scrambled eggs with cheese. He poured three vials into a bowl, mixing the ingredients into a gooey yellow mess. He grabbed the other two vials and mixed those as well. They cooked fast and then they were loaded onto his parents' plates evenly. Ken stuck to bacon, toast, and cereal.

He kept thinking about the instructions and how they told him to keep the eggs in a warm place which led to the inevitable thought process that the inside of a human body is plenty warm to act as an incubator. Right? Sometimes his poop was hot. And the insides of bodies are wet. That's all the instructions called for. Warm and wet.

***

Coming home from school, Ken expected vibrating walls from Ozzy Osbourne or Robert Plant screaming their ass off, shaking the movie posters and Mom's framed artwork that she so proudly pointed out every time they had guests over. To Ken's surprise, the house was quiet. No sounds to push the durability limits of his eardrums. In fact, it was so quiet that he heard a moan from both the upstairs and downstairs bathroom.

"Mom?" he said, looking up the staircase. "Dad?"

He found Dad in the downstairs bathroom; door wide open because the family mantra was they didn't believe in hiding during the natural process of taking a dump or leak. An acrid smell punched Ken in the nose and settled on the roof of his mouth. Vomit covered Dad's hand that clutched the toilet tank, while his finger flicked the handle, trying to flush away his clumpy wet mess. Ken's stomach twirled, forcing him to step back until he reached the bottom of the stairs. A few feet separated the top step from the bathroom. It sounded like Mom was dealing with the same thing as Dad. That made Ken smile. The smile quickly turned into concern. He had to make sure she wasn't puking up the eggs.

Mom's slurred words crashed into each other like drunkards trying to smash private parts. As Ken approached the threshold of the bathroom, he could only make out four words. "Puke... bugs... squirming inside." That's all she said, and then stuck three fingers down her throat, releasing a waterfall of red-tinged fluids. Her head fell back like an unbalanced newborn, and she landed on her side.

Ken waited, studying the hitch in her chest. When he walked over to the toilet and studied the aftermath, his smile returned.

There were no tiny white floaters.

***

Another day passed, only this time, Mom and Dad were no longer in either bathroom. They must've slunk out in the middle of the night. Nobody cleaned them, so Ken treated those two rooms like a crime scene and stayed the fuck away. When he heard them scream for the first time, he allowed that trapped laughter to finally escape.

He made his way to his parent's room. No noise. When he peeked in, the musky smell of piss and shit greeted him. Neither one turned their head to look at him. Their arms rested on their sides, pushed outward slightly from a chicken-egg bump in their armpits.

He'd come back later to check on things.

***

In the middle of the following night, his parents' bloody screams ripped Ken out of a deep sleep. He could hear buzzing from the other side of the door before he entered his parents' bedroom.

Flaps of slime matted flesh and opened paperbacks littered the carpeted floor. Ken could barely make out the Ronald Kelly on one of the book's spines. Strips of skin hung from a hole in Dad's right cheek. Wasp eggs filled the inside of his mouth like a hamster's cheek. Running out from the eggs was a network of translucent fibers, draped down his neck, shoulders, and chest.

A black needle-like leg punched through one of the eggshells.

One of the zombie wasps buzzed in Ken's ear, he swatted out of instinct, and watched its iridescent torso and beautiful reflective wings trail away in afterimages. A burst of pain exploded in the nape of his neck. A chill expanded from the injection, his heart thrashed, and for the first time, he thought that maybe this wasn't such a good plan after all.

"Dad!" Ken said, shaking him. Dad and Mom wouldn't budge. One of the bugs pulled its stinger out of Dad's neck. A few more swarmed to the open wound, fighting over the leaking juices like thumb-sized raptors.

Ken screamed in pain as the stinger in his neck pulsed. He reached back and grabbed the insect in a clenched fist. It bit the inside of his thumb. Ken slammed his palm against the drywall splatting its clumpy, sapphire guts over a framed piece of art Mom fancied. Zombie wasps circled Ken like a helpless seal in the middle of Orca-infested waters. His hand swatted and connected with one, while another nibbled on his ear. Ken ran out of the room and straight into the bathroom across the hallway.

He could barely catch his breath, staring at his own reflection in the mirror. He closed his eyes, and all he could see was their death-dark face with jaws longer than its body. Jaws that did not stop clacking. Chomping. Hungry, oh so hungry for a warm and wet meal.

"I'm a warm and wet meal," said Ken.

His eyelids opened halfway, and then slammed shut. The wasps were winning. Their venom was bringing on this fatigue. But it was a good feeling. It reminded him that he needed this sleep. His fingers brushed the base of the stinger protruding from his neck. It sent a jitter through his nerves. The thing about the stinger, though, was it calmed his mind, forcing a smile in the corner of his mouth. While the physical effects of the venom pumping through him numbed the point of contact, what spread throughout the rest of his body, mind, and soul, was euphoria.

He had no reason to pull the stinger out. Had no reason to bother the wasp still gnawing at his ear. Eat well, little buddy. Ken hadn't the slightest compulsion to do anything but listen to flesh tear away. He felt the others crawling over him, slurping, and gnawing with their demonic mandibles.

"I'll be good to my babies. I'll be a good daddy."

Hot blood dribbled down his neck. His skull felt like it was filled with helium, creating the physical sensation of floating like his children. The new Ken enjoyed witnessing all these marvelous sensations. Like the wasps sinking their pointy ridged teeth throughout his body, filling their stomach with his nutrients.

Ken would leave this place when the wasps were ready. Every movement and every thought moved sloth-slow, yet it was the most tranquil experience of his short life. Without understanding why, he began to lick himself. It felt good. It felt right. When another wasp landed on the top of his skull, he smiled at its reflection in the mirror. He thought he raised a hand to wave but realized both arms dangled by their sides.

Thin sticks marched over his tongue and down his throat, he wanted to close his mouth but didn't. Ken couldn't remember opening his mouth, but he had to have at some point, right?

His reflection showed an open mouth welcoming eager wasps to enter. To feed on more wet and warm meat. Some dug underneath his tongue, while two others created a hole through his right cheek. One chode of a wasp forced its way up a nostril, tunneling until it joined the others down the esophagus. Pain signals were in overdrive, but tingling, biting, shredding, and tearing only caused him to laugh. Tears shed, but he wasn't sad, this was some kind of sick new thrill.

The feasting wasps tugged him by the ear until he was out of the bathroom, guiding him like a lazy dog on a leash. Ken's legs zombie-lumbered forward. The bugs pulled at his arms, contorting every motion to open the bedroom door, and when his legs didn't seem to work any longer, the wasps sunk their razor teeth into his knees and manipulated those too.

Look at me now, Mom and Dad! You're both dead and I'm a meat puppet!

The soft carpet felt nice on the soles of his feet. They forced him in his bedroom, in the corner, releasing him to join his pile of bug plushies. Somewhere in the back of his mind, a voice questioned if he'd ever be able to feel their soft hugs again.

One wasp landed on his limp hand. Ken's head lolled to see it crawl up his thin bicep and force its way underneath his armpit. Another skittered behind his left knee, while a third forced its way behind the other knee. Ken knew what they were doing, and part of him wanted to ask them to stay a while and talk, but they weren't interested in that. They made their way out of their skin flap egresses.

Ken heard them make their way to the screen window. It only took a few moments before the horde of buzzing made its way to the neighbor's home. He wondered if his zombie wasps from hell would kill their newborn and puppy.

***

Two hours later, he registered the sound of hatching. He *felt* it behind his knees, in his chest, and in the back of his head. The larvae moved with the agility of a slug. The first one that appeared in view had a snow-white maggot torso with a pitch-black head and tiny clacking mandibles. A secretion oozed out of its mouth, When it moved, he felt they had too many legs to count, it didn't make sense.

It was hungry, like a little vampiric parasite. They feasted on Ken's eye's first, then his nose, lips, and what remained of his ears and fingers. He wondered why there was no longer pain.

It took a few days for the baby zombies to pick away at most of the fat, flesh, and muscle. They too eventually left him—a mutilated abomination, so hollowed out that there wasn't a single laid egg in him.. He sat in the soiled mess he left a few days prior, and soon, the flies came.

Ken didn't care for the flies. They weren't *his*. He missed his little zombie wasps and wondered what they were doing now. If they missed him too.

Why would the things he brought into this world, the things he considered his children, do this to him? Did they know what they were doing? Were they even sorry for killing him? Did they not love him?

His door opened, and Ken felt floorboards give way to something ambling toward him. Breathing grated whatever was left of his ears. He didn't need eyes to know what stood next to him.

"Kenneth," said Mom. "We... missed you."

Arms wrapped around him, picked him up, and they left his room.

"Your father..., " it took great effort to spit out two words at a time for her. "Can't speak." His father's arms were hard, rough, boney, yet... comforting. "No tongue."

"What..., " Ken tried to say. His tongue lolled from his mouth. It wasn't easy to speak. "What happened?"

Mom's harsh voice returned, only, that irritating tickle he always felt wasn't the same. It wasn't annoyance, wasn't excitement. "New life... " Mom sucked in a death rattle, and coughed up, "together."

That feeling...it was happiness.

DEAD GANGSTERS

BY JIM RULAND

"She was such a liar."

It's true, my mother was an incredible liar, particularly toward the end of her life, but that's not why Lisa's upset.

We're sitting around the dining room table of my mother's house in Brooklyn, sorting through boxes of her belongings. Someone found her favorite CD—a compilation of Ruthie Morrissey songs—and put it on. We'd spent the day going through closets, dragging boxes out of the attic, figuring out what to do with all the stuff she'd accumulated. Now we're drinking tea spiked with honey and Irish whiskey.

Shortly after her diagnosis my mother said her greatest wish was to go back to the Emerald Isle. We pounced on this.

"You've never been to Ireland!" we reminded her, but she insisted she went to Ireland between marriages to her first and second husbands, which was news to us, her three children.

"Liar's too harsh," Frankie says. "I prefer the term 'fabulist.'"

Frankie flew in from San Jose with his wife and two children. Frankie was the only child from my mother's marriage to her first husband, who died in Vietnam and never laid eyes on his son, though Frankie once told me he dreams about him all the time.

"Bullshit," Lisa says, splashing Jameson's into her empty teacup. "Nothing she said was reliable. Nothing!"

We are all getting a little buzzed, but Frankie and I can't keep up with Lisa, a Washington, D.C. attorney and the self-described alpha bitch of the family. With Frankie in California, she's the one who organizes our family gatherings and is in charge of mom's finances.

"What do *you* think?" Lisa asks me.

I'm the youngest, the only one who stayed in Brooklyn. I was my mother's caretaker through her long illness. I was the one who sat with her while she took her last breath.

My siblings aren't in the habit of asking my opinion, but now they're full of questions, most of which they already know the answers to:

Was she in pain?

Did she pass quickly?

They never ask about my father. I'm his caretaker, too.

"It's not like she was hurting anyone," I say.

"The woman lied about everything!" Lisa insists. "Books she'd read. Movies she'd seen. Who does that?"

That wasn't true. She didn't lie about *everything*. She never embellished the truth when it came to her kids. She was clear about who and what we were—even when we had doubts about ourselves.

The box on the dining room table is a mish-mash of family photos, ancient letters, newspaper clippings, and tax documents from decades ago. There's no logic to any of it. We put the photos and important papers in separate piles, but most of it is going in the trash, which is sad. The ordinary sadness of a parent's death.

Lisa curates a separate pile of newspaper clippings and articles from travel magazines in the hope of gathering evidence that will unravel the mystery of her alleged trip to Ireland. I wish Lisa would let it drop.

"Remember the gangster?" Frankie asks.

"Oh my god," Lisa says.

I'd forgotten about the gangster even though she told the story often when we were kids. It went something like this. When she was a teenager, a low-level gangster started following her around at night. Her father was a bartender in a predominantly Irish and Italian neighborhood. According to my mother, it was one of the safest places in all of Brooklyn because the mob bosses who lived there didn't want any trouble. My mom was fond of saying, "You could drop a five dollar bill in the middle of Third Avenue and no one would pick it up!"

"Wow," we'd say, but thinking back it makes no sense. What does a five dollar bill have to do with how safe a city is? What does it have to do with anything?

Three nights in a row the gangster followed my mother home from the diner where she worked part-time after school. On the fourth night he was determined to get her. This was how my mother always told the story. Now I can see how unlikely it is. What did "determined" mean? What about "get"? And how did she know he was a gangster?

My mother took a different route home, or so the story goes, past Luigi's, an infamous Mafia hangout, where two of her father's cronies were standing outside. Both named Tony.

"Both guys were named Tony?" Frankie asks.

"Yep," Lisa says.

"I didn't know that," Frankie says.

"It gets better," Lisa says. "Their names were Buttacavoli and Carracciola."

"Tony Butts and Tony Crotch?" Frankie asks.

"How did we not know she was lying to us?" Lisa asks.

"She wasn't lying," I insist. "She was telling a story."

"Same difference," Lisa says.

"What was the gangster's name?" Frankie asks.

"The gangster didn't have a name," Lisa says. "He was just the gangster."

According to my mother, she informed the two Tonys about her predicament and they told her to wait inside Luigi's while they took care of it. When my mother told the story, she went into great detail about the restaurant. "They sat me down at their best table and served me a plate of lobster ravioli. I'd never had it before and it became one of my favorite dishes. You never tasted anything so delicious!"

"What happened to the guy?" we asked.

My mother always responded the same way. "What guy?"

"The gangster!"

"They wouldn't tell me," my mother insisted, "they just said he wouldn't be bothering young women anymore."

"Do you think they killed him?" I ask.

Frankie and Lisa shrug. My mom changed the ending of the story depending on who she was talking to, and how old we were. The second time I heard her tell the story, she intimated the Tonys cut off the gangster's balls. We all have a laugh about that.

It's getting late and Frankie announces he has to go—he's got the kids to wrangle and a flight to catch in the morning. Lisa orders a car and packs up her stack of papers. We say our goodbyes and I stay behind. At least that part hasn't changed.

Determined to finish the box we'd been working on, I sit down at the table with a fresh cup of tea—no whiskey this time. I'm starting to worry that I'll never make it to the bottom of the box when I pull out a *New York Post*—

not a clipping but the entire paper. It's dated September 11, 2002—the one year

anniversary of the attacks on the World Trade Center. I'm about to toss it in the

trash when a name jumps out at me: Anthony Carracciola.

Holy shit, I think. Tony Crotch was real.

It's a small article about how the former Mafia strongman was being

released from prison forty years after he'd been charged with the murder of

Rudy Tomaselli.

According to the article, my mother would have been fifteen when

Rudy was killed and Tony was put away. Was Rudy the gangster in my

mother's story or was it all a bizarre coincidence?

I click off the light and go upstairs and try to fall asleep. Between the

television that was always on and the oxygen machine that kept her alive, the

house is so much quieter now.

I text my siblings about what I'd found, but they're skeptical.

"Just because Tony is real doesn't prove that mom knew him," Lisa

argues.

"The fact that it was a well-known crime makes her story even less

likely," Frankie adds to the group chat.

I can see their points, but why did she keep the paper all these years?

No one has an answer for that.

Why does anyone keep anything? Why did mom keep our third grade

report cards and old book reports and duplicate photos of blurry buildings from

around the neighborhood?

I close my eyes and get on with the business of grieving.

***

When I wake up in the morning and go downstairs there's a dead gangster sitting in my mother's living room. Technically it's my living room now—she left me the house—but I still think of it as hers.

The gangster is dressed in an old grey suit with wide lapels and a matching felt fedora cocked back on his head at a rakish angle. I don't know why I think he's a gangster but this is how gangsters dress in those black-and-white films they're always showing on Turner Classic Movies. Boxy coats, high-waisted pants, door-kicker shoes.

The gangster looks like he's been dead for a long time because he's all withered skin and raggedy bones, barely any flesh to speak of, and his eyes look like nails that have been hammered into his skull.

When I step into the living room he turns and glares at me.

"What the..." My heart is galloping in my chest, but the gangster doesn't say a word.

I edge toward the front door and the gangster slowly pushes its body out of the chair.

I stop, go back to the bottom of the stairs, and the gangster sits down again.

There's an animated corpse sitting in my living room. It doesn't want me to leave but is okay if I stay, which is crazy.

We stare at each other for so long that I start to get tired. I can smell the coffee brewing in the kitchen. I always make my coffee at night and set it on a timer. Gives me something to look forward to in the morning.

"You want some coffee?" I ask.

His mouth hangs open, exposing long yellow teeth. His hands grip the armrests like claws. When the gangster doesn't answer, I say, "I'm going to get a cup. Be right back."

The gangster watches me slink into the kitchen but doesn't follow. I could slip out the back door, but where would I go? Who would I tell?

I return to the living room with my coffee and sit down next to the gangster.

"Who are you?" I ask.

Nothing.

"What do you want?"

Nada.

Eventually I figure out that he can respond to yes or no questions by moving his head.

"Are you alive?"

No.

"Dead?"

Another no. So something in between.

"Is there anything I can do for you?" I ask.

The gangster nods.

Interesting, but I have to go. My father has a doctor's appointment. He's dying and there's nothing anyone can do about it, but I need to get him dressed, change his linens, and get him to eat something before we go.

I turn on the television and the gangster turns its head toward the screen. I put on Turner Classic Movies and we both sit there for a few minutes and watch. It's not a gangster flick but Edward G. Robinson is in it and I'm able to slip out the back door.

***

The undead gangster is still there when I get home. I think about picking up the phone and asking Frankie or Lisa for advice, but they have their own families, their own messes. I think they low-key resent the fact that our mother left me the house, but that's not something any of us is ready to admit.

Me, I take care of people. Not the way Tony Crotch took care of people. Right now I'm taking care of my father, who is dying of bladder cancer. The gangster doesn't scare me—cancer scares me—but he's starting to get on my nerves. The gangster doesn't know who the president is or who the next one will be. The gangster doesn't know anything. I thought having him around would be like having access to a walking Ouija board, but it has no knowledge from the beyond. The gangster only knows what it knew when it was alive, which seems like bullshit. What's the point of the afterlife, even one as fucked up as this one, if we don't have access to the wisdom of the world?

On most days he follows me when I leave the house, but no one else can see him. Passersby walk right through him. Dogs sense something and raise their noses in the air as we go by. When I go visit my dad, who only lives a few blocks away on the other side of Third Avenue, the gangster follows me down the street and into my father's apartment.

The first time it happened my dad opened his eyes as soon as we entered the room.

"What's that smell?" he demanded.

I couldn't smell the gangster, but it was easy to imagine why he could. I looked at the gangster who seemed to be studying my father, though who could say?

"Maybe it's the pizza I had for lunch," I said and my father let it drop.

***

A week later when I come down the stairs I can see the gangster has something in its hands. It's the *New York Post*, the very same edition my mother saved. I have no idea where he found it.

"What do you have there?" I ask.

He points to the article about Tony Crotch.

"Is this you? Are you Tony?"

The gangster shakes its head, puts its finger on a name farther down the article.

Rudy.

"Nice to meet you, Rudy."

Rudy stands. He shakes the newspaper and points to the door.

"You want to see Tony?"

Rudy nods and maybe it's a trick of the light but I swear there's a twinkle in his eyes.

If I was like my mother I could pick up the phone and call one of the neighbors and find out all there is to know about Anthony Carracciola. In a few calls I'd know everything about the man. Where he lived, how his health was, whether his children or grandchildren—if he had any—were looking after him. If I worked the phone long enough I could find out everything I wanted to know about his connections to the neighborhood and its relationship to him, but all that ended when my mother died.

I am not my mother. I go days without speaking to anyone who isn't a medical professional but I have the internet and it tells me Tony Carracciola is alive and well in Sunnyslope, the assisted living facility across the street from Monahan's funeral home. I know all about Sunnyslope because Mrs. Manningham lives there too. She was one of my mother's oldest friends.

I call up the facility and inquire about visiting hours and when the woman who answers the phone asks who I'm visiting I tell them Mrs.

Manningham. At the mention of the name the receptionist perks up and tells me visiting hours are every day between lunch and dinner.

"I'll be there this afternoon," I say.

I walk around the neighborhood with the gangster. We go to see my father, who sleeps while I tidy up and wash his sheets and towels. He goes through a lot of towels. When the day nurse arrives we go to the good Italian deli for some cookies. Even if Mrs. Manningham can't eat them they won't go to waste. Rudy seems enchanted by the display case with its jumble of meats and cheeses, baked good and prepared dishes. It might be my imagination but when it's time to leave, it feels like Rudy doesn't want to go.

It's a beautiful day, the sun is out, and the wind off the Narrows blows through the trees. On days like today I can see why people never leave this place. Although I've lived here my whole life, I always assumed I'd leave someday, like Frankie and Lisa, just sell the house and go. But maybe not. Maybe I'll stay, like my parents did, like most people from the neighborhood do. After my parents split up, we assumed one or both of them would leave, but they both stayed, living their new lives a few blocks apart. I never asked my mother why she stayed. Maybe my father knows, but he isn't talking much these days. That's when it dawns on me that I can ask Rudy about my mother.

"Did you know my mother?" I ask him.

Rudy nods.

There's no easy way to say this so I just spit it out. "Were you going to hurt her?"

Rudy shakes his head. He doesn't answer the question with any more or less enthusiasm than the others. The gangster doesn't care about my feelings. It knows what it knows, wants what it wants. Which is what exactly?

I guess I'm about to find out.

The staff at Sunnyslope is happy to see me. Who doesn't love a cookie tray? The receptionist summons an aide to take us up to see Mrs. Manningham, who will be so pleased to see me, she says. We follow the aide down a hallway and then into an elevator. The aide keeps looking from the cookie tray to me and back to the tray again, like something isn't adding up, all while standing inches away from the gangster's putrefying corpse.

On the fourth floor we pass what looks like a TV lounge. Rudy stops and stares at a man watching a *Law & Order* rerun. My mom loved *Law & Order*. So does my father. I suppose everyone does. The old man wearing slippers and a robe over his pajamas turns and looks our way. Apparently, he recognizes Rudy because he starts screaming.

"Get him away from me!" he shouts.

This must be Tony.

Some of the residents look at me, the only newcomer they can see, and the aide steps in front of me, as if to shield me from their stares. He's got a walkie-talkie in his hand and he's calling for assistance, but it's too late. Rudy advances on Tony, who has fallen out of his chair and is trying to crawl away from him. He can't take his eyes off the gangster.

"No," he shouts, or tries to anyway, but there's no power to it. He's having trouble breathing. He's in more than a little distress. A swarm of nurses and aides rushes into the lounge as the various systems inside Tony's body stop communicating with each other. I know where this is going. I've seen it before and will see it again, but when I turn to leave, to take Mrs. Manningham her cookies, Rudy is nowhere to be found.

THE DEPRESSION OF JOHN STONEBROOK
BY
AARON PAUL SCHAUT

John arrived at the cabin late afternoon after a long trek into town to pick up some goods from Polanski's General Store. Beans, corn, coffee, whiskey, and tobacco would be enough to get him through the next couple of weeks. Beans, corn, coffee, whiskey, and tobacco had been enough that year. The season was early spring or late winter, depending on the day. The ground was a mixture of mud and snow, and John slid in the muck a little bit when he dismounted Timber. His boots were still good. A worn-out red flannel and a pair of denim pants had also served him well this past year. He had learned to stitch and patch the holes in his garments on his own, without Mary around to do it for him. The stitching was crude but sufficient enough. He recalled wearing this same outfit a year prior when typhoid fever claimed the lives of his wife, Mary and their daughter, Jane. The both of them passed only seven years after he had returned home from the war. Seven years was not long enough.

John had been a cavalryman with the Iron Brigade at the Potomac. A fierce pack, he fought alongside men of immense bravery, men of valor, and even men of color. He fought for the Union, at Gettysburg, alongside names like Meade and Pickett and Johnson. John even had the honor of attending the funeral of Abraham Lincoln. What a funeral 'twas.

While Mary raised Jane and did what she could to survive at the home front, John wrote many letters to her. Letters of the war, letters of the men, letters of loss and letters of hope. He wrote letters of longing and letters of hunger and letters of any other things on his mind. Letters of Boots, rations, bullets, and amputated bits. He watched many men lose their lives defending freedom, defending dreams, defending ideas, defending this and defending that. After all the death, losing Mary and Jane, less than a decade later, was too much for any man to bear.

After putting a log in the stove and sitting down at the table, John glanced at the newspaper he had brought with him from Polanski's store. The front page was littered with ads for watches, dry goods, fancy clothes, and land for sale. There was no mention of what they were calling "the panic" and no mention of war. Either way, John didn't give a good goddamn about a war or the panic. The panic. John's world had been a constant state of depression and isolation since Mary and Jane had passed.

The lumber on his property had dwindled, and money was thin. Whiskey, tobacco, and beans were his lifeline when he wasn't holding the barrel of his revolver in his mouth. He knew that any given night's whiskey would either put him to sleep or put him down. Up to now, the whiskey had only put him to sleep — brief, nightmare-ridden sleep. He knew it was only a matter of time; the whiskey would see him pull the trigger and reunite him with his family.

The early morning sun had started pushing the icicles from the shingles to the ground. The noise woke John from his slumber. He drew his revolver. He got up, threw another log in the stove and made some coffee. Placing his coffee on the newspaper that was left on the table, a stain left behind from his tin cup circled a story about a gold miner's migration to the American Southwest. John didn't bother reading the story; he didn't care for stories. Howe'er, from this headline, a seed was planted. John squinted and began rolling a cigarette with one hand, crouched over, his left elbow on his lap. He licked the rolling paper and glanced around the empty cabin, imagining himself departed, imagining himself removed from the isolation and loneliness that was this homestead without Mary. He was desperate to not relive, o'er and o'er again, the memory of his beloved wife and beloved daughter dying there, in that bed. He was lost in a gaze toward the bed.

Mary was the most beautiful woman John had ever seen. She had long black hair, brown eyes, and a strong jaw. She was tall and lean and had no problem swinging an axe but could delicately prepare a meal. Watching her cook in the summer heat was one of John's favorite memories. Her white dress falling off of her shoulder, revealing her dark skin, glistening with sweat from the heat of the stove and the humidity in the air. She'd smile and quietly sing while floating over the pine wood floor like a hummingbird around a pond. Every now and then, he could smell her around the room. When that sensation hit him, he'd nearly pass out from the euphoria of it. He was never sure what the sweet floral fragrance consisted of. She never told him. Nevertheless, every now and then, this sweet aroma would consume him, leaving him useless for a brief amount of time.

"The American Southwest," John pondered as he spat some loose tobacco leaves from the tip of his tongue. He stood from his chair and began gathering small necessities into a pile. He laid out a small blanket roll on the table. On it, he placed the beans, tobacco, and whiskey. He produced a second pair of long johns and a second pair of briefs from near the stove. In a sack, he put the tobacco and his whiskey and a water-filled deer hide flask. He placed his rifle and his revolver and a small map next to the sack and filled another small sack with what little ammunition he had. One by one, he carried these items out to Timber. What little snow was left glistened in the sun as he mounted the horse and headed down his property's trail toward town and the American Southwest.

Four days and four nights had passed. John hunched o'er a small fire, brewing some coffee. The spot was next to a small lake just off the trail he'd been riding. Along the way, he'd come across some clove. He sliced the clove up with his hunting knife and put it into his coffee. This is something that Mary would do on occasion and was another trigger of pleasant memories for John. As he took a sip from his cup, out of the corner of his eye, he caught a shimmer across the lake. He squinted so to focus on its direction. He could make out a man standing next to a horse. Tall feathers floated above this man's long black hair. His chest also adorned with feathers that draped down to his belly. His steed was painted in blue and yellow and was also adorned with feathers. The man held a large staff in one hand and a rifle in the other. He lifted the staff into the air, and his body leaned in such a way that it lowered the rifle toward the ground. John looked down at his coffee and back up toward the man while squinting again. The man was gone. There was no movement in the woods, nor any sound to be heard.

"I reckon those cloves have me seeing things. Timber, you see that?"

Timber bobbed and nodded in return.

"Ah, Jesus, you didn't see nothin'," John replied in his quiet, deep voice while spitting tobacco from his lips. "Some traveling partner you are." The tobacco never really left John's lips.

John took another sip of that 'reminder of Mary' and tossed the rest of the coffee onto the fire. "We better set out, ol' boy," he said to the horse as he flicked the remnants of the cup and started to load up his gear.

So far, the trail had been void of any travelers. John hadn't thought of turning the gun on himself since leaving the cabin. He thought about it a little. He hadn't toiled in sadness or longing. He felt free and his direction gave him some kind of purpose, a little peace.

A hawk circled above their head as they continued west. Leaves left over from fall were still scattered over the ground. John spotted something odd sticking up from the leaves, shiny and foreign. "Whoa, boy," he said as he pulled back on Timber's reins. He got down and crouched over the object and spit tobacco from his lips.

"What in sam hell is this you reckon?" The object was square and red or maroon or red. John was half color blind and didn't know colors so well so it's red or maroon. One side of the object had several small holes in it, in unison and symmetrical. It had the word "Regency" written on it, fancy-like and reflective. It also had a pair of dials with numbers on each. He turned one of the dials and it clicked. A noise was released through the small holes, a noise like nothing John had ever heard. He could only compare it to the noise that might come from putting your ear up to the hole end of a lead pipe. Seems John had done such a thing at some point. He rotated the other dial, which caused the noise to change its shape, warble, and hum. Suddenly, while continuing to turn the dial, the voice of a man came through the small holes, causing John to throw the thing back onto the ground. It continued to speak to him as he backed away. It was speaking sternly, with importance and directness. It was father-like.

"I have today ordered to Viet-Nam the Air Mobile Division and certain other forces which will raise our fighting strength from 75,000 to 125,000 men almost immediately. Additional forces will be needed later, and they will be sen–."

John, frightened of the object, slowly reached for it and turned the small wheel back to the zero position. He backed away a little but continued to stare at it silently. He picked up a stick and nudged it a few times, as though he were poking a dead animal or a dead body. It didn't breathe or emit anymore sound so John slowly reached down and picked up the box. He dared not touch the knobs but rather just stared at the thing in his hand. He looked over at Timber and back at the thing. Timber snorted and nodded in anticipation to leave. John quickly put the object in his sack, and the two continued on their journey west. John hadn't thought about his pistol just then.

"What you suppose of that thing, Timber? Who was that talkin' in it? Sounded like a call to arms, ol' boy. You supposin' something happened we don't know about? Somthin' not in the papers? Maybe this thing is from the big exposition in France."

Maybe.

The trail widened and a large city appeared in the distance. Smoke rose from the roofs of buildings and houses and into the air and over the sun. John slowed and checked his map. "Des Moines, Iowa," he said aloud. "The city is no good to me, but she's in our path. Figure we'll fetch some supplies and stay the night in a brothel with a bed."

He rode in and hitched up in front of what was Hierb's Brewery. "I reckon we'll spend the night here, Timber. What say you?" Timber gave a nod, and John proceeded into the saloon.

Inside the parlor was rowdy and loud. While a piano played itself, people were playing cards and dancing. John, avoiding eye contact with the commotion, made his way up the bar rail and sat down on a bar chair.

"Howdy, friend, names Joe Hierb, what'll you be havin'?"

John looked softly at the barman. "I'll have a nice whiskey, sir."

"Sir, nobody calls me sir around here. Save it for your commander. Either way, one nice whiskey, comin' up! Catch your name, pal?"

"Name's John."

John set his sack on the bar top and removed the small, square device and set it in front of him. Once spotting the device, Joe couldn't stop looking at it, causing him to over-pour the whiskey. The object was colorful and weird. Joe was also colorful and weird. A small mustache sat trim just above his upper lip. He wore a fancy hat and a bow tie. His voice was kind but loud. It was obvious, on first observation, why he was a barman.

"What you got there, John?"

"I dunno what this thing is, Joe. I found it on the trail just up a ways and can't make nothin' of it. It's like nothin' I ever seen. I turn this little wheel here, un voices come out of it. A call to arms come out of it."

"Can't be," replied Joe. "Maybe you ought visit Doctor Parnassus up the street. Ain't no war and ain't no magic boxes in Iowa."

"Really, lemme show you this here."

With hesitance, John turned the first dial revealing the pipe sounds. Joe stood back a little and John proceeded to the second wheel. It warbled and hummed until, just like that, through the little holes, some crazy music was playing, and somebody was screamin' like they was dying.

"Matty told Hatty, That's the thing to do.
Get you someone pull the wool with you.
Wooly Bully, Wooly Bully."

The loud noise and crazy singing frightened both men. A few other patrons joined the two of them around the bar. John quickly turned the first dial back to zero. Joe poured both of them another whiskey and set the bottle on the bar. After drinking his shot, Joe looked seriously at John and quietly said, "You don't mention none of this to nobody. You got me?"

"You don't say?" replied John.

"I don't say," said Joe.

"I say, what is that thing?" said one of the men who had gathered around the commotion.

"Look here," continued John. "I need a stable for ol' Timber out there and a bed for me. Where should I lead myself for such fine, Des Moines, accommodations?"

"Cross the road there, you'll find a stable and a room," replied Joe, "You gonna keep it?"

"Ain't decided yet. I'm fixin' to sleep on it."

"Okay, I won't be telling nobody about this."

"Thank you, friend."

"I shall not tell a soul," mumbled a noticeably inebriated man from two stools down. "Not a soul or nobody nothin. Cross my heart," he sloppily waved his hand around his chest, "and kindly pour me another one, kind sir."

John left the saloon and walked Timber to the stable across the road. While crossing, he was startled by what looked like two very bright moons heading toward him. As they drew closer, he realized they were coming at him with the speed of a locomotive. He dove to the side, did a bit of a somersault, and felt a breeze of dust and sand hit him as whatever it was had passed. He looked in the direction of the object, forearm above his brow, but nothing was there. Others had seen it. Folks had a look of awe on their faces as he looked around. Timber stood near the side of the road, somewhat anxious about the scene. He must have seen it too. John shook it off as did the others. He kept his wits about him and kept moving.

Once he had Timber settled in at the stables, he made his way to the hotel, settled up, and headed to his room. He pulled his boots off his feet, lay on the bed, and stared at the object. He thought of the Injun man by the lake, and he thought about Mary and he thought about his pistol. He thought about Mary's lineage. She was part Ojibwe and was proud of it. She always said it was why her maple syrup was so sweet and why John slept so well. Before long, John was asleep.

John awoke the next day to what sounded like thunder rumbling overhead. He could feel it in his heart. He noticed that beams of sunlight shone through the slats in the window's shutter. He ran over and flung the slats open, expecting to see a storm. There were no clouds in the sky, but the constant rumble of thunder could still be heard. It was trailing away from him. He scanned the sky toward the direction of the sound, but it revealed little. There was a glint in the sky, a diamond, an unusual-looking flicker. A whistle, white light, smoke and fire and screams and–nothing. He shut his eyes. He opened his eyes. Everything was as it was.

He threw on his flannel, pulled up his boots, grabbed his things, and made his way out of the room. He felt uneasy about everything that had been happening to him around this town. He wanted to get moving and put all these weird scenes and crazy thoughts behind him.

John headed into the dining hall next to the saloon, sat himself up at a table, and looked at the sack that contained the red or maroon, probably red, object when, out of his right ear, he was startled.

"What can I get the galley to make up for ya, lad?" He glanced up to a woman, strong and round, with an Irish accent, ready to serve.

"I'll have a coffee and some eggs, if ya don't mind, las," he responded.

"Funny guy, are ya now? Don't bodder me none. I'll have those out for ya in no time t'all. Don't mind me askin', what about that ting ya had in the pub. You e'er figure out what that ting was?"

"What are you talking about?"

"That ting. You know. Everyone is talking about yer ting."

"Wouldn't be the first time."

"Still a jokester, huh? Not that ting, boyo. Don't flatter yerself. Is the udder ting I'm talkin' about, da one in your sack there. The boys were sayin' that it had some kinda magic and spoke ta ya."

"I'd rather not talk about my ting any longer, ma'am. I'm starved. My eggs?"

"Okay, boyo, loud n' clear, I'll get yer eggs. Just be knowin' that we all be wonderin' about yer ting."

John glanced at the newspaper that'd been left behind on the table. More advertisements 'bout land for sale, clothing for sale, and watches and trinkets, and fancy suits and other things. Nothing about "the panic" was mentioned, at least on the front page.

The waitress brought him his eggs and his coffee and again mentioned "somethin' about his ting." John, quickly, without talking about his ting, nodded at his waitress, ate his food and set back to Timber.

The city was now behind him as he crossed the river and disappeared into fields and farmland. He was glad to have the space and silence back. After a certain amount of time with only your own thoughts keeping you company, that kind of noise can feel like a windstorm after a drought. Nothin' but dust and wind and more dust and more wind. The kind of dust and wind that'll make you think about your pistol.

Suddenly came the sharp sound of gunfire from John's nine o'clock. The corn was pierced to his left and his right. He threw himself off of his horse and drew his revolver. He darted and skidded and slid into the rows of corn. Another shot rang out from across the trail. Instinct set in. Although he couldn't see anything, John returned fire into the corn. After a brief silence, another shot was fired. Some stalks of corn were pierced right next to him. John dashed through the corn toward the front side of Timber. He caught a little movement of corn stalks just the other side of the trail. He drew and fired, and a man howled out a cry. John moved slowly toward the sound with his revolver still drawn. He inched into the corn until he reached a man on the ground, rifle at his side, a bullet in the side of his belly.

"Ya shot me. You done shot me!" Yelled the man.

"I shot ya? You were the one shootin' at me. Care to 'splain?" John pushed the rifle off to the side with his boot. He recognized the man as the drunk from the bar.

"That thing of yours. I couldn't stop thinkin' about it is all. I had to see it. I had to have it." Tears were in the man's eyes.

"You mean you tailed me all the way out here because of the thing?" John asked with a frustrated dismay.

"I couldn't stop thinkin' bout it. I just couldn't."

"Where's your horse?"

"Back a little way, in the corn. Not far. Ya gotta help me."

John started walking back down the trail. After a minute, he spotted the horse through some rows of corn. He grabbed its reins and headed back to the man. John helped drag him out of the field and helped get him on his horse. He took the guy's hand and pressed it tight against the wound in his belly.

"This is on you, pal. Pray you make it back to a doctor."

John headed back toward the city with his passenger in tow. This was the last place John wanted to go; back to where they knew about the thing and where nobody talked about the panic.

They rode up to Parnassus' office. John hitched up both horses before glancing at his treacherous compadre who was now hunched over the neck of his horse. John let himself into the doctor's office and was greeted by the receptionist.

"Welcome to the office of Dr. Parnassus. What brings you in today?"

"Feller out there been shot. He needs tending to."

"Shot, you say? Oh my gosh! I'll get the doctor straight away!"

"So, I reckon we're good here? He'll be tended to?"

"Sir, please wait here," she said as she headed toward what must have been the doctor's office."

"You all can handle this," John muttered to her ghost and the doorway.

John headed back out to Timber and began unwrapping his reins from the post. A nurse and the doctor burst out and began examining their new patient.

"What on earth happened to Mr. Dowd?" The doctor anxiously asked.

"He must've been sticking his nose where he ought not," replied John.

"You're that fella with that thing; I heard about you."

"Yup, I'm the fella with the thing. I take it ya'll have what you need? I'll be seeing myself off."

"Mister, you need to wait here for the sheriff."

"Mister, if the sheriff needs me, you tell him I'll be o'er at the brewery. I didn't ask to be shot at and I'm not fixin' to be asked about it."

"Mister—"

"I'll be at the brewery. Good day, good doctor."

John mounted Timber and headed to the brewery. Joe was still tending bar and lit up on seeing John enter.

"My friend, it's awfully good to see you return. Did you bring the thing?"

"I'll have a whiskey, Joe."

"One whiskey, comin' up. How's about that thing?"

"I've grown tired of my thing."

From behind, a billowing voice asked, "Are you John?"

John turned to a large man who was obviously the sheriff, seeing he had a badge and all. "I am," said John.

"You mind telling me what happened with Mr. Jacob Dowd?"

"I mind that he tried to take my head off on the trail."

"Tried to take yer head off, huh?" The sheriff spoke in a calm, baritone voice.

"That's right. Took a shot at me from the corn. Nearly hit my horse."

"Now why in god's name would Dowd take a shot at you?"

Joe intervened, "I know why sheriff, it's got to be because of that thing John found in the woods. Dowd seen it yesterday, here, in the bar."

"Ah, yes, I heard about your thing. It's not like Dowd to shoot at anyone over anything. Was he drinking?"

"He was drinking, alright. The sight of the thing and the whiskey in his blood must have driven him to it."

"Okay, Joe. Alright, John. John, I didn't catch your last name."

"Stonebrook."

"Okay, Mr. Stonebrook, I reckon you best not leave town until this gets squared away. Mind showing me that thing of yours?"

"I mind."

"Completely in your right, Mr. Stonebrook. Stay in town and report back to me at sunup."

The Sheriff left the saloon while Joe and John finished their whiskey. Shortly after, John headed back to his room. As he sat on his bed and removed his boots and socks and lowered his suspenders, a flickering caught the corner of his eye. In the direction of a dresser, a wooden box appeared. There was a man in the box. No color in him. John stood slowly and carefully backed away to the far corner of the room. The man was talking at him.

"Finally, whether you are citizens of America or citizens of the world, ask of us here the same high standards of strength and sacrifice which we ask of you. With a good conscience our only sure reward, with history the final judge of our deeds, let us go forth to lead the land we love, asking His blessing and His help, but knowing that here on earth God's work must truly be our own."

John watched as this man spoke. He felt comforted by his words, his face. He was mesmerized by it all. The other thing and this new thing had saturated his comprehension. He slowly approached the box and gently touched the glowing glass. He pressed a switch, and the glow faded and was gone.

John put his boots back on and escaped to the hallway. An unnaturally bright light was emitted from orbs on the wall. Carpet was soft below his feet. Down the stairway, the entry looked somehow different. People were in strange clothing and music played, magically, in the air and all around. Nobody looked at him and everybody was hurried. He exited to a street filled with noise and bustle and lights and horseless carriages like the one he'd seen the day's prior. He tried to cross the paved road while falling and weaving and dodging and while loud yells came from the carriages. Yelling and screaming and "get out the road," and "what's the matter with you, pal," and loud horns and suddenly — it all fell silent.

Between the rows of carriages, now not moving, stood our friend from the lake, horse at his side, calm. The man raised his staff again as John approached, barely able to stand.

"Why? Why is this happening? What is happening to me?" John cried out as he fell to his knees and reached out to the man from the ground. The native removed a locket from a pouch at his hip and threw it to John. Trembling, John reached for the locket and opened it. In it, a photograph of Mary.

John cried and stared at the locket as the man spoke.

"She is my great-granddaughter, John Stonebrook. Our people are proud. She left this earth but brings you strong medicine, John Stonebrook. Yes, the panic will come, the war will come, the sicknesses will come, the depression will come. John Stonebrook, you must move forward, aware of what lies ahead. You will have a wife and a child. The child will have a child. They will live in the future you've witnessed. They will be born into the panic and the depression and the war and the violence and the bigotry. They will be of Mary's blood and the blood of our ancestors. A blood forever tied to our people. Do not retire to your pistol, John Stonebrook. You must carry this spirit with you. You must carry our strength."

Still sobbing and still on the ground, John stared at the photograph of Mary. He looked back up but the medicine man had vanished. The town was as it was before, and a small crowd had gathered 'round.

"Mr. Stonebrook," the sheriff stood over John with his hand outstretched. "Mr. Stonebrook, let's get up and out of the road now."

John stood with the help of the sheriff, locket still in hand. The sheriff led John into the dining room and helped set him down at a table.

"John, dear boy, here is a cup o' coffee ta help bring ya back ta life."

John looked up at his waitress, then glanced around at the other faces looking at him. He reached into his bag for the thing, but it was not there.

Scanning the room again, he did catch another glimpse of his medicine man, but only for a moment. Where the man had appeared, a woman sat. Her hair was long and dark, her brown eyes pierced John Stonebrook's soul. He glanced again at the locket.

"That there is Margaret Mitchel, Boyo. She come in here 'bout two, maybe tree times a week. Always be by herself if ya catch what I'm trowin' atchya."

John glanced up at the waitress, then down at today's newspaper on the table. There it was, in big bold typeset, "The Panic – Excitement on Wall Street."

John fixed himself up a bit and walked o'er to Margaret's table and nearly fainted as he approached her scent.

"Miss, my name's John Stonebrook. Would you be so kind by sharing with me what scent you are wearing?"

"Hyacinth. Is that what you mean Mr. Stonebrook? Hyacinth is the scent that I am wearing."

RATS

BY PHILLIP THOMPSON

It's four-thirty in the morning, and I'm in the back of a van going down the interstate at eighty miles an hour.

It's not what you think.

I'm in the van with the Shake and Bake Twins because Cam was a rat. And not even a very good one, mainly because when push came to shove, Cam didn't have the stones to straight-up lie to Smoke, after crossed him in the worst way possible—over Smoke's money and his woman.

* * *

Of course, I knew Cam had the hots for Terry. He was about as discreet as a nuclear blast, which was stupid on his part because the only two things Smoke cared about was his cash and his gash. It's not like that was a secret to anybody who knew him.

So, when Cam got around to banging Terry and, with her help, stealing from Smoke, I knew that it was going to end only one way: with Cam begging for his life, probably while standing in his own grave.

It took Cam less than a day to figure out the magnitude of his fuckup and another day to tell me about it. As I said, Cam was stupid. I don't care how tempting that much money is, you don't steal fifty grand from a drug dealer with Smoke's reputation unless you are insane or a Terminator. Cam was neither.

Smoke had been kicked out of the Marine Corps *and* the Hell's Angels. Before the age of thirty. He'd also killed three men as he built a dope operation that covered two counties that straddled the Mississippi-Alabama state line. And he kept the rest of us—his street dealers—in line with a pair of fists that hit you like bricks. I knew from that first-hand experience.

"Lip, you got to help me out here," Cam said when he called me. I agreed to meet him at a barbecue place on the edge of town that night.

He showed up on time, twitchy as a scared cat, and we ordered our meals and settled into a booth near a window that gave us full view of the highway that coursed through low hills and kudzu past the barbecue shack and into town.

"I'm in a shitload of trouble," he said over a basket of fries. "And I'm seriously worried Smoke is going to fuck me up."

And then he told me how he and Terry hooked up and, after the dirty deed, decided to swipe some of Smoke's meth money.

"How much?" I asked as I worked on a plastic mug of draft beer.

"Fifty thousand. But we left something like two hundred grand."

I tried not to spit beer across the table at Cam's admission of an act of sheer lunacy. I wiped my mouth, shook my head.

"How'd Smoke find out you stole it?" I said.

Cam looked at me like a confused puppy. "Terry."

"Seriously?" I said, though it made sense to me. Of course Terry ratted Cam out—Smoke probably got suspicious, and Terry instinctively covered her own ass.

"I know," Cam said. "I can't believe it."

"Why only fifty?" I asked. "In for a penny, right?"

"Terry knew where the fifty was and could get to it," Cam said. "The rest of it—Terry said it was two hundred fifty grand—was locked up in their bedroom in a strongbox, and she didn't have a key. We figured fifty was enough for us to take off somewhere."

"Somewhere like where?"

Cam shrugged. "California. Las Vegas."

"Not good," I said before biting into my sandwich, processing this information, wanting to tell Cam he'd signed his own death warrant, but he already knew that. Otherwise we wouldn't be having this conversation. "What are you going to do?"

"That's what I'm asking you," he said, his voice becoming a whine. "What the hell *am* I going to do?"

I chewed, swallowed. "You need protection. Top cover, you know?"

Of course Cam knew what I meant—or thought he did. Whenever we sold Smoke's meth, we always covered each other, because meth heads are squirrelly, unpredictable sons of bitches. If I got into trouble with one of those idiots, I knew there was a gun hand nearby—sometimes Cam—to handle the situation.

"You mean to keep Smoke from killing me?"

"That, too," I said. "But what you need is real protection. Like cop protection."

Cam's eyes widened. He nearly choked on his fries. "You can't be serious."

"He can't kill you if he's in a cell, can he?"

Cam stared at a spot over my head for a solid minute. He was thinking about it.

"I ain't no rat," he said, finally.

I shrugged. "Suit yourself. But he'll be coming after your ass, you can believe that."

Cam pushed his fries to the middle of the table, licked his fingers. "Fuck it, I'm not looking over my shoulders for the next few days."

"Few *days?*" I said.

"You know what I mean."

I couldn't help but laugh. "You really think you can duck a guy like Smoke for even days? He's going to be after you until you're in the fucking ground. I was you, I'd take some of that money and get the hell out of the country. One-way ticket to New Zealand. Or Nepal."

"I don't even know where Nepal is. Or what it is."

"It's country, dumbass. Loaded with hippies, hash, and crazy-ass gurus on a lifelong high."

"I ain't got a passport."

"Get one."

Cam dug some crumpled bills from his pocket, threw them on the table between us, then stood. "Not a goddam word about this, right? You don't tell nobody."

"Nary a soul." I wiped barbecue sauce from the corner of my mouth. I watched him scurry to his car like he was running through a hailstorm as I finished my supper.

When his car had disappeared down the cracked asphalt of the highway, headed toward town, I dug my phone out of my pocket. The burner all of Smoke's dealers use to conduct business. Smoke answered on the second ring.

"It's me," I said.

"That don't tell me much."

"It's Lip," I said, staring through the greasy plate glass window of the restaurant.

"What do you want?"

"We should meet later on tonight," I said. "I need to deliver some proceeds and some news."

Smoke grunted, which sometimes meant agreement. "Ten o'clock."

He didn't need to tell me to not be late. He clicked off, then I called Jorge.

"You with your brother?" I said when Jorge answered. He and his twin, Guillermo—the Ramirez brothers—were known as the Shake and Bake Twins. They weren't part of Smoke's crew—or anybody else's. They were more like a freelance operation. Muscle on demand.

"He's here," Jorge said.

"Put me on speaker." I waited a couple of seconds, then Jorge said, "Go ahead."

"How does splitting a quarter mil sound?"

"Where's it coming from?" Guillermo said.

"Smoke," I said.

A long pause—the kind that makes you think even bullet-headed psychos with a penchant for ax handles and nail guns might have limits. I wadded up the wax paper that held the remains of my supper.

"We're in," Jorge said.

* * *

Smoke moved faster on Cam than I thought he would. Two days later, Cam called me in a full-blown panic, screaming that Smoke had put the word out.

"Whoa man," I said. "Where's Terry?"

"Gone. Can't find her. Not answering her phone."

That meant Smoke had already taken care of his Terry problem. "What are you going to do?" I said, hoping he was going to give me the answer I wanted.

"Nothing I can do," Cam said. "He's coming over tonight."

Not the answer I was hoping for. "You got a gun?" I said.

"Yeah. Got myself some protection."

"Good. You'll need it."

"That ain't all."

My breath caught. "What do you mean?"

"Cops. And I already told them he's going to kill me tonight."

"Goddam, Cam, that's a huge gamble," I said. I was surprised that Cam would actually rat on Smoke, but relieved at the same time. Even after his declaration at the restaurant, Cam must have realized that being a live rat is better than being a dead drug dealer.

"Maybe, but Smoke's a maniac," Cam said. "You know that. I'm not going up against him alone. So I dropped a dime to a cop, like you said I should. They'll be here, too."

I checked my watch. This was happening way faster than I'd planned. "Jesus, Cam, you sure you know what you're doing?"

"Yeah, I'm taking care of my own ass."

"When's all this going down?"

"Soon as Smoke gets here. In about an hour." Cam hung up, and I called the twins.

When Jorge answered, I said, "Change of plans. Time to roll."

* * *

I'm sitting in the passenger seat of Jorge's newly painted olive-green van. It had been white until I convinced him that white vans draw attention from the cops.

"Where's Guillermo?" I say.

"Watching Smoke's place," Jorge says, eyes on the road.

"Cool."

Typical Jorge. Speaks only when spoken to. I watch the pine trees whiz by in a dark green blur. The summer night has encased us in an ebony blanket, wet and warm, making our operation feel even more urgent than it is. Jorge drives the six miles to Smoke's small house in the woods in silence.

We're rolling down the highway, about halfway to our destination, when Jorge's cell phone chimes. He answers with a "yeah." Then: "Got it. Okay." He lays the phone on the console and looks at me.

"Smoke left. House is empty."

I check my watch. By my calculations, we have a solid hour. That would give Smoke time to get to Cam's apartment, take care of business and return—if he returned at all.

"You better be sure about this," Jorge says as he drives down the wide blacktop. Feels like he's reading my mind.

"I am," I say, with slightly more confidence than I feel. There are a lot of moving parts in this caper. Jorge and I are working off the assumptions that Smoke *would* go to Cam's place to confront (and probably kill) Cam. And that the cops *would* be there waiting to arrest Smoke when he did, if Cam ratted him out to the cops as I'd hoped. Still, a lot is riding on those two assumptions.

Jorge wheels the van onto the gravel strip that is the driveway to Smoke's one-story cabin set in a copse of fifty-foot pine trees off a nearly forgotten county road. The headlights reach out ahead of us into the darkness and finally land on the house. Jorge parks, and we jump out and step through a gray cloud of dust toward the side of the house, heading for the screened-in back porch.

Among Jorge's numerous criminal skills is his wizardry at picking locks. He has us inside in less than a minute. As our eyes adjust to the darkened interior, I glance at him. "Where's Guillermo?"

"On his way to Cam's apartment. Where's the cash?"

"Bedroom."

Smoke's bedroom is surprisingly tidy for a man with such a fearsome reputation. Terry's work, I reckon. Bed made. Curtains hung well and partially open. Nightstands and lamps on either side of the queen-size bed, each with a neat arrangement of alarm clock and phone charger.

"Closet," I say as I point to the door opposite the foot of the bed, next to a sixty-five-inch wall-mounted TV. "It's in a strongbox."

"How you know all this?" Jorge says.

"He trusts me." Even badass drug lords like Smoke can be a bad judge of character. I'd seen Smoke pull the box down on some of my cash deliveries. "Top shelf."

Jorge grunts, stands of tiptoes, and grabs a battleship-gray metal rectangle. Grunts again at its heft, then hauls it into his arms. He looks over his shoulder at me.

"You sure?" he says.

"I'm sure."

Jorge drops the heavy box on the bed, and the weight of it makes the mattress bounce. He tugs a small black leather kit out of a pocket and goes to work on the lock. He pops the lid open after about thirty seconds.

"Holy shit," Jorge says. It sounds funny in his Salvadoran accent, but I don't laugh. I'm goggle-eyed at the stacks of cash in Smoke's strongbox. Banded stacks of various currencies crammed into the thing.

"Let's move," I say, suppressing the urge to touch that much money, count it, rub it on my face.

Jorge slams the lid and we trot to the van. Jorge even locks the door behind us. He has the key in the ignition when Guillermo calls. Jorge answers, looks over at me, brow low over brown eyes.

"Yeah," he says. "Cool. Meet us at the spot." He hangs up, nods toward the back of the van. "Get in back."

"Why?"

"Guillermo always rides up front."

Jesus Christ, I think as I clamber out of my captain's seat into the bench seat behind the cockpit. Not wanting to argue in the middle of this operation, I oblige Jorge. I wait until we're sailing down the highway before I say anything. When I do, Jorge lets loose with an uncharacteristic grin.

"It's going down just like you said," he tells me, making eye contact in the rear view mirror. "Guillermo tailed Smoke to Cam's place, then hid. About a minute later, he heard a gunshot inside the apartment."

Cam had bought the farm. Just as I'd figured he would. I just didn't think it would be there.

"Cops showed up three minutes later," Jorge says. "Like four cars, eight cops, all carrying shotguns. Busted in, lots of yelling."

I'm amped over the news, but also apprehensive. "Yeah? And? Smoke?"

Jorge grunts. "Cuffed and stuffed. Three cops hauled him out of the apartment and shoved him in a car. Guillermo waited until things settled down, then hauled ass. He's meeting us up ahead, as planned."

I slump back in my seat, relieved. Jorge checks the rearview, then swerves off the highway into a convenience store parking lot. He swings the van behind two vehicles parked at the gas pumps, drives to the side of the store, near the ice machine and propane tanks. Guillermo steps from the side of the ice machine and climbs into the passenger seat. Jorge is back on the road in less than a minute.

I lean forward as Guillermo settles in next to his brother.

"Tell me how it went down," I say. Guillermo shrugs. "Like I told Jorge, ese. I scoped it out. Smoke rolled up to the place, went inside. Heard a shot. Then the cops show up. Lights everywhere."

"And you're sure Cam is dead."

"Pretty sure," Guillermo says. "I mean, I didn't see the cops take him out. Just Smoke."

I face the windshield. If Guillermo's version is accurate, Cam had damn little time to blab before Smoke put one through him, which is all the better for me. I point to a side road up ahead. "Turn here."

Jorge gives me a sidelong look. "There? Why?"

"I stashed a vehicle by a lake. I told you this van is way too obvious."

Guillermo makes a noise in his throat. "You just now telling us this, man?"

I grin at him. "What do they call it? Operational security? It's cool, though. We switch out our ride, then split the cash."

Jorge locks eyes with his brother for a long second—long enough to make me tell Jorge to watch the road. Guillermo nods.

Jorge slows, wheels into the right-hand turn onto the narrow gray macadam road that falls away from the highway through a stand of tall oaks. After a quarter mile, Jorge follows my directions and turns onto a dirt road, and we bump down a gentle slope until a sparkling lake opens up before us. Six acres of flat black water glittering under a crescent. Off to the right, next to a concrete boat ramp that disappears into the lake, sits a Honda sedan. Jorge pulls next to the car, parks.

I pull my nine-mil from the back of my jeans, lean forward and shoot Guillermo in the base of his skull. The pistol sounds like a howitzer in the closed-in space, and the bullet decorates the windshield with Guillermo's blood, brains, and hair. I swing my arm to the left and fire again, this time into Jorge's stunned face as he watches his twin brother's body slump over the dashboard, soaked in blood. The bullet hits Jorge at point-blank range under his right eye, blasts through his skull and shatters the driver's side window. He falls backwards against the ragged edge of the busted window, as dead as his twin.

I huff out a breath, then slide the big cargo door open and hop out. I drag the box of cash from the floorboard and drop it. It lands two feet from the van with a thud. Run to the driver's side. Fragments of glass glitter like diamonds on velvet in the soft brown soil. I scuff dirt over them with my shoe, note pulpy masses of Jorge's head, and stifle a gag as I fling dirt over the mess.

I yank the driver's door open, then haul Jorge's body from behind the wheel and push him to the floor between the seats. It takes longer than I expect, and I'm drenched in sweat from the exertion of wrestling two-hundred-plus pounds of dead weight.

I crawl behind the wheel, crank the engine, and maneuver the van to a low spot at the water's edge. Point the nose of the vehicle at the lake, then stand on the running board on the driver's side.

I drop the van into drive and steer with one hand, jumping free as the van rumbles into the water. I land in a mushy apron of algae and slip several times before my shoes find purchase on the bank.

The vehicle sinks fast, with a gurgling sound that turns into a hiss before it disappears below the surface. I wipe sweat from my forehead as I watch concentric circles of ripples fade away, returning the lake to its placid natural state.

I grab Smoke's strongbox from the ground and heave it into the Honda's back seat. Twenty minutes later, I'm in Alabama, headed east, into a lightening sky, doing the speed limit and listening to the radio.

Nepal is too far away and too cold. Plus, I don't speak the language.

But I do speak Spanish.

FAIRY TALE MISSION

BY TERRANCE LAYHEW

On September 20, 1969, Henry Welles was summoned to the office. He'd been at the family farm, helping prepare for the apple harvest when the call came. His brother complained Henry was using an excuse to get out work, but his parents understood. The office came first. The office didn't care about fairness, it didn't care about the apples, it didn't care about the blight, it only cared about the mission.

The nondescript building looked like any other in Washington, DC. A place for government functionaries to be miserable making the lives of others miserable. In a way, this department had the same commission. With his clearance checked, Welles passed through the maze of hallways towards his destination. Unlike Theseus in Greek myth, his tour through the labyrinth wouldn't end with meeting a monster. That came later.

Behind her desk, Emily Carter guarded the doorway to Chief Williams office. She looked at Welles with a sphinx's smile, all mystery and self-satisfaction.

"Heard you were playing Johnny Appleseed." She said.

"Your hearing is as perfect as the rest of you." Henry replied.

"If I'm so perfect, why haven't we had dinner yet?"

He leaned in and gave her a peck on the cheek. "Let's blame my eyesight, I don't see you often enough."

She crossed her arms. "He's waiting."

Pulling back, Welles sighed. "Once more into the breach, dear friends, cry 'God for Harry, England and St. George."

Waiting behind the door, seated at his desk was Chief Williams. His operations experience stretched back to World War II where he already had his fingers in dozen of intelligences pies. Now, he was head of the Office of Operations, known by the cheeky title of "Triple O."

They were operatives. Intelligence was collected by various other agencies, if actions needed to be taken which was sensitive or off-books, it became the purview of Triple O.

As Welles seated himself, the Chief pushed a file across the desk. No foreplay tonight. "We've intercepted chatter the Soviets have uncovered something big in Siberia while drilling for oil. They've been cagey about details, but have taken whatever they've found to a military complex in Soyangi." The Chief explained.

Flipping through the pages, Welles saw scant details. "Pardon me sir, but this doesn't sound like an operations concern. There's nothing actionable here. Let the intelligence boys do more research before sending us into heaven knows what."

"Look at the bottom of the report."

Turning to the final page, Welles scanned the last paragraph. After a moment of silence, he nodded. "I understand sir."

He had the name of his monster to slay.

Dr. Mortimer Burbach had been an elusive quarry for the Triple O department for more than two years now. Formerly a ghoul of the Nazi party, given carte blanche to experiment in the concentration camps, Burbach escaped justice in the fringes of the world. If he had kept his head down, he might have succeeded. Instead, he was found at the center of a human trafficking ring Welles broke in South Africa. He slipped away by the skin of his teeth.

Finally, after months of whispers and failed searches, Burbach reappeared in Soyangi. His presence reenforcing the danger of whatever the Soviets were developing behind their gulag walls. The mission was simple. Welles was to finish the job he'd started and eliminate Burbach by whatever means necessary. While there, glean whatever he could about the secret project.

Two weeks later, in the early evening, Henry heaved against the lid of his coffin. A crate labeled as canned goods, his entry point into the facility. The tacks above gave way and he was breathing fresh air again. Stretching his shoulders and back, he inspected the pantry he'd been deposited within. His stomach growled. He picked an apple from a bag on the shelf. It might have been a gala. Taking a bite, he grimaced. Instead of a pleasant snap, it was mealy. He dropped the offending fruit in disgust.

Checking his firearm, Henry made sure it was loaded and ready. If he did his job right, he'd only need one shot. Holstering the M1911, he was about to leave, when he decided to grab another apple.

The report said the facility was a refurbished factory. Living quarters placed in the upper levels and surrounding wings, the original fabrication and manufacturing replaced with laboratories. Intelligence guessed that was where they'd stored whatever had been taken from the ice.

The signs on the walls read danger, caution, and other warnings of dire consequences. Welles ignored them. As Dr. Burbach would soon learn, Welles was the dire consequence. Around the corner, he expected to find the main laboratory. Instead, he found two soldiers guarding a set of double doors. Each carried an KM assault rifle and stared at Welles with narrowed eyes.

"Pass?" One soldier asked.

Fumbling, Welles patted his pockets. Shaking and shrugging when he couldn't find one, he threw the apple into the face of one soldier and grabbed the rifle of the other, slamming him into the wall. With the element of surprise on his side, Welles dispatched both men without a shot.

Drawing his gun, Welles stepped over the bodies and through the double doors. He found another hallway. No laboratory in sight. Perhaps he had read the signs wrong?

Opening the door, he found himself face to face with two very alive soldiers standing above two very dead soldiers. They stared at each other for a breath before they started shooting. Welles ducked behind the door, throwing the deadbolt and started running. Behind him, he could hear the thud of bullets hitting the door.

Darting down the hallway, Welles turned at the first corridor he met. Picking a door, he yanked on the handle. It was locked. He cursed. The next door he tried was successful. He plunged through. Closing the door and slipping the lock behind him.

Leaning against the wall, Welles caught his breath. He'd expected to find himself in a storage area or a laboratory room. Instead, as his eyes adjusted to the darkness, he was greeted by a bed, closet, and all the makings of a spartan apartment. If he was in the housing wing, he was in the complete opposite side of the facility. He cursed the schematics in the file, but to be fair, he had never been good with maps. The office joke was if Welles didn't return from a mission, it was more likely he was lost than dead.

Stepping towards the closet, Welles scratched his chin. Maybe this wouldn't be a complete waste. He might find a uniform to disguise himself with.

He'd just started rifling through the hangers when he heard the door unlock. Ducking inside the closet, he shut himself inside before the door opened.

Outside the closet doors, Welles heard the sound of footsteps. He didn't doubt he could overpower the man who lived here. A quick shot and it would be over. He made up his mind to charge out when the sound of the shower started. Even better, he could escape while the guy was in the shower.

There was no telling who was more surprised when the closet doors opened. Henry Welles, or the beautiful blonde staring at him. Acting fast, he sprang forward. Covering her mouth with his hand and pushing her against the bed. Wide eyed with shock, she didn't attempt to scream.

"I'm not here for you," Welles growled in Russian.

She nodded wordlessly. Her large eyes staring into his. Standing so close to her, he could feel her breath: rapid and excited.

Slowly, he lowered his hand from her mouth. "What's your name?"

"Anya Romanov," she said softly.

Dropping from her eyes to appraise the rest of her body, his look was anything but indifferent. She was only partially dressed, wearing a skirt and a somber utilitarian bra. Despite their drab setting, Henry couldn't help giving her cleavage an appreciative gaze.

He forced his eyes upward. "My name is Henry Welles, I'm looking for Dr. Mortimer Burbach."

If Anya found his gaze unpleasant, she didn't show it. In fact, she leaned back on the bed, causing her chest to jut out further. "I could tell you where he is." She said, calmly.

"Directions would be appreciated." He said, throwing her a small notepad from his pocket.

"You are an American?" She guessed, waving the notepad.

Before Welles could answer, someone was pounding at the door. Raising a finger to his lips, Welles grabbed a robe from the closet and tossed it to her. He gestured towards the door with his gun.

Nodding, she threw on the garment. Stepping towards the door, she took a breath before opening it a crack.

"Yes?" She asked, her voice betraying nothing out of the ordinary.

"There's a security breach," the soldier explained, "Have you seen anything?"

Gesturing towards the bathroom, the shower still running, Anya said, "I'm about to shower, I've seen nothing."

The soldier offered her a lecherous smile. "I could join you comrade,"

From behind the door, Welles prepared for the shot which would end the soldier's life.

Devoid of emotion, Anya said, "Never Vadim, don't make me say it again."

She slammed the door shut. When she heard the sound of footsteps walking away, she faced Welles. "When you leave, take me with you."

"Why should I?" He asked. He was sympathetic, but could already imagine the apoplexy of Chief Williams if he returned with her on his arm.

"I will give you the directions you want. If you don't agree, I will tell them you are here."

"What makes you think I'll let you live?"

The hint of a smile played at Anya's lips as she seated herself on the bed. "You are American. You don't kill women, not in the movies."

"I'm afraid life is more complicated than the movies." Welles muttered, tightening his grip on the the gun.

Stepping into the hallway, Welles ignored the recriminating voices which played in his head. He made a choice. If there were consequences, so be it. They could wait in line with the rest. What mattered was he had his directions. Marching towards the lab, Welles felt the hunter's instinct of closing in on his prey. Whatever else happened tonight, Dr. Burbach would die and the world would have one less monster.

The laboratory doors were unlocked and unguarded, Welles stepped inside and raised his gun. The room was dark, illuminated by a single candelabra burning on the work table. A figure in a white lab coat hunched over the desk. Stepping forward, Welles broke the silence with a crunching step.

The white figure's movements froze. Slowly, the body straightened upright. The white of the lab coat filling Henry's vision like a snow-covered mountain capped by the bearded face of Dr. Mortimer Burbach. Known for his mental genius, but remembered for the sheer size of his body.

"Agent Welles," rasped the cultured voice in accented English. "I thought they would send someone who didn't fail the first time."

"If at first you don't succeed and all that," Welles replied, his gun aimed squarely at Burbach.

"I assure you, there won't be another opportunity to try again."

"It won't be necessary. Before I put you down like the beast you are, care to tell me why the Soviet's airfreighted your bulk here?"

A smile grew beneath Burbach's broad mustache. Before he could say anything, the sound of charging men came from behind the door. Distracted for a split second, Welles was unprepared for Burbach rushing him. The mountain fell. Welles' head cracked against the solid floor. The image of soldiers surrounding him was his final sight before fading from consciousness.

Waking surprised Welles, the shackles on his wrists did not. He was handcuffed to an upright table of some kind, but inside what? The gurney was encased in a half cylinder of steel and copper. The open lid reminding Welles too much of a coffin for comfort. The speculation didn't last long, Welles attention was seized by the oversized bulk of Dr. Burbach staring at him with undisguised glee.

"He's awake!" Dr. Burbach announced.

"Excellent," said another man. Welles turned to look at him. The uniform ranked him as a Colonel in the Soviet army. The paunch ranked him as a functionary bureaucrat. To his right stood a lieutenant nearly as tall as Burbach, but with a face twice as menacing.

"Tell me," the Colonel said, "What does your government know about operation *Skazki?*"

Henry looked at him blankly.

"I will loosen his tongue," The Lieutenant spat, stepping forward.

The Colonel raised a restraining hand. "Silence Lt. Egorov."

Burbach cackled. "He doesn't know a thing about *Skazki*, wouldn't believe it if you told him. He's here to assassinate me, nothing more."

"No doubt, he was ordered to interrogate me." The Colonel insisted.

Henry shook his head. "I was sent here to terminate Dr. Burbach. Do us both a favor, let me finish the job and I'll get out of your hair."

Burbach leered at the sneering Egorov. "*Skazki* is nothing without me, the good Colonel would love to order his attack dog to put a bullet in my head himself, if he could figure out how to explain such an accident to his masters."

Clearly crestfallen, the Colonel coughed. "Agent Welles, you have shown, what's the word?... Bravado," he enunciated the word slowly, each syllable said like a word in itself. Shaking his head, the Colonel turned his back on Welles and walked out the door.

Lt. Egorov remained. His eyes boring into Welles.

Burbach stared at Egorov expectantly. "You may go too."

Egorov hesitated.

"Lt. Vadim Egorov, if you want to hover over my nurse, you can do it later. Go away." Burbach dismissed.

After giving both Welles and Burbach a final glare, Egorov obeyed.

Tutting aloud, Burbach watched the retreating soldier. "Egorov would happily tear the flesh from my bones. Toadstools like him meant nothing to me in the reich, and mean even less now."

"Before we begin, care to clue me in on the *Skazi* project?"

Welles was playing for time, both knew it.

"I'd have laughed it off as a fairy tale, if I hadn't seen it myself. Somehow, it's real enough. Real enough to require my services to bring it to fruition. Real enough to have my every whim granted."

"I find that hard to believe."

"Precisely, which is why there is no point in prolonging what comes next."

"You'll be disappointed to discover how little I have to say." Welles assured him, "Whatever your torture, I won't talk."

Burbach didn't laugh, but he grinned wide enough to see his teeth beneath the bristling beard. "I do not care about your secrets, your government or your personal affairs. Disappointed though Lt. Egorov was, the Colonel was easily convinced to surrender you to my keeping. The alternative would have been to cull one of his soldiers for research. Your presence is an unexpected gift."

A new sense of panic possessed Welles, his hands straining at the restrains.

"They are quite secure. Do you notice the tubes?"

Welles nodded.

"Cryogenics, agent Welles is the secret to immortality. By placing the body in a state of suspended animation, we can extend lifespans by decades. Nothing more than sleep to the body, allowing you to wake in a whole new future."

"Sounds like a fairy tale,"

Burbach chuckled. "It does, does it not? Unlike Sleeping Beauty or Snow White, I'm afraid there are no curses and no true love to wake you from this slumber."

"Don't sell yourself short, you're quite the witch-doctor."

Burbach grasped his hands behind his back and lectured. "We've had some success with cold blooded creatures, but mammals have been... difficult to revive. Understand, it is not enough to freeze the body, but to slow down the metabolism and stabilize the..."

"Is boring me to sleep is the first step?" Welles interrupted.

Ignoring Welles, Burbach continued. "I have created an anesthetic gas to mix with the oxygen. Each breath, combined with the decrease in temperature will place you in a deep and dreamless slumber. Without this drug, you would freeze to death within minutes. Although," he paused, stroking his beard,

"There's always a chance you will freeze to death anyway. Cryogenics is not yet an exact science."

Welles tried to come up with a witty retort, but his words were taken away when the doors of the laboratory opened again.

"Nurse, prepare the patient." Burbach ordered.

"Yes Herr Doctor," Anya said.

Burbach's ranting continued while she went about her duties. Welles ignored the ravings. If he was about to die, he was grateful to have a beautiful woman as his final memory. It was a more pleasant image to carry into the hereafter than the beard of Dr. Burbach.

"He's ready Doctor." Anya announced, fitting the oxygen mask to Welles face.

Rubbing his hands with glee, Burbach said, "Close the chamber and start the gas."

Anya closed the hatch. Stepping to the row of canisters, she twisted the nozzles and the hiss of air began making its way into Henry's mask.

"Herr Doctor," she said, "Activity has been reported from the monitoring room."

Burbach's face puckered. Glancing from Anaya to Welles and back again. He flipped a switch and liquid nitrogen began pumping into the chamber. "Goodbye agent Welles, by the time we return you will be fast asleep. Remember, if we are successful, we will meet again. Sweet dreams." Before leaving the lab, he waved to Welles. Following, Anya gave Welles a forlorn look, but added the whisper of a smile before disappearing.

Despite the creeping cold, Welles' forehead had broken into a sweat. In a matter of moments, he would be gone. The anesthetic gas would drag his consciousness away. His body left either dead or next to dead. When sleep came, it would be the start of his ice age. Only sleep didn't come. In fact, he wasn't feeling drowsy at all.

He realized Anya must have only started the oxygen. The relief was mixed with horror. Without the gas, he was guaranteed to freeze to death. Completely conscious as the frostbite ravaged his body. The temperature was dropping rapidly. Already, he could feel a creeping numbness pressing into his extremities. Staring at his bonds, Welles tried to find a weakness in the leather strap or chains.

Liquid nitrogen poured into the chamber from twin tubes on either side of the gurney. Cold was filling the space inside like rising water. Invisible to the the naked eye, the cold would kill him as surely as drowning. Although it wasn't invisible, not completely. Like warm breath on a Fall day, the liquid nitrogen clouded briefly. That was when Welles saw it: The Leak.

The chamber wasn't completely sealed. If Anya hadn't turned on the sleeping gas, what else hadn't she done? Raising his legs, Welles pushed his feet against the lid. His fingers and toes were numb. He kicked against the lid. It rocked open an inch, letting a surge of room temperature air inside before rocking shut again. It was a moment, but it was enough to give him hope.

He braced his legs again. Welles kicked at the lid with all his strength. It swung open, the liquid nitrogen spreading like a fog throughout the room. Welles had an idea. By stretching his hand at an angle, he could expose the chain to the freezing gas.

The hand, temporarily relieved by the open lid, screamed from the burning cold. Despite the pain, he held fast, watching as frost gathered on the chain. He was losing feeling in his hand, the crying of his nerves growing fainter by the moment. He yanked upward and the chain broke with a satisfying crack.

Instinctively, he stuck the ice cold hand under his left armpit, trying to warm feeling back into it. With a dull ache, he flexed the fingers. He didn't have time to waste and pulled the hand out and fumbled with the strap on his left wrist. Launching out of the chamber, Welles quickly closed it. To a casual glance, it would look like he was still on ice.

Breathing heavily, Henry felt like he had just finished trekking through a snowstorm in the dead of a Dakota winter. He was frostbitten, but he was free.

There were no missteps when Welles stepped into the monitoring room. Dr. Burbach was sitting at a control panel, staring at an erratic chart. Over his shoulder stood Anya. Both turned at the sound of the door opening. Anya smiled, Burbach did not.

"You were right Doctor, success meant we would see each other again." Welles said, raising the rifle he'd taken from a soldier along the way.

Burbach started to reply, but the rifle spoke first. Two shots roared in succession. One to the head, one to the heart. Dr. Mortimer Burbach was dead. Mission accomplished.

"We need to get out of here," Welles said, gesturing towards the door.

She nodded. Stepping to the control panel, she began to flip switches and press buttons. "This will give us a distraction." She explained.

Impatiently, Welles glanced from her to the door. He could see Anya was ignoring the large red button. If he had to guess, that would give them the biggest distraction. He pressed it.

Anya swore. Her large eyes flashing at him in anger. "What have you done?"

"Come on," he said, grabbing her arm.

He felt her trembling as the sirens began ringing over the loudspeaker.

"You shouldn't have pressed that." Anya said as they stepped into the halls.

Welles ignored her. The results spoke for themselves, literally. The loudspeakers were instructing everyone to vacate the premises, providing them the perfect way to slip into the crowd. He was already calculating the distance to the exfiltration point.

"Where the garage?" He asked.

The pair arrived in the facility garage in time to discover is wasn't an original destination. Soldiers were already swarming over whatever had wheels and an engine to escape, some leaping into moving vehicles as the drove through the open bay doors.

Wordlessly, they joined the rush, scrambling to an unclaimed jeep. Anya leapt into the driver's seat and cursed. "No key!" She grumbled.

Before Henry could reply, he found himself in a fist fight.

When Lt. Vadim Egorov saw Welles in the garage with nurse Romanov, escaping himself became a lower priority. Shooting the American would be too easy, too clean. He wanted to hurt him. Grabbing Welles by the collar, Vadim threw him from the passenger seat of the jeep and to the ground. Landing on his shoulder, Welles grimaced.

In the jeep, Anya tore off the panel beneath the ignition to hot wire the vehicle into submission.

Adding to the sirens screaming overhead were tremors shaking the facility. Welles didn't know what was happening, but shaking concrete meant it was time to leave. Vadim didn't give him the chance to stand, kicking him in the stomach sending Welles rolling away from the jeep.

When Vadim kicked again, Welles was ready, catching the foot. He pushed the Soviet off balance, rocking him to the ground. He recovered quickly, but it was long enough for Welles to stand too.

Raising his hands like a boxer, Welles crouched for the brawl. Vadim smiled. It didn't make him any prettier. He struck out with a left jab, Welles ducked and delivered a rabbit punch. He got too close and Vadim's arms encircled him in a crushing grip. The oxygen was forced from Welles lungs breath by gasping breath.

Anya threw the small metal panel. It bounced off Vadim, who laughed. When he'd finished with the American, he'd come for her next.

"Henry, we have to go!" Anya yelled.

The agent's eyes bulged in a response he couldn't speak. Under normal conditions, he'd have happily bantered, suggesting she get out of the vehicle and help him take the Russian strongman. Instead, he was drowning on dry land. Dying in a fight was better than freezing to death, but given the option he'd rather keep living. After all, he still had to help with the apple harvest.

The sound of the jeep's ignition roared and Welles was vaguely conscious of the sound as he struggled against Vadim crushing hold.

Anya watched in dumbstruck horror. She had the vehicle running, she could escape. Defection to America wouldn't be possible without Welles, but living in Russia was better than dying in Russia.

Before Welles could fall unconscious, the floor heaved. Vadim kept his footing, but dropped his captive. Released from the vise grip, Welles gasped desperately on the ground.

"Goodbye American." Vadim said, raising his foot to put the fallen Welles out once and for all.

The wall behind them broke, shards of concrete crumbling to the ground. Anya's decision was made. She put the vehicle in gear.

Vadim turned and cursed as he was faced with the most terrifying sight he would ever witness. From the ground, Welles stared in abject disbelief.

Crawling through the broken wall, wings retracted to fit through the space, claws marking the floor where it stepped, shaking the world with each footfall, the monster rushed at Vadim. The soldier couldn't react fast enough, his scream had only begun when the beasts jaws closed on him.

With every ounce of remaining strength, Welles rushed from the floor to the moving jeep. Halting could mean her death, but Anya paused for the longest heartbeat of her life. He leapt for the jeep. The moment he landed she gunned the engine, racing forward out the door.

Finishing what remained of Lt. Vadim Egorov, the monster roared and the facility shook. An issue of flame leaping out from between bloody fangs was the last thing Welles remembered before blacking out.

From the balcony of his hotel, Welles admired the night sky and lit a cigar. A doctor might argue the recent damage to his lungs, near freezing, oxygen deprivation, and bruising, would mean he shouldn't smoke. His nurse wasn't arguing.

Glancing back inside, he gazed at her in the bed. The sheet barely covering her glorious figure. Welles puffed the cigar, watching as the tip grew red. It was a miracle either of them were alive.

The office wanted him to come in for debriefing. After he notified them of Burbach's termination, they still had questions. They wanted to know what he'd learned about *Skazki*. Henry Welles knew they wouldn't believe him. They wouldn't believe Anya either. He took another long draw from the cigar and removed it from his lips, releasing a billow of smoke into the night sky. He still hadn't decided what to tell them. Would anyone really believe he'd survived meeting a dragon?

THE COLDEST TRADE
BY C.W. STEVENSON

"That's all of it," Kirkman said, and the tail box at the end of the hover-cycle whirred shut. From their location on the Plains, they couldn't see McCoy's Rock, but he could see the luxury zeppelins of the social elite drifting over the city.

Zarif hadn't been listening. He studied the orchard that he and his partner had just plundered. Before, even while they'd gone through each nest throughout the orchard, Tarifree's squawked at the men, plaguing their intrusion with continuous birdsong.

Zarif turned an ear to the orchard.

"Hear that?" he asked.

Kirkman scoffed, dismissing the man's paranoia. He was always too careful. Kirkman had gone along with Zarif's ridiculous spending on equipment they didn't need *solely* because Kirkman had no intention of going in on the deal alone. He found their contact too intimidating to handle alone.

Hover-cycles are an escape plan. Just try running on foot through the snow and see how far you get.

And, *We'll need the guns for protection. We don't know who or what the hell could come across us out there.*

It'd been Kirkman's idea to hike up to the Plains—only called the Plains because it was one of the only flat regions on all of Vindorr, aside from the two port cities of McCoy's Rock and Sherrfield, the rest of the planet was covered in mountains of black rock. Hover-cycles, though convenient in the winter months, were an expensive commodity. As for the fusion pistols, Kirkman wasn't opposed to having *some* protection, but they too came at a hefty price. Zarif had opted to purchase the HKII, only the second most expensive piece of weaponry the underground gunsmith possessed.

Altogether, Kirkman imagined that Zarif's protective measures had cost them about a quarter of the take.

Kirkman sighed. "I don't hear a damn thing. Now let's go, they'll be waiting at the Shiv already."

Zarif held up a finger. "Quiet," he said.

"For fuck's sake, Zarif" said Kirkman, and he climbed on top of the hover-cycle.

"Listen. Nothing at all, right? You don't find that eerie?"

Zarif didn't wait for a response. In a panic, he yanked the pack clung to his shoulder off and onto the frosty ground. Unzipping the pack, Zarif's hand dipped inside and began digging around.

Kirkman shook his head as Zarif came up with a fusion pistol tight in his grasp.

"*Enough,* Zarif. Let's get out of here, we've got all—"

"*Shut up!* Shut up and listen."

Kirkman sighed, annoyed more than anything. He didn't have the patience for this. Not now. Not when they were so close. An hour ride back to Sherrfield and they'd be off planet on their way to Jericho by tomorrow, retired.

He rubbed his eyes, looked back up and was about to call out Zarif again when he heard it. Distant, and difficult to comprehend what he was listening to, the more he focused on the lone sound the more it became clear.

Humming.

Kirkman saw it first, blotting out a part of the sun as it made its way over the ridgeline. His eyes grew twice their normal size.

"Ship!" Kirkman yelled, but Zarif was already on his hover-cycle.

A glance at the ship was enough to make out the insignia etched in bronze across the body of the incoming ship. A mountain bearing the Federation "F" below its peak made it clear it wasn't local law enforcement.

The Federation warden's thrusters blew up snow and ice from the ground as it descended, turning it into slush as it rained down upon Kirkman's head.

Hopping onto the other hover-cycle, Kirkman held tight as he sped back inside the orchard.

The ship turned sharp as dozens of Tarifrees flew frantically from the orchard's branches in all directions, desperately trying to make their escape from the zooming craft on the ground.

Kirkman glanced back to check if his plan had worked. No warden would risk the deaths of such a rarity. The yacking birds only existed in the few dozen orchards across Vindorr.

A second later, the ship was overhead, speeding higher and higher, further north of his current course.

Leaving?

It was impossible to say.

As the ship reached the ridgeline, suddenly it stopped. A dark figure came down from the stationary ship, repelling down until Kirkman lost sight of the figure behind the ridge.

Kirkman turned course again, jerking the hover-cycle to the east. It'd be a longer route to Sherrfield, but he'd lose the warden through the tight canyons and craggy rocks along the way. Then, there was a flash in front of the hover-cycle's nose and an explosion as debris from the ground coated his face. Snow, ice, rock, and dirt covered his eyes, making it into his nose, and mouth as well. He spat, wiping away the snow so he could see and squinted, just narrowly missing a tree, forcing him to swerve. He was losing momentum.

Another explosion, this time closer. The rock and hard ice bursting from the ground smacked him in the face even harder than before. His face stung, and he was sure he was bleeding.

Warm blood filled his eyes. It would've been soothing against the freezing wind if his face wasn't in such pain. Now he truly couldn't see. Kirkman tried to wipe his face, but he felt tired, and weak, swatting at air until he became limp. As the hover-cycle came to a stop, he fell face first into the snow.

***

Oden Grey inched closer to the figure buried in the snow. Placing his thermal rifle against the icy bark of a tree, a few of the panicked Tarifrees squawked overhead.

Then, the still figure turned over on his back with a groan. As he came to his senses, Oden watched as the man wiped the snow and gunk from his face before making eye contact with him. The man panicked. Oden saw him reach for his side, and as his body turned, Oden saw what appeared to be a pistol of sorts.

In several lightning-quick strides, the warden was over the man, katana in hand. The steel gleamed even more spectacularly against the white of the snow. It was the weapon of choice for the wardens of old, when dignity, honor, and perseverance mattered. Oden belonged to the old breed.

Kirkman squealed, closing his eyes as he brought the fusion pistol up to fire. His finger on the trigger, he squeezed.

Nothing happened.

Opening his eyes, Kirkman saw the indigo, black-bearded face of the warden looking down upon him—a pigmentation generated from a myriad of experiments, when the enhancing of one's physical and metal capabilities was still facing trial and error. Now, anyone with the credits could change their appearance. But...to enhance one's instincts, their senses, their physical strength...only the Federation could approve such an operation.

He'd expected the warden to be snarling-mad, brows furrowed, or at least cursing at him for having attempted to kill him. Instead, the man looked down on him without any sort of emotion, like some machine programmed to only concern itself with the next task.

He looked at his pistol. It'd been cut in two, not far from where his index finger clenched the trigger.

"You can put that down now," the warden said matter-of-factly. Reaching into his coat pocket he produced a pipe, masterfully carved with swirls and vines, and the wood—Elder Tan, the largest of Corsaga's trees.

"I—yeah, okay," and Kirkman dropped the remains of his pistol in the snow.

"The eggs are with the hover-cycle?" the warden asked, looking off into the distance at the overturned transport. Lighting the pipe, the contents inside singed and crackled, shrinking as the leaves turned to ash. Oden released a heavy cloud of smoke.

Kirkman thought about going for the warden's legs right then, but something stopped him. The warden had been confident armed with only a sword when Kirkman pulled the fusion pistol. The warden could've gone for the rifle, but he'd chosen to diffuse the situation without it. And here he was now, not looking at him, appearing distant and unconcerned with Kirkman at his feet, and smoking.

The thought of this man thinking so little of him caused Kirkman to feel quite offended. Kirkman thought himself not one to be trifled with, and yet this man was treating him little more than an insect.

"The eggs," warden Grey repeated. "Are...they...on...the bike?"

Now he was just being condescending, Kirkman thought, but he answered without complaining, "Inside the tail box."

"And your partner?"

"He doesn't have any."

Now the warden looked down on him. Pressing a boot hard onto his sternum, the warden's face finally showed a tinge of anger, but not much. "Lie to me, and I'll leave you up here to walk back to Sherrfield. Let's see how far you get with that," the warden said, gesturing to his legs.

Confused, Kirkman propped himself up a little to get a better view. He nearly passed out at the sight of a white bone poking through his trousers.

"Oh! My fu—what?" Kirkman said, even though he hadn't a clue what he was saying.

"I'll set your leg, stop the bleeding, put you onto my ship and onto the next transport out to McCoy's Rock. There are doctors who can have you walking good as new in a week's time. Now, *tell me*, where is your partner going with the rest of the eggs?"

Kirkman was sobbing now, not just from the pain, but from the whole situation. "I can't! I...I need to know—oh god—I need to know I won't be locked away."

Oden then gave Kirkman a slight nudge with his foot against Kirkman's bad leg. Seeing white from the pain, Kirkman screamed.

When he'd calmed, Oden squatted down beside the panting Kirkman, placing one of his large indigo hands on his shoulder.

"Let's assess the damage, okay? You've caused a biological tragedy to a species that takes nearly two standard centuries to hatch their young. As soon as you and your partner touched those eggs, they became stillborn, they'll never hatch now. I won't forgive you, but I can save you if you decide to save yourself. The Federation will decide what becomes of you. So, your next sentence will be either you tell me what I want to know, and you live! Or, you say nothing, and you stay here in the snow to bleed out. The Tarifrees will most likely come scavenge you before you pass on," then Oden stood. "I guess that'd be some measure of revenge for killing their young. Now, decide."

Of course, Kirkman told him everything.

***

Sherrfield's Exotic Specimens and Pets was no longer in business in Sherrfield. When Kohl had inherited the store, she'd taken on her grandfather's exponential debt as well. Not long after his death, McCoy's Rock appealed as the more suitable place to do business thanks to Sherrfield's taxes, but still, she kept "Sherrfield" in the stores name. It had a sentimental value, she supposed.

But now things were quite different. No longer were there heaps of children running through the aisles laughing as they clutched Soymian Puffballs to their chests. No, the store's clientele had changed dramatically.

Kohl rubbed at her eyes as the young man babbled on about the viquarium he'd been preparing for his twin Darkori Basilisks.

"—and if the temperature changes even *ten degrees* Fahrenheit, the darkoris become territorial. They'll actually fight each other until I adjust the temperature back! Then if I—"

"Ah fascinating," Kohl said absentmindedly. She had a shipment coming in less than fifteen minutes. She'd need to lock up the top of the store, and this...*enthusiast* was going to make her late.

The young man adjusted the quadfocals on his face and shot a look of disappointment.
"If I'm boring you, I'm sorry. I thought you'd care, being you're the owner and all."

"Nope. Don't give a shit," and she pointed to the entrance. "Now scram."

"Actually, I was hoping you could help me?"

"I can help you leave if that's what you mean," replied Kohl. Then, taking the young man by the crook of an arm, she began to lead him toward the door, but before they reached the door, the young man planted his feet.

"C'mon! I hear you've got a whole treasure trove of exotics beneath us. Skogur Jackal cubs, Blue Hephlins, and...I heard a week ago you smuggled an actual Kanovarr. That true?"

Twisting the youth's arm back behind his head, Kohl hissed in his ear. "If I did...why...*in the fuck* would I tell you about it? Now...get out." She released him, watching as he went stumbling back.

His hand on the door, the young man stopped again. "Sell me a few of the jackal cubs, I'll pay whatever you want!"

"Why, so you can throw them in with the basilisks and see who comes out alive?"

"So, you *do* have them! Just two, please!"

"You sick little bastard. If I catch you in here again, I'll follow you home and throw *you* in with the basilisks. Then we'll see how long you stay alive when I adjust the temperature."

Glaring at her now, the young man turned to leave.

"Freak!" he spat, and then he was gone.

Kohl thought about running after him, dragging him back inside, and actually doing what she promised, but just as the thought finished crossing her mind, the door opened again. At first, she thought the young man had saved her the trouble of coming after him and here he was to spout more shit.

What entered was a tall figure in a cloak, a dark hood wrapped around its head.

"I don't sell any fucking dream resin," she said. "You'll have a better time finding that in the alleyways by the square. Now get the fuck out, I'm closing shop."

A hand came out from under the cloak. It held something, but he was too far so she stepped closer. Though his skin was dark, in the dim light she could make out his indigo complexion.

An egg.

"Shit, I..." she trailed off.

"Your sellers won't be coming by," and the thing, that she could clearly see now as a tall, wiry man, placed the egg on a shelf.

"Been a long time since a warden has shown up around here. My grandfather told me things about you lot."

"Herman, mmm. The man wouldn't have stooped down to your level though."

"You knew him?" she asked. Cautiously, she took a few steps back.

"I've been around for a time."

"A Federation warden?"

The man pulled his cloak open enough for Kohl to see the badge pinned to his chest. She could also see he didn't have a gun, only a sword sheathed in its scabbard hanging limp against a leg.

A katana.

She looked to the back of the store for the hidden space in the wall where she kept the blaster. She'd never make it there in time.

"You'll never make it there in time," he told her, as if the fucker could read her thoughts. He continued, "You do this for a few centuries and some situations always play out the same."

"What do you want?" asked Kohl.

"These guys were small time. What's next? Tell me what and tell me who."

Kohl was already ruined, she knew it the second she saw the badge. All of her hard work...for nothing. Nearly a *decade* spent paying off her grandfather's debt, just for everything to come crumbling in shambles. The following decade she just...got greedy. Maybe some of the sales were inhumane, but while they were in her care at least they weren't abused.

Kohl figured, once the sale was final, and the purchase in the hands of the buyer, she no longer felt responsibility toward it, sales both legal and illegal. You can't *force* a person to love a pet or take care of it properly.

Her grandfather claimed, "I can always tell the good owners from the bad ones."

Kohl didn't think the gift had been passed down. Who was she to judge good from bad? Giving an organism a better chance at a higher quality of life was better than *no chance*.

"I was just trying to do the right thing," she mumbled.

Oden Grey produced a rare grin, rarer than most of the creatures Kohl held here, he suspected.

"Well, you've got a funny way of showing it. So, you want to lead me down below, or do I need the marshal to have his men tear this place apart to find the hidden door?"

Kohl wheeled an empty two-hundred-gallon aquarium out of the way until the cellar door was completely uncovered. Kohl hit a switch against the wall and the door buzzed open until through the darkness a set of winding stairs could be seen.

Oden followed her. Down here it was much colder. Oden figured this enterprise was much more lucrative than he'd imagined. The floor was nothing but loose rock and soil, but the space was enormous. Most of the space sat unused, but what Oden could see was nothing short of impressive. There were large pens with steel bars a foot thick, some enclosed and some not. There were vats and aquariums, some full, recently used still filled with bits of floating excrement, while the majority were rusted and falling apart. There were terrariums containing a variety of alien atmospheres, aquariums filled with ice, kaleidoscopic soils, and some that appeared to be lava.

"What's down here now?" Oden asked, still searching the room, observing the creatures that she might have kept prisoner at some point.

"Nothing," Kohl replied.

Noticing the aquarium that held the lava, Oden saw a hole in the upper right-hand corner of the glass.

"A Golden Pike...*escaped?*" Oden asked.

Kohl couldn't believe this was happening, but she soldiered on. "Yes. I had to put her down. Either that or the whole city would've been in jeopardy."

"So noble of you. I've always wanted to see one."

Kohl shook her head. "Try killing one and then living with yourself."

"Somehow it appears you've made a miraculous recovery. How many creatures that you've sold this way do you believe actually have better lives?"

"I don't know," she said in shame. "I shouldn't have started any of it. The money...it was just...it...it got out of hand."

"And people wonder *why* wardens prefer the company of other species beside their own..." Oden then tapped on one of the steel bars of a pen. "These look new."

Kohl nodded.

"For what?" Oden asked

"Iron-Tails," Kohl said.

Oden strode steadily to where Kohl stood, and she began to tremble as he came closer. Oden looked down upon her.

"When will you go extract them?"

"I...I won't. Like the two who were supposed to deliver the Tarifree eggs, they deliver what my customers order. Tomorrow, my usual contractor is heading up to Ystantagar Mon."

"What for?" the warden asked.

"Why go up to the mountain?"

"No. Why capture the iron-tails?"

Kohl sighed. "For the sport. They'll go after juveniles, then train them for the fighting pits inside the Wall of Seraphim."

"Contact the contractor...tell them they'll need another means of board and transport for the iron-tails once extracted."

"Okay," said Kohl.

Oden Grey turned to leave back out the way they'd come but stopped. He looked at Kohl, standing in the dim light of the cavernous room. There was fear in her eyes, that was plain enough to see, but what he noticed most of all was her shame.

"Your grandfather loved all creatures. Did you know there was a time he thought of becoming a warden? He was a boy when I promised I'd take him to the academy. When he was a little older, and running the store on Sherrfield, he became my most trusted source. He knew the underground business of the animal-trade."

Aghast at what the warden was telling her, Kohl shook her head. "I didn't know. He never said anyth—"

Oden continued, "What begets me is how his own flesh and blood would resort to the same level of scum he helped put away."

Making his way up the stairs, he left Kohl sobbing where she stood.

***

Kohl waited an hour after the warden had left.

She'd hoped the sobs had the effect she'd wanted—a little bit of pity might go a long way, creating an opportunity to strike. But Kohl couldn't help but dwell on the facts the warden had presented. The shame in her actions cut her to the core, and she found *real* tears beginning to well.

Steeling herself, she slammed a hand against the wall. What her grandfather did or didn't do had no impact on the present situation. There was still a way out of this yet.

Using the viewscreen in the center of the store, she scrolled down the bluish hue of the screen until she found the contact information she'd been searching for.

 Paul didn't answer *hello* like a normal person, just breathed, waiting for Kohl to muster the courage to speak.

If she did this now, if she failed, then this was it. She'd go away forever, locked in some Federation prison, floating through the black of space. No fresh air, not even a rock to look at. Nothing but metal, chains, and empty space. Cold, lifeless colors would be her future. Her life would be spent around the sort of people she did business with, but that wasn't her. No. She was better than that. But she asked herself what other choice did she have? Give up? Now? This warden...he was the only one who could jeopardize her business aside from those two fools she'd hired, Kirkman and Zarif, but they'd be easy enough to keep quiet. Paul would see that too she wagered. That is, if he didn't keep her quiet first.

Finally, Kohl found the words, "There's a warden. He hasn't called backup. It's just him, alone. I'm...I'm sending him to the mountain, Ystantagar Mon."

Paul sighed, then asked, "Why? Couldn't you have taken him out at the store?"

She could have. But there was that fear. Maybe she would've slipped and never reached the gun in time. Underneath the store, there were several weapons stashed. But a million things could've gone wrong, and anyhow, she wasn't prepared to do murder. Zapping a couple of thieves in her shop after finding them in the back huffing Al'drafian scud with a taser was one thing, but shooting a man in the head because she let herself get caught up in her own greed was another.

"I..." she began, "There wasn't a chance. Anyways, this one is different. He's one of the old wardens. Still uses a damned sword," scoffing at the last bit.

"He uses a *sword*, and you couldn't take care of him?" Paul asked.

"That's not what I do."

"No," Paul said, "It's not, obviously. But we're going to have a long conversation about this when it's done."

She wanted to explain herself, to tell him how it was that damn Kirkman and Zarif who were responsible! But before she could speak, he was gone.

***

Oden Grey sent the recorded message of the traced call to the local authorities. Annoyed as they were by Grey's interference with planet law, they did not question or complain. Afterall, the warden was in charge here, a representative of Federation law, his word reigned supreme in such matters.

Standing in the darkness of the alley, the warden lit his pipe, waiting. The fragrance of the local tobacco proved a delicacy, and he made a note to replenish his supply on Vindorr before returning home as soon as his business here was complete.

Home.

Four centuries as a warden, and before that, a *normal* life...home wasn't anywhere, not anymore. The cabin on Corsaga had served him well, and he wasn't lonely there. The verdurous surroundings provided him with a plethora of diverse company. And Chief Warden, Ling Abiko was always making an appearance — no doubt sick of the claustrophobic, polluted streets of Jericho's capital, Horizon.

Noticing several figures emerge from the shop, Oden dumped the ashes of the pipe, releasing a final plume of smoke along with his despairing thoughts of the distant past. There'd always be time to indulge in reminiscence.

Oden watched from the alley as Kohl kicked and squirmed in the grasp of the marshal and his deputies. Carrying her away in shackles, they threw her into the back of an aircar.

Oden's transponder pinged as the trace completed, showcasing a route on the screen along with a name associated with the transponder used to answer Kohl's call. The letters shone a bright blue, glowing above the route.

Pauluk Xolteer.

Emerging from the darkness of the alley, Oden approached the aircar.

Kohl's head hung low, she didn't bother moving the tangled mess of multi-colored hair covering her face.

When Oden knocked on the back glass of the aircar for the marshal to roll the prisoner's window down, Kohl jumped in her seat.

Lines of purple stained Kohl's cheeks where tears had mixed with makeup. As if on cue, Kohl's eyes began to well up once more.

The warden spoke without remorse, without emotion, keen on the next task. But there was guilt, deep down. A guilt that saw emotion allowing a criminal he'd some distant connection to catch a break. A lighter sentence perhaps? He could see it done. He could even see her go free at this very moment. Instead, he focused his thoughts on the trafficked animals kept in the mangy cages beneath Kohl's shop, locked away in the darkness, tormented lifeforms without the means to fend for themselves. The warden then decided he would see her sins atoned for in the most meaningful sort of way.

Oden kept his composure as Kohl cried pleas of mercy, then held up a hand.   "Enough," he said. "I want Pauluk Xolteer. Tell me what I need to know, and one day, you may see the light once more. You'll go free. Maybe today... *if* I'm told what I want to hear."

The deep hitching sobs ceased at once as the prospect of freedom loomed before her. Pouring out the truth, she told him everything, from her own illegal operations and that of Paul, to the operations of mutual associates.

"That's all I know, I swear it," Kohl said, hanging her head in reverence. Then she pointed to one of the zeppelins hovering in place over the city. "Paul is there. And there's a shipment of iron-tails...in the cargo hold."

The marshal released her then, much to his dismay, uncuffing the shackles around Kohl's feet and hands.

Oden Grey escorted his newest informant back to Sherrfield's Exotic Specimens and Pets, stopping when they'd reached the entrance.

"There may come a day where I need more information. You'll be here...ready to give it. You will not be paid by the Federation for such information. This information will be an exchange for your freedom. What I do offer is protection—no one will come to harm you for what knowledge you exchange. More so, I offer you redemption."

Kohl nodded her head profusely, managing to spit out a "Yes," before Oden Grey turned to leave.

"I never meant to!" Kohl called out, referring to her crimes, heading down one bad road to the next, until it'd become routine, blind to the destruction of her grandfather's legacy and all she cared for, for the money.

Oden mumbled to himself as he walked away, "They never do."

***

Oden Grey opened the zeppelin's cargo hold via the hacked remote control the marshal provided for his unannounced visit to Paul Xolteer.

As the ramp opened, already a plethora of yellow eyes gleamed back through the darkness. Oden could make out the cages now and he determined there wouldn't be enough space inside to land the cruiser.

Positioning the aircar the marshal had provided near the ramp, Oden opened the door to jump.

Below, dense clouds hid McCoy's Rock from view. Oden jumped a moment later, unconcerned with the deadly heights he leaped through, landing gracefully within the cargo hold.

The iron-tails came alive as the intruder passed along their cages, howling through raspy jowls where six sharp looking tusks jutted from each side.

Oden ignored their warnings, observing their living conditions instead.

A dozen cages littered the cargo hold, filled with two or three iron-tails a piece—mostly juveniles. In each cage, excrement and hay lay strewn beneath each specimen, and with no water or food present. Some appeared sick, without the strength to stand.

Oden Grey glared as he proceeded toward the entrance of the zeppelin's living quarters. Placing one hand on the knob, Oden unsheathed the katana.

Two stories, the luxurious confines of the zeppelin spoke volumes to Oden Grey of the amount of capital this *Pauluk Xolteer* was able to rake in through the illegal trafficking of a native and alien species.

Black furniture, appearing more like priceless pieces of art than a comfortable place to rest, adorned the living room. In the middle of the room, a holo-map beamed vertically, so much so that it was almost touching the vaulted ceiling.

On the west wall, shoulder mounts and heads stuck out—*trophies*—showcasing more than a dozen different species, some of which Oden hadn't the slightest inclination of what they were.

In the center of the room stood a large marble table, carved in the shape of an Earth continent, Africa. On it, tactical gear lay spread out, and a haversack hung from one strap on the back of an attached seat also made from marble.

Even from the other side of the room, Oden Grey could make out the proton hand cannon. Judging by the glow of golden energy sparkling within the pistol's cartridge, the weapon was fully charged.

Walking into Paul's trap, the warden looked up as the ion blasts leaving the pulse rifle lit the room a stupendous blue.

Paul surveyed the scene below from his position on the second story balcony overlooking the room. The warden was nowhere to be seen. Then, Paul felt a hot twinge of pain starting a fire within his guts.

He looked down at his stomach, dropping his pulse rifle to the deck.

Paul grabbed the hilt of the katana as Oden Grey calmly came forth.

"I could smell you," Oden said, the product of horrific experiments gone right inside the laboratories and vats of Earth for the purpose of making Federation wardens a cosmic force to be reckoned with.

His heroics deemed legendary on the worlds of Jericho, Soymia, Corsaga, and a dozen others, Pauluk Xolteer had just received the very worst of introductions to the warden, though he'd never know it.

Paul stumbled forward as he groaned in agony, hanging onto the handrails by some miracle.

He stared into the warden's eyes.

"You've killed me," he said, surprised at the words coming from his mouth, more so as he fell to the deck on his side.

The warden looked down at him, no trace of remorse as the dying man lay bleeding out at his feet. The threat neutralized, he took out his pipe and began to smoke.

"Tends to happen when someone tries to ambush me," Oden explained, and gestured down to the gun.

"Just let me go," Paul said, already forgetting the sword stuck through his guts. His breathing slowed then, and suddenly he was freezing... which was strange since he always made it a point to keep the internal temperature of the zeppelin comfortable. He decided he'd fix the temperature settings as soon as he was done sleeping. Then, a voice brought him back to the present—a deep one—if only for a moment, hoping then that it wouldn't be his last.

"You vie to stay away from the eyes of the Federation in too cold of a trade — the coldest if you ask me."

Pauluk Xolteer never had the chance.

Corpse at his feet, Oden Grey leaned over the railings and dumped the ashes of his pipe, watching as they floated away to the deck below. Then, turning his neck to face the great window of the zeppelin, soft rays of sunshine from a distant Red Giant shone through the small gaps of dense clouds. He gazed down at the rocky surface of Vindorr, taking in its dull color, and craggy, black rocks that stretched as far as the eye could see. With such a view before him, the augmented eyes of the warden could see quite far across the ocean of black.

Aching for home; his cabin, the small population of colonist who dwelled nearby, his neighbors... the green jungles of Corsaga would be a welcoming sight.

Turning to leave, he made it a few steps before he turned back around. Pulling the katana free, Oden wiped his bloody steel clean with a portion of the dead man's pantleg until it was gleaming back with the reflection of the sun.

BET

BY MANNY TORRES

"Listen to the flies," Vamecia said.

"Atlanta is becoming pure trash," Cosmicola, aka Cola, said.

"Becoming? It's done been trash for a long time. Girl, I ain't even gonna talk about it right now."

Cola sat without speaking for a full minute. The silver Honda Accord was warm, and Vam had lowered the windows. But the dumpster smelled so bad, she rolled them back up and turned on the AC. They could still smell it.

8:30 and the sun had set. The back alley behind Peach Jungle was as quiet as it would be for the evening.

"You do whatchoo want, boo," Cola said. "But I'm going to Vegas when we get done here."

Vamecia, with the short black hair that was all hers, unlike Cola's extensions, shook her head. Every quiet stare into nothing while shaking her head meant she was figuring it out. It's why Cola trusted her with her life and ATM password.

"That's counterintuitive," Vam said.

Cola twisted left to get a better look at Vam. Her majestic black hair fell just below her shoulders. *Like Betty Page or Cleopatra,* the woman at the wig store had said.

"You always saying that," Cola said. "What exactly does that mean?"

"I'm working this out in my head, girl. Too much to explain right now. All I know is there ain't shit in Vegas and what I want to start up is right here. How am I gonna trash my city when if I'm not staying around to help fix it?"

"Girl, it ain't your place. It ain't our place to save anything but our jiggly asses. And I got my own shit I need to start up too."

Vam looked at her. "Escort game off the chart right now. There's an ocean of pussy out here but ain't nobody paying for it. You all about *that*, I'm a dance my way out this bih."

"It ain't just about my ass or pussy, girl. I'm serious about the nail shop. My girl Camie gonna help me started up."

"The Vietnamese girl?" Vam said.

"Nah, she Laotian. But that's down the line. We already on top, Vam. I made a knot tonight and you did too. Like we do every night clapping our cheeks on that pole."

"Yeah, that ain't shit compared to the thing Imma start up. But first…"

"Huh. You going through with it? 'Cause it's do or die, boo. Once we in it, we in it up to our titties."

Vam nodded. "Ain't the first time I shot a nigga for money."

"Ain't gonna lie: it's not the best or brightest side hustle."

"Cosmicola, we go big, or we don't go."

Cola sighed. Her eyelashes fluttered like hungry Venus flytraps. She checked her glitter-tipped pink nails. Not too long so her trigger finger wouldn't get caught. She'd put on silver short-shorts and tank top that showed off her natural rack, her lean, muscular arms and map of tattoos.

"We going tonight?" Cola said.

"Got to," Vam said. "Further delays will just back things up. We can't sleep on this shit. How you dressed?"

Cola sucked her teeth. "How you dressed?"

Vam wore a dark denim onesie with short sleeves that revealed her strong arms and a long snake tattoo that went down to her wrist on her left arm. Her other arm was a work in progress of a dragon with big breasts strangling a man whose pant pockets were drawn and devoid of currency.

Guns on the dashboard. Glocks.

Vam pulled out a black and lit it. The smell of grape juice and marijuana temporarily erased the stench of the dumpster.

"We'll just roll up," Vam said. "Far as *they* know, *we* all friends."

"We about to set fire to they shit."

They were getting out of the car, guns in their small purses, when Turk Winslow caught them by surprise. He was an older man with a snap cap and sandals. He stopped in front of the Accord, slamming his palms on the hood.

"What I tell you?" Vam walked close to him, arms crossed. "Our shift is over, nigga."

Cola approached from the other side. "Cheap mufucka. Tip me $5 after my dance. Bastard."

"Fuck you want?" Vam said.

"Ladies," Turk said. "Is that anyway to treat your favorite customer?"

"Yes," Vam said. "Yes it is."

"Come on, now," he said. "I told you I'd show you ladies a good time. You know my motto: wine, dine, and sixty-nine."

Cola got closer. Made sure he saw the gun at the waist of her short-shorts. He looked her up and down lasciviously.

He took a step closer to Cola. "Got yo' tip right here..."

"Whatchoo get your EBT reloaded?" Cola said.

Vam showed him her palm. "Nigga, we got real work to do. Go on home to your wife."

"Hold on, now." Turk started dancing and spinning.

Vam and Cola stood beside each other watching him go at it. When he finally stopped, he was out of breath.

"Ya finished?" Vam said. She turned to go. He grabbed her shoulder and Vam turned swiftly with a short knife. The 4" blade went into his side and Cola kicked him onto the hood of the car. He slid to the ground where they proceeded to kick him until they were satisfied. And maybe he was too because he went down with a grin.

"You just gonna leave him there?" Cola said.

Frustrated, Vam sighed loudly. "Better put his stupid ass in the dumpster. Worst he could do now is leave us a one-star review."

Major Lee's was only three buildings away. They could easily run back to the car it if shit got hot. It was dark and humid tonight, water dripping from the afternoon's rain onto the cobblestone alleyway. The rest steamed up around them.

A long wooden deck had just been installed and small tables were set up with umbrellas.

"Feels like a goddamn pirate ship up in this piece," Vam said.

"Girl." Cola looked at her and chuckled.

The tall beefy guy at the back door was Papa Bear.

"Uh huh." He looked them up and down. "This city is open carry, but you can't come in here with those. Leave your *jammies* out here.

"Jammies?" Cola said.

"That what you call 'em nowadays?" Vam said. "Is that what the kids say?"

He took their Glocks and tucked them behind his waist, under his jacket. They were shown the entrance and long hallway. The interior was the total opposite of the outside of the building. The hallway glowed red and smelled of incense and marijuana. At least it wasn't mildew. Antique light fixtures and velvet paintings lined the walls.

"Fuck we gonna do now?" Cola said. Teeth clenched. One of the gold ones gleamed with a diamond.

"We fynna talk, that's all," Vam said. Cooler and calmer than Cola. She was also very high. She'd burned through the entire joint.

They reached a small, narrow foyer where the doorman there searched them again. The suited creep took pleasure in groping them.

"Nigga, put your hand there and you better leave a tip," Cola said.

The suited doorman grinned. "I got a tip."

They entered a private, smaller bar, as opposed to the bigger bar upstairs. This was small and quaint but with enough room to accommodate a small party. It was smoky and aglow with neon lights. The DJ was a white boy so white they called him DJ Albino. While everyone in the room wore sports jackets and party dresses, he wore an Atlanta Falcons ballcap and t-shirt, which made any white boy look like a clown. He made eyes at Cola as they crossed the room. She rolled her eyes and flipped him off.

Vam's eyes were wide, pupils dilated, making Cola lose some confidence in her. She stuck close to her girl though. She'd never lied to her or let her down.

"Where he at?" Cola said. She leaned into Vam's right side so she could be heard over the sweaty funk playing from the overhead speakers. "You know we aborting this bitch on account they took our guns. Unless you hiding something in that magical pussy of yours."

Vam stood still for a moment, letting the room's energy cyclone around her.

"Yes, my pussy is magical," she said. "No, I ain't hiding shit up in there."

Majors Lee was a tall, muscular black man with a big face, big wide nose, big lips, and big ears. His head was not unlike one of those Japanese floating head gods. He moved majestically, entering the room like a princess. Dressed in a gilded blouse, pleated pants and a pink boa around his neck, he pranced around, smooching and saying hello. Circling the room until he reached where they were standing. He stopped, then dramatically turned to DJ Albino, and gave him a sign to shut the music off.

He walked off with a look of distaste on his face.

"Ma—" Vam said but he kept walking. Floating around, flirting again until he felt it was time to address the two ladies. The music started again. Something smoother. Nina Simone singing "The Look of Love".

Majors got everybody active again, interested in whatever they were doing. Mostly business talks. Propositions, invitations, etc. When the interest faded away from him he stood in front of them again. It was then they realized that three of his best men had their guns drawn. They held them low, below the waist but triangulated around the two ladies.

Majors stepped up so their conversation could be semi-private.

"What they paying you to kill me?" he said. His eyes were hard, shifting between the two of them.

Vam opened her mouth and then closed it. She looked down, sighed. Took a deep breath.

"You would think that," she said. "But we came to tell you...*reveal* to you that someone has in fact paid us a good amount of cash to remove you from the lineup, if you know what I mean."

Majors looked at her the way her angry mother used to. He said,

"Uh huh. It was that mufucking Greek, Yorgus paid you to do it."

Vam nodded. "But we a family, Lee. When it come down to it, our tribe sticks together."

"Correction: when it comes to money, our tribe sticks to the highest bidder."

"Can't argue with that," Vam said. "What's your bid then?"

"My bid is that you both get your stank asses away from here, kill Yorgus and then come back and kiss my ass. I might extend my forgiveness then."

Someone brought Majors a drink in a wide champagne glass. It was something fruity and fuzzy. Vam and Cola could both smell it. He sipped, gulped it down and threw the glass on the carpet where it shattered. The room stood still again with everyone staring and Nina Simone still crooning under all of it.

"You have until the morning to take care of this," Majors said. He began walking backwards away from them, sashaying in his coattails and boa. "My mens will come looking for you. When you return, I'll be expecting the head of the Greek in one of those bootleg Tory Burch purses y'all sport around with."

Vam opened her mouth to say something but kept it to herself.

Unlike Majors and his cast, Yorgus lived outside the perimeter and was a good thirty-minute drive getting there. And then to be black and driving at night into a prominent neighborhood often posed a challenge. It usually took his guards a long time to reach the front gate, check their credentials and let them walk in. Vam was forced to park at the roundabout, and they had to walk up the curving road uphill until they made it to the front entrance to be checked over and searched. Once inside the mansion, they waited in the marble foyer that was right out of a movie with its marble statues, columns, and spiraling stairwells.

"You know, one day, I'm going to find my place," Cola said. "This ain't it. Majors' ain't it either."

"Girl," Vam said. "Me too." No matter how hard she tried, she couldn't instill anymore confidence in her gal pal.

Yorgus had a young sister named Lil Kat. She was stunted, about 4'3". A child's body but with a haggard woman's face. Tired face, stringy blond hair that had seen too many dye jobs. She leaned against one of the columns and stared at them, smoking a long black cigarette.

When Yorgus came down he was wearing a silk robe and pink fuzzy slippers. Neon sunglasses. Silver lame' pants.

"What are you doing?" he asked Lil Kat. "You just standing there? Give them a soda pop or whatever they want."

Lil Kat rolled her eyes and left. Never did bring them drinks.

Yorgus clapped his hands. "No party tonight, ladies. Did you get it done? Is that why you're here?"

Vam smiled. The biggest, whitest smile in the room. "Well... There's been complications, boo."

The room got tense. Lil Kat peeped from around one of the columns.

"No, no, no!" Yorgus threw his fists against his thighs. He circled them, kicked furniture. It took a hit off his meth pipe to stabilize him.

"He found out about it, to be honest," Vam said. "So, we made a deal after he paid us twice what you gave us and told him we'd do you."

"Wait...what? You came here to kill me?"

"Pretty much," said Cola.

"Look, you obviously have more loyalty to me than to him. Right? Otherwise, you wouldn't just be standing there."

"Now that you mention it, Yorgus," Vam said. "We actually work for ourselves. For the highest bidder. No one ever wanted to put us on their side. Maybe it's because we're dancers. Our living is made by getting naked in a gentlemen's club. Maybe it's Cola's degree in science that intimidates y'all mufuckas. In any case, we're just contracted workers. 1099er's, if you will. And if they made an offer, and you're countering, maybe y'all should sit down and hash it out. Pay Cola and me a finders fee."

"You mean a consultation fee?" Cola said.

"Yeah, whatever."

"So...talk it out?" said Yorgus. "He's skipping the line and going for my high-end clientele. I can't have that. He broke the treaty."

"Yorgus, in this country, we have a thing called free enterprise," Vam said. "And Americans are notorious for breaking treaties. Just ask the Indians."

"I fucking know what free enterprise is, I went to school here. How do you think I got established?"

"Alrighty, then. You understand that this is just business, and we can't just go on and go killing our competition. For instance, lotta girls I work with got mad jealousy because of what I pull on my shifts. But that's got nothing to do with them. It's what I got that gets the gold. So, you just gotta show up right and then it's business as usual."

Yorgus stood staring for a while. "No. In this business, you kill to get ahead."

"Well, go on then."

"That's why I paid you. I'll double—no, triple what he's paying you."

"Maybe," Cola said. "Notice we ain't take our guns out, right?"

Yorgus nodded.

"So, if you want to go talk to him, we'll accompany you," said Vam. "Bring a few of your boys with you. Settle in. Bring your little sister too. She look like she can fight. We roll in like we fynna talk and then—*ka-klah!*"

Yorgus thought it over, scratching his chin. "Okay. Let's take the party to him. But this is just talks. Lil, grab a couple of bottles of vodka. We'll take separate cars. Let's go."

"Yeah Lil," Vam said. "Grab the vodka."

"I could use a fucking drink," Cola said.

A three-car caravan drove out of the suburbs and back toward Majors Lee's compound in Old Fourth Ward. Lil Kat rode in the backseat behind Vam and Cola, hugging several bottles of vodka she was told to bring.

Vam and Cola were silent. Vam's high had faded but her mind was racing. Shit just got real. Could her bank account handle the checks she'd just written? She would turn and make eye contact with Cola and silently, they both agreed.

Yorgus was in the car ahead, packed with four other men and their guns: Tech-9's and Glocks. The car driving behind them was an SUV with about eight more henchmen, fully loaded. Vam looked at Cola again like telling her they'd be returning to their apartment as bodies riddled with bullet holes.

"Like Christmas," Lil Kat said. Vam and Cola were momentarily stunned having forgotten she was back there. She spoke with a mild accent.

"The line of cars, going to party," Lil Kat said. "It's like Christmas at home. We bring good things. Gifts. It's not ouzo, so, eh…"

"Yeah," Vam said. She sounded more elevated than she was, affecting a jolly-good time smile. "Gifts for everybody. We got Ms. Santa Claus riding up in this bitch."

They arrived as things lit up around the strip. The cars all parked behind Peach Jungle in the alleyway.

Yorgus, his men, Vam, Cola, and Lil Kat stepped out of their cars like celebrities at a premiere. Yorgus got a good look at the newly installed raw wood deck and said,

"Looks like a goddamn pirate ship."

Majors Lee and his crew rose from behind the wood rails and tables. Waiting for them with open arms. That is, arms aimed at them in the open. Yorgus' men aimed back.

"Hol' up!" Vam stepped up between Yorgus' men, the cars, and Majors. Majors crew had the higher ground, every one of them, even the shot girls had guns pointing down at them.

"They come in peace," Vam said. "Like I told you. They here to talk."

Nodding her head, and knowing she was risking it all, Cola stood beside her.

"Majors!" Yorgus called. *"Bruddah!"* He came up carefully behind Vam and Cola, shielded by them.

"Ain't your *bruddah,* mufucka," Majors said. "You want me dead!"

"You want me dead! But you forget, this is all just business. No need to get so sensitive."

"You ain't hurting my feelings... fuck all that."

"You want me dead, I want you dead," Yorgus said. "What is it they say, if you can't beat them..."

"We already tried that. And look where we at, bruh."

Cola whispered to Vam,

"How are we getting out of this again?"

Vam took a step closer to the deck. "Why don't we all just go inside the bar and talk some sense to each other. Hash it out. Otherwise, we turn to cold bodies in this back alley. I don't know about you, but I'm too pretty to get dusty."

She could see Majors really considering it. Thinking hard. Releasing the trigger of his revolver.

"Y'all can come in and we can talk," Majors said. "Drinks ain't free."

Most of Yorgus' men staid outside. They were allowed to mingle on the east side of the deck. Majors left several of his crew outside as well. Everyone else went inside to talk. Vam was allowed in. Cola was not. Lil Kat was allowed to bring the vodka in. Majors wasn't about to pour from his own wells.

They gathered inside one of the u-shaped bars on the second floor. The lights shined brightly, overhead disco ball spinning, shooting thin lines of lasers over their faces. A pyramid of liquor bottles topped the back of the bar. Vam thought she noticed a whiskey fountain but wasn't sure.

"Stoney, make some drinks," Majors ordered. Stoney only made drinks for his boss and his minions. Vam separated from Yorgus, really trying to figure it out. She knew the mind would answer most questions if she just learned to relax and wait for the answer. Something she didn't have time for right now.

Yorgus stood among them smiling, outnumbered but looking cheerful, ready to toast and drink. Maybe not immediately forgive the death of several of his men and the loss of merchandise, but at least drink a toast to the future.

"This will be a day—a night that goes down in history," he said.

Vam felt pressed in the enclosure. They were suffocating her on purpose.

Majors and Yorgus faced each other at the bar, whispering. Majors was much taller, having to lean to speak into his ear.

DJ Albino put on some music and made eyes with Vam. For that moment that their eyes were locked she saw the fear in his. Majors' and Yorgus' conversation grew louder and heated. Territory disputes, men they'd lost, shipments that were lost or highjacked. Spittle traded between them when they announced how much they hated each other and that they should be dead. Vam was stupid to set this up, and maybe it was her fault, and she should be dead too. She realized she may have been underexperienced to take on such a job.

Vam turned around, squeezing her way to the exit for air when she saw Lil Kat standing in the doorway. She wore her gaudy blouse with sharp shoulder pads but below the waist had only white thong underwear. Her skirt had been converted into thin strips of fabric soaked into the mouth of the vodka bottles. Huge bottles, now that Vam noticed. Almost as big as Lil Kat herself.

Vam waited a moment, blocked from the exit. They stared at each other. Vam saw the light go up in one of Lil Kat's hands and had to duck to miss the overhead flaming cocktails.

Her immediate thought was, *oh, this is how I die...*

Two flaming vodka bottles somersaulted over her and next thing she was feeling the heat and flames that engulfed the back of the bar. A ball of fire rolled across the bar from the back to the front that pushed her into Lil Kat all the way to the back exit. Good thing she hadn't worn a wig because it would have gone up with the rest of the bar. Gunshot after gunshot followed, glass exploding, wood burning.

Next thing she knew she was out on a flaming deck and there were dead bodies surrounding her. She looked up from covering her head to see the last of the men and women from both sides shooting and stabbing each other to death, finishing each other off. She rose low to the ground. Flames rudely licked her back. She eased down the stairs. One of the men dying on the steps grabbed her thigh and she whipped out her knife and stabbed his neck, leaving his liquids pouring down onto the cobblestone. She stepped over the bullet-pocked bodies and saw Cola leaning on the hood of the Accord. Lil Kat stood beside her sharing a joint.

"Hey," Vam said. She coughed, vomited and spit.

"You ain't gotta do all that, now," said Cola. Lil Kat, fire-singed around the edges, nodded. Sirens in the distance. Firetrucks.

"We best go," Cola said.

"Where?" said Vam.

"My place," said Lil Kat. "Afterparty."

"You killed your brother back there," Vam said. She let Cola drive her car.

Lil Kat shrugged. "He was only my half-brother."

SNOWBIRD

BY ALEX SLUSAR

June 2018

John Randall stood in his backyard listening to the night. His low bungalow backed onto a dry wash and from somewhere down it came a sonata of high-pitched yips and howls. He closed his eyes, listened, opened them again. The source was somewhere further south, where the wash curved under the faint jagged purple outline of the San Tan Mountains.

"What's that, then?" Spencer said from a deck chair under the patio awning. He had his ear cocked to the night and a sweating can of San Tan Devil's Ale perched on his broad knee.

"Coyotes," Randall said. He sipped his tumbler of Old Pulteney 12-year. It was cool and briny, an ice spear in the glass stoking a scent of frosted straw which mixed with the spicy mesquite carried on the desert breeze. "They're eating."

"Fantastic. Eating what?"

"Maybe a jackrabbit. Maybe someone's little dog. There's a yappy poodle five houses down that way."

"Think it's done for?"

"I can hope," Randall said.

Spencer stroked his thick grey-black beard and chuckled. "I didn't believe it when I found out you turned snowbird and flew south in the winters," he said. "I thought, our Johnny Canuck, the thinking man at the tip of the spear, gone soft and bald, pissing around in a fuckin' golf cart? But now, mate, I think I get it."

"Get what?"

"Arizona's beautiful, is what."

"Sure," Randall said. "But that's not why I come down here. You thought I'd gone soft and bald, Spence?"

"Briefly worried. Pleased to see you're still sharp enough. Christ, that why you come down? The health benefits?"

"If that were the reason, I'd be in better shape than Church."

"Fair point. I don't know how he does it."

"Probably because he stays kinetic," Randall said. "I mean, I'm active, investments keep my brain going. But he must be squeezing more life from the business of death."

Spencer smiled wryly. "If that's how it is," he said, "we're about to gain some time."

"You're ready, then."

"Aren't you?"

Randall sipped whisky and exhaled. "Yeah," he said. "Though we could still bring in more men for this. Up the odds. Sanchez and Morris are hanging around Coronado. It's a quick flight. They'd get it, you know. They'd understand."

"Can't risk it, mate. I'd love to bring more lads in, but the Americans can't know."

The coyotes yowled. Randall sipped whisky. "One question, Spence," he said.

"Of course."

"If I weren't down here already, would you have told me?"

Spencer swallowed a pull. "At the least, John. Granted, it's a bit of luck for us that you've got your place here. Close to where we need to go." He stared out at where the ripple of mountain met the night. "But even so, I'd have wanted you on this one."

"Even though it's Karlsen."

"*Because* it's Karlsen."

"You think if anyone can take him out, it's me? Us?"

"I think if a man has it coming, better his friends bring it to him."

The patio door slid open. Becker came out carrying a glass charged with cloudy yellow ale. He took a free chair next to Spencer and stretched out, lean, sinewy and pantherine. He looked out at the wash and frowned. "What is that noise?" he said.

"Coyotes," Spencer said.

"How are the kids?" Randall said.

"Ah," Becker said, rubbing his blond buzz cut. "Awake, and off to school. They know they won't hear from me for several days. Matthias doesn't like it, I can hear it in his voice. For Felix, no issue. I think he will be the soldier. He has my temperament." He smiled and drank.

"That's all we need," Spencer said. "Another Becker getting his sausages around things that go boom."

"The world could use another."

"Johnny's got a beautiful piece of globe here, don't you think? Hot days, cool nights, easy access to firearms. A pocket of the Wild West all his own. A man can be a proper cowboy down here."

"I wanted to be a cowboy," Becker said. "As a child. Probably because of a movie. I had a straw hat and a stick horse. Then one day, I wanted to be a police officer, like my father. Finally, I wanted to be a commando. Now I am in Arizona, and I want to be a cowboy again."

"Here's your chance," Randall said.

The patio door slid again. Church came through, his beefy frame wedging through the narrow slot, a whisky glass with a thin smear of caramel-amber liquid in his tapered hand.

"Finally, his nibs," Spencer said. "Becks finished his nasty little firecrackers and talked to his kids in the time you spent with that goddamned thing. Did you clean it, or take it to dinner?"

"That goddamned thing's seen more sea air and salt water in the last four months than a gull's arsehole," Church said. He sat on the end of a deck chair. "Plus six days of range time in this scorching hell. It's like me grandmam's donkey, a reliable beast I'll take no chances with."

"Scorching hell, he says. D'you not enjoy being somewhere other than an oil platform or container ship for once?"

"Maybe Randall likes it, but it reminds me too much of other places." Church swept the fringe of his sandy surfer cut out of his eyes. "You said there was business on dry land, I didn't think you meant America's fuckin' driest."

"When we're done here, mate, you'll have as much water and as many pissed-off Malaysian pirate skiffs as you want."

Church grinned. Becker chuckled. Randall smiled.

"Well, lads," Spencer said.

The coyotes yipped and howled again.

"Tomorrow's the day. Last thoughts, doubts, misgivings, I'd rather hear now so we sleep with clear heads."

Randall eyed Becker, then Church. Then Spencer.

"I wish we didn't have to," Becker said. "But it's better that we do."

"Seconded," Church said. "Not proud, but. Best it's us."

"Same," Randall said.

Spencer nodded. "That it?"

"It's a bit 'ours not to reason why.'" Church said.

"Always is," Randall said.

Spencer leaned forward in his chair. "You know what I reason?" he said. "Karlsen's not who we knew anymore, and by his own choice. He's not strung out or mental, lads. This isn't fucking *Apocalypse Now,* and it sure isn't *The Deer Hunter* – we're not trying to get him to come home. He went to Los Forajidos of his own volition. He chose blood money to help murderous fuckers get better at murder. We can rationalize it, wonder if we were ever on the right side to begin with. But we know the truth, lads. Karlsen's the enemy now."

They sat silent a moment. Randall turned it over in his mind. Knew the others were doing the same. He nodded.

Spencer raised his glass. "Cheers, lads," he said.

"*Slainte,*" Church said.

"*Prost,*" Becker said.

"Absent friends," Randall said.

They finished their glasses and went into the house. Spencer and Church went to collapsible cots in Randall's office and Becker went to the guest bedroom. Randall set the glasses in the sink and went in the living room, where three encrypted laptops slept silently on the coffee table beside maps and grid references. The far wall was covered in images he'd committed to memory. Satellite printouts, swatches of arid desert pockmarked with sun-blasted brown structures, marked up with routes of ingress and egress. Grainy drone photographs of men and vehicles in the desert – the men slender and prodigiously tattooed, their assault rifles and pistols and submachine guns rattling as they fired at a row of targets or practiced hand-to-hand combat in the sand.

In most of the photos a man was circled in red. One had him emerging from a truck. In another he directed the gunmen. One picture showed his face – a vulpine, sallow head with receding black hair shaved close to the skull, eyes obscured by thick black wraparound sunglasses, mouth cantered to the side as he showed the vicious men how best to sight and kill. The face of a friend, once.

Randall turned the lights out and set the security system. He checked his garage where the garbage can was full of stained swatches of gun cloth from Church's cleaning session. Guest etiquette, he thought. He saw their weapons cases and backpacks stacked next to the grey SUV he'd bought with cash earlier in the week. One small black case was Becker's, newly filled with special charges of his own design. Germans and engineering, he thought.

He went to his room, stretched out on his bed in the dark and ran reasons why. Words danced between his ears – honour, duty, principle, brotherhood, revenge. He cancelled the last one. It wasn't revenge. It was enforcing atonement. Extracting a price from blood. When a debt is incurred, someone must collect it, honour the inalienable construct forged in fire and mire.

We know the truth, he thought.

That out of sweltering heat and blinding sun and swirling choking dust and screaming metal, from out of ground shattered by explosion and painted with toil emerged an ethos: no matter colour or blood or aims there was one fight, not for country or coin but for the man at your side in the fray. An ethos understood well by those who went to war. Unforgotten, embedded in the bones of those with Task Force K-Bar in southeastern Afghanistan from October 2001 to April 2002. Nearly three thousand special operations personnel from seven coalition nations. Including:

Lieutenant John Randall, Canadian Armed Forces Joint Task Force 2 assaulter.

Captain Colin Spencer, UK Special Air Service intelligence specialist.

Feldwebel Jonas Becker, German *Kommando Spezialkrafte* demolitions expert.

Sergeant Padraic "Church" Maguire, Irish Army Ranger Wing – *Sciathán Fianóglach an Airm* – sniper on exchange with the SAS and looped in as a "trainer" under the UN flag.

And now Løytnant Jørg Karlsen, Norwegian *Forsvarets Spesialkommando,* rejected that ethos. Deemed it unimportant. Decided that what mattered was the coin of those who wanted motley gangbangers molded into paramilitary assassins. Money made from flooding entire countries with toxins craved by the sickest and most forlorn, virulent poison which had taken good men he knew away when they came home from the fight, destroyed families, upended lives, threw society and community and brotherhood into the gutter.

The ethos is rejected at your peril, Randall thought. And in your peril, you will be judged by the company you keep. By the company you kept.

So there, he thought, closing his eyes. Embracing the shadow.

Once more unto the breach, etcetera.

***

They left Randall's house in the grey SUV as the sun crested the distant Superstition Mountains to the northeast and bathed the spread of suburban homes and tarmac in burning amber. Randall drove with Spencer riding shotgun. Becker and Church filled the back seat. They wore polo shirts and khaki pants, like middle-aged businessmen on a golf trip. The weapon cases and gear were in the rear of the SUV though they kept holstered pistols with them, jammed between seats with the grips accessible.

They drove southwest over the trickle of the Little Gila River to where the 287 and the 87 converged at Coolidge. In the rising morning the sheltered ruins of the Hohokam structures at Casa Grande were illuminated on their eastern sides.

"Thirty-third parallel," Randall said.

"Oh?" Spencer said.

"Latitude thirty-three degrees north. Goes right through those ruins to the west."

"Really?"

"Yeah. Follow the earth's curvature long enough and you'd end up near Baghdad. Beyond that, Shah-i-Kot Valley. The Armas."

Spencer, Becker and Church eyed the ruins. The car merged onto the 10 and joined lines of southbound semi trucks and long haulers.

Randall turned on the radio. The news narrated the spike in border violence. Larger cartels fracturing amid leadership disputes and arrests, scrabbling for control. The old guard were hiving off into different factions – Aguilas Negras, Caballeros Asesinos, Los Forajidos. Pundits opined that more was needed, more money, more action, more *toughness* to keep this kind of barbarism out of the States.

"If they only knew," Randall said.

"Change it," Church said. "Find something that fits the scenery."

Randall found a Latin station. The speakers sounded a vibrant *corrido*.

"Pick up any of the language, John?" Spencer said.

"I can get a decent margarita."

"That sounds like all you'd need," Becker said.

"I have no idea what they're singing about, if you're asking."

"I've a guess," Church said. "Something about four outlaws, riding south on a mission of providence."

Randall grinned. "Yeah, I know this one. It's called 'Los Lost Causes'."

They left the highway north of Marana. The road narrowed. The desert was sparse but for tall saguaros like Roman legionaries marching up the stark tan ranges and halting under the summits. South of Three Points the radio faded to static. Randall switched it off. The weaving road cracked in places where the desert rejected its imposition.

They coursed toward the thin horizon, beyond which lay Sasabe and the Mexican border. Randall found the side road he was looking for and nosed the SUV toward the hills. They rolled over a cattle guard and into dirt and dust along filamentous stretches of barbed wire though they saw neither horse nor cattle kept behind the fences. The car faintly bounded over rises and grades. As the sun reached its apex in the pale blue Arizona sky Randall saw a low house and corral and barn at the base of a rumpled mountain.

They pulled up to it, passing under a trellis with a brand forged in rusting black iron. They stopped the SUV outside the barn with the engine running.

A man came out of the barn. He was old, potbellied, sun-browned. He wore a stained white cowboy hat, a blue shirt, dark jeans with a broad gold belt and had a Henry Yellow Boy repeater slung over his shoulder.

Randall lowered the window. "Mr. Salinger?"

"Yeah."

"Afternoon. I'm Smith."

"Yeah," Salinger said. "Park that next to the house," he said.

They parked and exited, tucking their pistols in their waistbands. Salinger waited, then brought them over to the barn. Four horses were inside, tacked and saddled – a sorrel, a pinto, an appaloosa, and a paint.

"This here's Ace, Joker, Bingo, and Deuce," Salinger said. "They're good 'uns."

"They look it," Randall said.

Salinger had them bring the horses out of the barn. Randall took Deuce's lead. Becker grinned and patted Bingo's neck. Spencer led Ace out, mounted him cleanly and sat high in the saddle – Randall wondered if some education in his youth had been triggered. Church regarded Joker warily as he led him away from the barn.

They brought the horses over to the corral. Salinger watered them. While the others loaded their gear on them Randall went to the car, found a small canvas bag inside and brought it to where Salinger sat on his front porch.

"You said y'all can ride," Salinger said.

"We can," Randall said.

"And you know to keep 'em on those flake packs. They'll graze on desert grass fine, but the hay's best."

"We'll keep them fed and watered."

Salinger pushed his hat back. "And you ain't those militia dipshits playin' soldier."

"No. But if you've got any concerns with us using your horses, you can tell us no right now, no harm done. It'll take us a little longer to get where we need to go, is all."

Salinger stroked his chin. "No concerns. You boys seem the right type. And militia don't have the kind of money you talked about."

"Speaking of," Randall said. He opened the bag and set it on a porch table beside Salinger. "You can count it up."

Salinger looked in the bag. He thumbed through bricks of cash.

"Fifteen now, another fifteen when we're back," Randall said. "Any of your horses don't return, you'll have compensation sent to you."

"And if you don't come back?"

"Another thing you don't have to be concerned about."

Salinger nodded. He picked up the bag. He carried it into his house.

Randall went to the SUV. The rear door was open. Spencer, Church and Becker had brought their gear out. They had traded their polos for loose combat shirts and shemagh scarves wrapped around their necks, and were readying combat harnesses and plate carriers.

"Randall," Becker said, "when was the last time you gave a local a bag of money for his horses?"

"Sixteen years," Randall said. "Back then I was buying, not renting."

Randall brought his case out, opened it and pulled out a Colt M4A1 carbine rifle. It had a suppressor threaded on the barrel and had a vertical foregrip, an EOTech holographic optic sight, and a SureFire tactical light mounted on the picatinny rails. He pulled out a multicam plate carrier and harness, put them on, checked the six 30-round magazines loaded with 5.56x45mm hollow-point ammunition and sent a seventh into the M4A1's receiver. He removed a ballistic helmet from the case and hooked it onto his harness. He put on a thigh pistol holster, removed his Sig Sauer P223 pistol from his waistband and secured it within, then checked the contents of his backpack – first aid items, canteen, gloves, comms mic and earpiece – and strapped it on. Finally he closed the case, heaved it back into the rear of the car, and turned to the others.

"How the fuck am I ready faster than you guys?" he said.

"What is it our frogman friends say?" Becker said and chuckled, "'Slow is smooth and smooth is fast.'" He sent a magazine into the receiver of his assault rifle, a Heckler & Koch G36C. Spencer hefted a suppressed CZ Bren 805 assault rifle he'd purchased earlier in the week – Randall had teased him about it, saying that in the land of the AR platform he couldn't refuse the one chunky profile that reminded him of the British L85A1. Church shrugged nonchalantly, the Accuracy International AXMC bolt-action sniper rifle he'd brought slung over his back and tucked neatly against his rucksack. When they were ready with all gear assembled they checked each other over, made sure all their kit was secure.

"Lads?" Spencer said.

"Let's roll," Randall said.

They mounted up and rode. They followed the powdery base of a wash toward the eastern mountains where tendrils of white cloud brushed the peaks. Becker took point. Spencer hummed the theme from *Lawrence of Arabia*.

They reached Salinger's fence line, bordering the Coronado wilderness. They crossed where it drooped low. As they rode, they clung to the low curves of the hills and wove through fields of desiccated mesquites. The only sounds made were the soft trod of hooves in rocky grass and some light nickering from the horses as their riders guided them.

Randall swiveled his gaze ahead of Deuce's bobbing ears. He took point, scanned for sharp rocks, snakes, anything out there which was dangerous and well-camouflaged. Before long the familiarity kicked in. As the hours passed, he synergized with the rhythmic pulsing of the animal under him, the gentle bump of the rifle against his body. The blazing sun above. The steady passage into the land of the enemy. It was a dangerous novelty the first time he'd experienced it, half a world and almost half his age away. Now the feeling welled up and clicked into place, like the return of a missing piece. Something his own and yet apart rode with him.

The sun dipped behind the far western peaks. Shadows rose as they came to an arroyo rimmed with scrub in the bosom of a hill and made camp. They secured the horses in low scrub, fed and watered them. They set their bedrolls out close together against the arroyo wall and under a cottonwood – like a row of coffins, Randall thought as he paid rope out around the bedrolls to repel snakes. In the shelter of the arroyo they made no fire but unpacked MREs which cooked with internal chemical packets. Randall scarfed down pasty macaroni and cheese.

"Christ alive," Spencer said.

"What?" Becker said.

"Picked the salmon one."

"Oh, fuck," Church said. Becker snorted.

They buried the wrappers. Spencer brought a chunky portable military laptop out of his bag and set it on a rock shelf. The others watched him work it.

"There we go," Spencer said. "Satellite passed over an hour ago. Averages every two hours, remember. And as you can see…"

Spencer tapped the navigation pad. It enlarged a grid reference and drew in closer. The image was imperfect, but discernible. Randall saw a cluster of small, ramshackle buildings, a handful of vehicles, small white spots – heat signatures against the cooling land.

"Not much change," Church said.

"No," Spencer said. "Estimate still holds. Fifteen, twenty strong."

"What happens if you go into that viper's nest and Karlsen's not there?"

"Then we burn the nest out, anything and everything we can. Put him in the wind. I'll find him again, and let you lads know when I do."

Church shrugged. "Well, you've thought about it."

Spencer shut the laptop. They settled into their bedrolls, Randall tucked in between Becker and Church. He remembered observation posts in the Armas, the warmth of friends in the trenches. The rifle lay across his body with his hands light on the grips. He checked his G-Shock wristwatch. It was nearly 2100. To the west the sky was bruise-purple over a blood-red ribbon which arced over peaks like great fins in a sea of sand.

"Two-hour watches," Spencer said. "I'm first."

Randall closed his eyes. It felt as though he'd only blinked. They opened to an endless obsidian abyss filled with tiny fires, a gauzy band of galaxy high and clear among the clustered twinkling western stars. Becker gently nudged his shoulder.

"Randall?"

"Yeah."

"Your watch."

"Thanks."

Randall checked his G-Shock, saw it was two minutes past 0300. He sat up slightly, bracing himself against the arroyo, while Becker stretched out in his bedroll.

"Becker," he said.

"*Ja.*"

"Real cowboys sleep like this. Under the stars."

"Yee-haw," Becker said.

Randall watched the Arizona night. He listened to the gentle, cool breeze run across the desert plain, the brief high-pitched yip of a coyote to the far west. He counted shooting stars, thin bright streaks like tracer fire in the sparkling dark above the distant rises. The thought occurred to him that he'd slept his last, was looking upon his last peaceful night.

There could be worse views to have, he thought.

***

They rose with the sun and rode deep into the hills of the Coronado wilderness. In the afternoon they found the place they sought. They dismounted, secured the horses by a rock outcrop under a mesquite thicket and ascended a steep hill until it tapered to a rocky ridge at the summit.

They flattened out, covered their heads with their shemagh scarves to break up their outlines and lay atop the ridge. It overlooked a wide basin rimmed with hills dotted with palo verde and mesquite trees. The floor of the basin was blanketed with thick pale scrub which grew up around rusted minecarts and lengths of ancient stovepipe, yellow grass straining around the hulls of weatherbeaten brown wooden buildings with rust-blotched steel roofs.

"There it is," Spencer said. "Opal."

Randall, Spencer and Becker scanned the ruins with field glasses. Church spied it through the AXMC rifle's scope. Randall counted the buildings – thirteen, just like in the satellite images. In those, the structures seemed geometric growths on some kind of fuzzy bruise or scab. From the ridge he saw Opal for what it was: an actual ghost town of the Old West. Closest to them at the base of the hill was a mining outbuilding set along a small oblong dry lake turned corpse-grey from turn-of-the-century tailings. Past the mine was a line of warped and corroded railway track, ragged and sunbleached shacks, and what remained of the center of town – hulls of buildings, a schoolhouse, a church which had caved in on itself when the steeple fell through, and a squat two-story hotel/saloon. Beyond that it was less antique – Randall eyed four construction trailers which were covered by camouflage netting and a matte steel quonset beside a firing range in the shadow of the eastmost hill.

"I just got it," Randall said.

"Got what?" Becker said.

"These guys are Los Forajidos. The Outlaws."

"Right."

"And their camp is in a Southwest ghost town. On the American side of the border."

They were silent a moment. Church said, "Fuck me, that's daft."

They heard gunfire far below – distant pops and snaps. Randall trained his glasses on the firing range. Seven men stood further up the range, firing pistols at mounted targets. A man paced behind them, observing.

"That him?" Randall said.

"Let's hope," Church said. "One shot and we can run for the horses." He peered down the scope. "No. Some lanky kid."

Randall heard keys tapping. Spencer had the laptop out. "Sat read inbound," he said.

"Two sniper nests," Becker said. "First bears three-three-seven, high. Second bears zero-six-two, high."

"Seen," Church said as Randall brought looked to the northeast. There atop a rise was a small hide of burlap draped over struts.

Becker squinted. "Three-three-seven, range three hundred twelve meters."

Church brought the AXMC forward, sliding it into position and tucking the stock tight against his shoulder. He exhaled and peered down the scope. "Seen," he said. "Christ. Ugly bastard."

"Zero-six-two, range four hundred nine meters."

Church shifted. A moment later he said "Seen. Karlsen's work needs checking. These boys are watching, but interested in their phones."

"Sat's up," Spencer said. "Heat signatures in the trailers, the centre of town – the schoolhouse, and the hotel."

"How many do you figure?" Randall said.

"More than we thought. Thirty, maybe."

"Fuck. What do you think?"

"He's down there somewhere. We figured the trailers for barracks, undamaged structures for instruction and command, yeah? That bears out. And that quonset's their armory, no question. He's here."

"What if he's left?"

"We're waiting anyway. He'll show."

They lay on the summit and waited. In the cover of the ridge, they ate energy bars and drank water from canteens and spied men coming out of the trailer barracks, rotating through to the range, doing jumping jacks in the shade of the ruins. They saw the range shooters exchange pistols at the armory for submachine guns – Uzi derivatives, compact H&Ks. They counted thirty-two – Spencer's estimate held. They saw the occasional patrolling *sicario*, sometimes two or three, weaving around the town limits, strolling in and around the shacks.

"Zero-one-five," Becker said. "By the hotel."

Randall looked. A man in a black combat shirt and pants had come out of the hotel entrance. He smoked a cigarette and watched the recruits.

"That's our buddy," Randall said.

"'Ello, Jørgey," Spencer said.

"Want him ventilated?" Church said.

"Don't fancy a running escape," Spencer said. "No, three of us are going down there tonight to ice him eyes-on, get out quiet as church-mice, then blow the barracks and armory like it's a mortar strike. While one of us stays up here, thumb in his bum and eye in his scope."

"Not here," Church said. "When I've cleared overwatch, I'm takin' that position at three-three-seven. And don't knock the thumb 'til you've tried it."

They watched Karlsen finish his cigarette, throw it in the overgrown street and go back into the hotel.

They waited. They watched. As the light faded and pulled away toward the far horizon behind them it turned the sand and grass purple and grey, as though the land changed colour while it cooled. Randall's eyes adjusted with the sunset, tuned to the night. The ruins of Opal below became a haven of shadow – he saw geometric edges and long stretches of dark. The stars came out slowly, almost coquettishly peeking out between masks of streaky cloud, until they were scattered pinpricks in a wispy moonless shroud.

"Zero dark stupid, lads," Spencer whispered.

Randall checked his G-Shock. It was time. He put on his ballistic helmet, readied his rifle.

"Sat picture?" Becker said.

"Last read was thirty minutes ago. We've got concentrations in the barracks and small patrol elements, maybe six tangos. It's as good as it gets."

"Then let's go."

"Movement," Church said over the comms. "Relieving the snipers. Two men switching out at each nest."

"You've eyes on?" Spencer said.

"Aye," Church said. "The old boys are going down to the camp. The new ones are seated. Started their last watch."

"All right," Spencer said. "Once you take them, we go get this done."

They nodded.

"Stand by for my go," Spencer said.

Randall felt a familiar tension rise inside. He exhaled slowly, focusing on it, bringing it to a needle-like thrumming in his body, picturing icewater running through his veins. The Colt M4A1 was comfortable in his gloved grip.

"Green light," Spencer said.

There was a barely perceptible *snap* on the desert wind. Church cycled the bolt on the AXMC. He found his next target, held, and fired again. "Two down," he said.

"Move," Spencer said. They rose up.

"I'm for better views," Church said, gathering his rifle. "Luck, boys." Randall saw him shift into the landscape, gliding ghostlike along the hill toward the sniper position he'd cleared. Randall followed Spencer and Becker.

They eased silently down the grade and came out at the base of the hill at the mine entrance. The opening was filled with loose rock, piled in. The mine outbuilding rested alongside, monolithic and barnlike with walls of sparse planking. They formed up in single file, Spencer leading, and crept toward the outbuilding. As they reached it their earpieces crackled.

"All, Church. I'm in position. Got boyo through the scope and in the eye."

"Oh, fuck off," Spencer said.

"I'll show yous a picture when you're back. Got you covered. Patrol coming your way up the path from town. Two with rifles."

They hugged the shadow of the mine building. Randall heard the soft crunch of approaching footsteps in old mine dust, low whispers of Spanish. Two *sicarios* came along the path. They wore black t-shirts and combat pants, and held AK-47s low and at the ready. One of them said "*Cuando crees que nostras* –" and Randall and Spencer stepped out and shot them. The men jerked slightly and dropped to the ground like cement sacks.

"Two down," Spencer said. "Moving."

They came low down the path along the scrub, keeping their formation tight, stepping as rapidly as they could as the path sloped toward the town ruins. It evened out along the weathered railway tracks which they crossed and followed until they came to a ruin of two low roofless walls and crouched behind it.

They peered around the wall. To the left was the centre of Opal with the hotel and schoolhouse, and beyond it the trailer barracks. Far to their right lay the firing range and the armory quonset.

Spencer keyed his mic. "Church, see anything?"

"One tango north of you, having a smoke. Two more further, between town and barracks. One sentry at the armory."

"Can you take the sentry?"

There was a pause. "Negative. I don't have a clear shot."

"Randall, close in on town, take that fucker out and hold position," Spencer said. "We'll clear the armory and rig it, come to you, clear the buildings, then proceed to the barracks."

"Roger."

"Ready to set some fireworks, Becks?"

Becker nodded. They slunk off into the night.

Randall came around the ruined wall and moved toward the edge of town. He drew closer to a building – some kind of small barn or feedlot, he figured – and saw a narrow shape leaning against the wall, the figure of a man working on the red glow of a cigarette cherry. Randall stopped and crouched low on his knee. He heard a cough, saw the man teeter, flick the cigarette into the dirt, move away from the wall and sling the submachine gun he held over his shoulder. Then he coughed again and turned to face the wall. Randall heard the faint sound of a zipper, the hard trickle of piss against wood, the muffled intonation of a song in Spanish.

Randall drew in with the M4A1 up, sighted the man and fired twice. The man made an unnatural sharp gurgle and hit the wall and slid down to the ground. Randall closed in and checked the crumpled body – a *sicario principante.* Not Karlsen.

"Tango down," he said into his mic.

"Roger," Spencer said.

He entered the town centre. He passed along the church, peered through a paneless window at the shattered beams inside which filled the space and covered the antique pews, and approached the main drag. Opal was silent but for a light breeze cascading from high up on the basin. It whistled faintly through the ruins.

Randall's earpiece buzzed. "Tango down," Becker said. "We are at the armory. Spencer is picking the lock."

"Becker, Church. I see you," Church said over the radio. "Randall, two *sicarios* north of town have moved toward the barracks."

"Roger," Randall said, and as he did, he saw the light across the street. A faint warm amber glow came from a window in the schoolhouse. "I've got activity. Light's on in the schoolhouse. Church, you see anything?"

"Negative."

"Roger. I'll check it out."

Randall checked the street, saw it was empty. He darted quickly across, cleared the street and braced himself against the schoolhouse.

"All, Spencer," his earpiece buzzed. "We're in. Nasty hardware. Gonna go up beautiful."

Randall sidled up to the schoolhouse window. He peered over the sill, scanned what he could through warped glass. The schoolhouse was one large room, dimly lit by a camp lantern. He saw no movement, nothing that betrayed anyone inside. He pulled away from the window, came back and around to the main door and tried it. It was unlocked. He braced himself, threw it open. He darted inside.

He swept the Colt across, seeing the room empty but for tables and steel folding chairs in a classroom setup, standing fans, a mobile whiteboard at the front with military formations scribbled out in dry-erase marker – X's, O's, circles – and something took him hard on the left side. It came out of his blind spot, a shape springing up from low and close to the door. Something fast, too fast. A hand pushed up against his rifle as the shape collided with him, throwing him back and into the schoolhouse wall.

Randall hit the weathered boards. His rifle dropped as the shape closed in. He felt an edge connect with his chest plate – a knife seeking the soft border between flesh and armor, nicking the protection just enough to stop it. He got his arm on the inside of the shape's knife hand and drew in, closing the shape's striking distance as the knife came up slicing over and the blade ran along his left cheek. A sudden warmth ran down his face. He closed the gap between them, brought his left arm down hard, heard the knife clatter to the floorboards as he drove his gloved right fist hard into the shape's solar plexus. He heard the *tock* of reinforced plastic knuckle on bone, felt something give. The shape yowled and exhaled hard. It attempted a strike with its left, but Randall gripped its neck and headbutted the shape, his ballistic helmet making contact at the brow.

The shape fell. It landed on the floor of the schoolhouse on its back, wheezing, hands raised in supplication. Randall unholstered his Sig pistol and trained it on the man at his feet as the lantern light cast across the man's face. Beyond the gunsight was Jørg Karlsen.

"No," Karlsen said. "No. Randall?"

"Karlsen."

"Randall. No. Hold on." Karlsen gulped and wheezed. "Please. I can explain."

"Not here to talk."

"Just...listen."

Randall stepped one pace back. He kicked the knife away.

Karlsen turned slightly and came up slowly on his side, grunting through gritted teeth. Blood ran from his brow, down over his right eye, trickling alongside his nose.

"I think you...broke my rib," Karlsen said.

"Try anything and you'll get worse."

Karlsen shook his head. "I'm...working for the Americans."

"Bullshit."

"With our history, I would not lie to you, Randall. May I stand?"

"Come up on your knees and show me your hands."

Karlsen rose, his hands raised. He sucked air in. He blinked, touched his bleeding brow and winced. "*Faen*," he said. "Who sent you?"

"Nobody."

"Someone told you...something."

"Someone told me you're training up *sicarios*, asshole. You gonna tell me you're not?"

"It's an operation. Which you're sabotaging."

"What kind of operation could have you working with Los Forajidos?"

"One that gives them what they need to fight each other, until they consume themselves."

Randall scoffed. "Shut the fuck up," he said.

"That was how they...developed it. Langley. The cartels along the border fractured and factionalized. So we...train them, harden paramilitary capabilities. Increase the rivalry. Then things happen, they said, to turn up the heat. They fight each other, America stays out."

"That's ridiculous."

"It's the truth. CIA couldn't use their own, so they brought in foreign experts. Like me. Like you. We hired out as trainers for the cartels. There are Germans, Poles, Foreign Legionnaires at other training camps in Mexico."

"Doesn't change what you've done, Karlsen."

"It's about the greater good."

"We'll see. Turn around."

"Randall, it's not too late. I can get you out of here before anyone knows." Karlsen wheezed. "Don't ruin this operation."

"It's a stupid fuckin' idea anyway. Turn around."

Karlsen turned around slowly on his knees. Randall bent down, picked up his rifle, and slung it over his shoulder. He stepped forward with the Sig trained on Karlsen's back and pulled a zip tie from his pocket. "Hands behind your back," he said.

"This is an arrest?"

"If you're CIA, I'll bring you in from the cold. Get the truth with you in custody."

"You won't get it that way. You'll get us both killed. And for nothing."

"Let's find out," Randall said. He bent down, looped the tie around Karlsen's wrists and pulled it tight. Karlsen winced. Randall grabbed him by the arm, helped him to his feet, then grabbed the back of Karlsen's collar and jammed the Sig's suppressed barrel against the back of his head. He swung Karlsen around and pushed him face-first into the wall. Karlsen grunted.

"I'm walking you out. Try anything and you're dead."

"I'll be quiet," Karlsen said. "What is Canada's interest in this, anyway?"

"Canada doesn't give a fuck. I told you, nobody sent me."

"You just...came down to Arizona?"

"I *live* here now."

"You couldn't have come alone."

"You're right, Jørg. Some of your old friends came down here for you. Spencer, Becker, even Church. Let's go see them. I know they'll love to hear your story."

"Spencer?"

"Yeah."

Karlsen stiffened. "Of course. He told you I was here, didn't he."

"So?"

"How do you think he knew?"

"An MI6 contact leaked it to him months ago."

"I wish I could laugh, Randall. The truth is, he's working for the Americans also."

Randall froze. He swallowed. "That's enough," he said.

"John?"

Randall looked over to the doorway. Spencer stood inside the schoolhouse. He had his Bren rifle up and shouldered.

"I got him, Spence. Where's Becker?"

"Setting charges everywhere he can. Now kill him or get back and let me, mate."

"Hello, Spencer," Karlsen said. "It seems Randall is in the dark as to why he's here."

"John. Let him go."

Randall eyed Karlsen, then Spencer. "What's really going on here?" he said.

"What did he tell you, mate?"

Randall tensed. He eyed Spence's rifle, recognized the intent – up at the ready, able to quickly dispatch two, if Karlsen was being truthful and secrets needed to be kept. He inhaled. The hell with it, he thought – better your friends be the ones to get you.

"That you're both with CIA, some horseshit plan to stoke cartel infighting."

"He was," Spencer said. "He's gone rogue. Now step away, John."

"Jesus Christ, Spence."

"He's turned, John. He sold out CIA assets in the cartels and got them killed. The money got to him."

"Look around you," Karlsen said. "Do I look like I'm here for the money?"

"I saw a beach house in Guaymas says you are, fucker."

"Goddammit, Spence," Randall said. "So this was never about honour. You roped us into cleanup on a burned op."

"It can be two things, mate," Spencer said. "I kept things from you, yeah. Everything you didn't need to know. We'll hash it out later, after he's dead."

Randall swung Karlsen around, putting himself between Karlsen and Spencer. He kicked the soft back of Karlsen's left leg, dropping him to his knees, Randall's grip on his collar choking out an annoyed gurgle.

"No, Spence. We're bringing him in."

"Can't, mate."

"You'll take him to Langley. Hook batteries to his nuts until he gives you everything he has on Los Forajidos."

"Not worth it, mate. No intel value on a loose end."

"Then shoot us both. He can die for principle. I won't kill him to cover up some mess."

"Get fuckin' real, John."

"We take him back, or you leave two friends here. And live with that."

Spencer's eyes narrowed. Randall saw the rifle jitter. The barrel dropped away.

"Fine," Spencer said. "God, you're a proper twat."

"You're the one that lied."

" *Withheld.* Your face is bleeding." Spencer keyed his comms. "Church, Spencer. Change of plans. Gonna need you sharp on cover, mate. We've taken Karlsen alive and we're bringing him back with us."

The radio crackled. "The fuck?"

"Just what I said."

"Rog. Be advised, I'm not sharin' that horse with him."

"Noted. Becker, how're those charges, mate?"

There was no response. Spencer keyed the mic again. "Becker, come in."

Something white flared outside the schoolhouse window. Randall turned, caught the glare of halogen from somewhere high, heard the distant *chunk* of electrical power initiation. He brought Karlsen over as Spencer covered the door.

"All, Church," he heard. "We've got lights up and *sicarios* coming out of the barracks."

They heard distant shouting, the rapid cracking and snapping of submachine and pistol fire from the direction of the trailers. Randall's earpiece buzzed.

"All, Becker!" It came out among the distinctive snaps of gunfire. "I've been spotted. I'm pinned down between the trailers and the town."

"Bring him outside," Spencer said, pointing at Karlsen, and keyed his mic. "Becker, Spencer. Can you blow the charges remotely?"

"*Ja.* Barracks, armory, and two buildings."

"Blow 'em, head for town, we'll cover you from the south. Church, cover Becks. Weapons-free."

"Aye."

Spencer charged out the door. Randall hauled Karlsen out and followed him into the night. He saw the main stretch of Opal and the barrack trailers beyond illuminated by cones of white halogen from lights strung along the roofs. He heard more gunfire, covered Spencer's six while dragging Karlsen, burying the Sig in the back of his neck. They moved toward the gunfire, stopped against the next building over for cover. Randall looked out over the scrub plain and saw a cluster of bent trees in the darkness, where the *sicarios* fanning out from the barracks directed their fire.

The ground shook suddenly. The barrack trailers erupted in balls of orange flame, one after the other – *pow, pow, pow, pow*. Randall heard screams, saw figures splay out from the explosions, one flailing along with tongues of yellow fire lapping up from his body before he pitched over and fell. There were two more explosions, thunderous peals with cracks of splintering wall and shearing cement as two ruined facades vaporized. Then *pow* – the armory went up in an orchid bloom of amber light and heat, pieces of steel rocketing out in twists and coils of sparks accompanied by the *rat-tat-tat* sonata of ammunition cooking off. In the firelight Randall saw Becker, coming out from the tree cluster at a run, cantered slightly over, firing his G36C at the winking flashes where the *sicarios* were.

Spencer leaned around the corner of the building and returned fire. Becker sprinted, came toward them, then gave out a cry and tumbled to the ground short of their position.

"Cover me!" Spencer said.

Randall pushed Karlsen into the dust, holstered the Sig, and swung the M4A1 up. He fired around the corner, sighting and firing at the submachinegun flashes. Spencer darted and grabbed a reinforced loop on Becker's harness. He fired the Bren low and pulled Becker along the ground into cover.

"Yee-haw," Becker said, wincing.

"You hit, Becks?"

Becker grunted. "Back of my right thigh. *Scheisse.*"

"Looks through and through. With me, mate," Spencer said and heaved him up.

Becker braced himself against Spencer. He eyed Karlsen on the ground. He spat.

"Very nice work, Jonas," Karlsen said.

"Why is he still alive?" Becker said.

"I'll tell you when we're out of here," Spencer said, reloading his Bren.

Randall reloaded the M4A1 and hauled Karlsen up. "On me," he said. He keyed his mic. "Church, Randall. Becker's injured. We're coming across the street and making for the mine."

"Rog, got you covered. Three tangos headed your way from north end of town."

"Take 'em and cover us up the hill," Randall said. He moved Karlsen toward the main street and peeked around the corner of the building, saw shadows moving around the lights to the further end of town near the hotel. He heard faint snaps of distant sniper fire, saw something burst in the shadows and a body collapse to the ground.

"Good old Church," Karlsen said. "That was in Sarajevo, yes? He shot another sniper in a church tower, the bullet rang the bell."

"Shut up," Randall said. He looked at Spencer and said "Ready?"

Spencer nodded.

Randall angled around the corner, fired a salvo to cover their movement, then grabbed Karlsen by the collar and pushed him ahead as he blitzed toward the other side of the street. They reached cover on the other side and Randall turned back, covering Spencer and Becker as they came over, Becker half-limping/half-being dragged with his arm around Spence's neck. Randall fired at lights, saw them pop and fizz and spark out. Spencer and Becker came to him. He reloaded.

They headed for the mine. They crossed the railway tracks, passed the building and ascended the basin grade. Karlsen strode up, panting with his hands behind his back. Becker grunted and grimaced alongside Spencer. Randall checked their six, saw the blazing shell of the armory quonset and tiny lone figures pecking and darting and shouting around the town where the ancient burning frontier walls crackled as the fire spread.

They reached the ridge. Church came over the radio.

"You're all clear. Proper mayhem down there. I'll meet you at the horses."

"Roger," Randall said. "Thanks, Church."

Spencer eased Becker down. He grabbed a kit from his pack and wrapped a bandage hastily around Becker's leg, saying "Lucky one, mate."

"I don't know that I'm the one that's lucky," Becker said, looking at Karlsen.

They came down from the ridge. They found the horses in the thicket. Randall helped Spencer get Becker up on his horse and riding to keep the impact off his bad leg. Then Spencer broke out his kit again and stuck butterfly bandages to Randall's cheek.

"That'll need stitches, mate," he said.

They waited until the scrub rustled and Church came down. Randall cut Karlsen's zip-tie. Church held a pistol at Karlsen's head as Randall tied a new one on with his hands at the front, then looped the rope he'd used for snakes around and through it. Randall secured the rope to the pommel of his saddle, and as they left the shadow of the hills at an easy trot he rode with Karlsen walking alongside and behind, kept moving by the tug of the line. Randall noticed that Karlsen made no objection, made no sound at all – a man resigned to be pulled along the horse like a bounty in some old Western movie. Randall turned to check on him as they rode, seeing Karlsen looking down at the length of sandy grass and scrub before him.

***

They rode all through the night and into the morning. They made brief stops to give Karlsen water or let him relieve himself, and to see that Becker was comfortable. The sun rose over the eastern Coronado hills behind them, and the dark plume that was burning Opal faded to a wisp against the Arizona daylight.

When they reached arroyo they'd camped in they dismounted. Spencer and Church checked Becker's wound, saw it was cleaned, and replaced the bandage. Randall brought Karlsen over to the arroyo wall and sat him down on the edge in the shade of a mesquite. Karlsen was dripping sweat and covered in grey trail dust. Randall brought his canteen out and sloshed it around – figured there was about a quarter left. He unscrewed it and gave it to Karlsen.

"Thanks," Karlsen said. He sipped at it, held a mouthful, and swallowed. He held the canteen back out to Randall.

Randall shook his head. "Go ahead and finish it," he said. "We're nearly there."

Karlsen shrugged and nodded. He drank from the canteen. He leaned forward, let it hang in his bound hands between his knees, then crossed one leg over the other, and balanced the canteen on his leg. He looked out at the distant plain.

"Months I've been out here," he said. "Mostly in the camp. The recruits brought in. The range. The program. Ugly. But it can be so beautiful in the desert. You said you live down here?"

"Mostly in the winters."

"That must be nice. Do you like it?"

"In a way."

"In what way?"

Randall sighed. "Most people come to escape the cold. Doesn't matter to me. What's down here is a lot of heat in the day, sometimes oppressive. Some nights get so cold there's frost on the cacti. Most nights I listen to the coyotes feasting on their kills. The terrain is vast and difficult to walk in. There are animals in the desert that have evolved pure lethality to survive. The history here is a history of war. The Chiricahua Apache resistance, the Coronado expedition. The Yaquis fought the Spanish near here for almost 400 years.

Before that, millennia of tribal warfare. This is a land that doesn't know peace. Kind of like some places we've been."

Karlsen nodded. "A hostile environment."

"Yeah."

"That's what you like about it."

"Yeah."

Karlsen chuckled. "I can understand this. I wanted peace after I left the service, but all I could think of was conflict, and I kept coming back to it. You know something? At a certain point it ceases to matter whom it is with, or what it is for."

"You said it was about the greater good."

"Come on, Randall. You were in this business almost as long as I. Do you really a difference was ever made?"

Randall sidled up to Karlsen. "I think we all did something to contribute to peace in some way, yeah. I think we paid a price so others could sleep soundly."

Karlsen smiled. "You never lost your idealism. I can respect that. But peace is only ever temporary, my friend." He sighed. "Spencer is right, in some way. I believed in the CIA plan until I saw it could not work. Fortunately, there was the money. Yes, from Los Forajidos. But it wasn't really about that, either. It was about...plying the trade. The art of it. It seemed the only thing that gave me energy. Similar for you, in the desert?"

Randall said nothing.

Karlsen drank. He sighed again. "I wish we had stayed in touch, Randall. I appreciate this kind of talk. Getting things off our chest. I wish we could have had a drink from time to time."

"Same here."

"Still, this is not so bad." Karlsen looked at the horses, at Spence and Becker, at Randall. He sloshed the canteen and chuckled. "A drink with old friends."

"Yeah."

"*Skål*," Karlsen said. He brought the canteen up. He drank.

Randall drew the Sig and shot Karlsen in the head. A black spot appeared between Karlsen's eyes as his head snapped backwards and a red mist blew out from behind. His body shivered as his eyes widened almost in surprise or muscular contraction before they went glassy and blank and he fell back against the rim of the arroyo. The canteen fell from his bound hands and spilled its remains into the sand as he lay there, open-mouthed, staring at endless cloud-filled blue above as dark rivulets of blood poured from the back of his head and his nose and mouth. He gurgled slightly.

Randall fired into his chest until the slide jerked back on an empty chamber. The horses snuffled and whinnied. Karlsen's body spasmed with each spurting impact and went still.

Randall reloaded and holstered the Sig. He picked up the canteen, shook grains of sand off it, wiped off the mouth and closed it and put it back in his harness. He turned and walked toward the horses.

"John," Spencer said.

"Something for the coyotes," Randall said. "It's what we came here to do, isn't it?" He looked at Spencer. Spencer swallowed and nodded slowly.

Randall went over to Deuce. He patted the horse's neck and heaved himself up into the saddle. "Mount up," he said.

They followed Randall along the dry wash. He spurred his horse on, picking up speed, displacing the ground underhoof and raising a trail of fine tan dust. He wanted to get to Salinger's and give the horses back, then drive north. Then see that Spencer, Becker and Church scattered to their corners of the world. Then he could sit and listen to the coyotes again.

ABOUT THE AUTHORS

CRAIG CLEVENGER is the author of three novels, including "The Contortionist's Handbook" (2002), "Dermaphoria" (2005), and most recently, "Mother Howl" (2023, Datura Books). His short fiction has graced the pages of publications such as "Black Clock," "San Francisco Noir 2," "Barrelhouse," and more. He spends his time divided between the desert and his job at a central coast library, where he runs a writing workshop for the local community.

JEAN-PAUL L. GARNIER lives and writes in Joshua Tree, CA, where he is the owner of Space Cowboy Books, a science fiction bookstore, independent publisher, and producer of Simultaneous Times podcast (2023 Laureate Award winner). He is the current editor of Star*Line Magazine, and deputy editor-in-chief of the soon to be launched Worlds of IF. He is the author of many books of fiction and poetry. https://spacecowboybooks.com/

TREVOR HOLLIDAY Trevor Holliday was born in Houston, Texas, and spent much of his life living on the Mogollon Rim in Arizona. His series of six crime novels set in 1980s Tucson start with *Trinity Works Alone* and feature private investigator Frank Trinity. Holliday's stand-alone novels *Lefty and the Killers* and *Ferguson's Trip* take readers to northern Maine. Another, *Dim Lights Thick Smoke*, explores Holbrook, Arizona, along Route 66. His most recent published work, *Ten Shots Quick and Other Stories of the New West*, is a collection of linked neo-western short stories. Holliday and his wife now live in Erie County, Pennsylvania.

SEAN JACQUES was born and raised in southern Missouri. Presently, he resides in Los Angeles with his wife, two daughters, and hunting dog named Rye. He is a literature teacher, screenwriter, and author of noirish crime and country gothic woe. His most recent short stories can be found in several literary magazines, and his debut novel, *Doe Run*, will be published in 2024 by Shotgun Honey Books. See more about him at seanjacquesauthor.com.

NOLAN KNIGHT is the Los Angeles author of *Gallows Dome, The Neon Lights are Veins* and *Beneath the Black Palms*. Peep more at nolanknight.com / Insta: @Nolan_Knight_

TERRANCE LAYHEW is a national man of mystery. A swashbuckler with a writing habit. He talks stories and storytellers with guests on the *Suit Up! With Terrance Layhew* Podcast. He lives in Des Moines, Iowa, and writes anywhere he finds himself.

BRODIE LOWE is the recipient of the Elizabeth Boatwright Coker Fellowship in Fiction and the Author Fellowship of The Martha's Vineyard Institute of Creative Writing. He is also a two-time finalist of the Ron Rash Award in Fiction. His stories have been published in The Broad River Review, Mystery Tribune, Eastern Iowa Review, New Plains Review, and elsewhere. He recently completed *Reaper of Oz*, a prequel to *The Wonderful Wizard of Oz*. www.brodielowe.com

PATRICK R. MCDONOUGH is an editor, writer, and the producer/co-host of the Dead Headspace podcast. His penchant for horror and history leads him down endless paths, growing his interest in forgotten stories. He's a New Englander that lives in South Jersey with his wife, two sons, and a small farm of adorable fur babies. You can find his short fiction in various anthologies through Dead Sky Publishing, Silent Hill Press, Cemetery Gates Media, and The Evil Cookie Publishing.

JIM RULAND is the *LA Times* bestselling author of *Corporate Rock Sucks: The Rise & Fall of SST Records*, which was named a best book of 2022 by *Pitchfork, Rolling Stone* and *Vanity Fair*. He is also the co-author of *Do What You Want* with Bad Religion and *My Damage* with Keith Morris, founding vocalist of Black Flag, Circle Jerks, and OFF! Jim is a longtime writer for Razorcake Fanzine and a frequent contributor to the LA Times. He is the recipient of awards from Reader's Digest and the NEA and a veteran of the US Navy. His new novel, *Make It Stop*, was published by Rare Bird in 2023.

AARON PAUL SCHAUT an Escanaba, Michigan native, Aaron Paul Schaut is the author of *These Americans, These Americans - Short Stories*, and *Modern Clothing*. When he's not scribbling his disjointed thoughts, he's writing music for *Dynaflo*, and riding a motorcycle all over hell

ALEX SLUSAR writes crime and Western fiction. His work has previously appeared in *Saddlebag Dispatches* and *Grain*. He is a member of the Saskatchewan Writers Guild, and in 2022 was selected for the SWG Mentorship Program. Apart from writing Alex works in national politics and serves as a reserve Navy officer. He enjoys exploring the northern wilderness, kayaking the St. Lawrence River, summiting peaks in the Adirondacks, or hiking in the Sonoran Desert. He divides his time between the Canadian prairies and Eastern Canada.

C. W. STEVENSON A native of San Antonio, Texas, C. W. "Clint" Stevenson resides there with his wife, son, and their retinue of furry companions. When he's not working at his textbook publishing job, you can find him spending time with his family, writing, and collecting more books than he'll ever be able to read in one lifetime. His work can be found in *Alien Dimensions, Illustrated Worlds Magazine, Samjoko Magazine, Tall Tale TV,* and the Tule Fog Press anthology: *Monster Fight at the O.K. Corral Volume 1,* as well as several other venues.

PHILLIP THOMPSON is the best-selling author of the Colt Harper series of four crime fiction novels set in his native rural east Mississippi. An Ole Miss graduate, he has served in combat as a Marine, covered capital murder cases as a journalist, and has written speeches for top military leaders in the Pentagon. He has worked as a reporter and editor at newspapers in Mississippi and Virginia, and his journalistic work has been featured in newspapers across the Deep South and the East Coast, and his short fiction has appeared in various reviews. He attended the Bread Loaf Writer's Conference as a fiction writer. He lives in Virginia.

MANNY TORRES is an Atlanta, Georgia transplant from Brooklyn, New York. He pens loosely connected crime-noir books, one of which made it onto the LGBTQ+ crime bestseller's list. His crime-noir novels and novella's include Dead Dogs, Father Was a Rat King, Perras Malas, and Cabrones Perros. Binaural Records, an online record store, has featured several of his articles and reviews. He was a programmer for Step Outside: The Strange and Beautiful Music program on WMNF 88.5FM in Florida and enjoys painting and photography, the music of King Crimson, and taking care of several cats. You can find him on Twitter @_MATorres_ and Instagram @_m.a.torres

BRIAN TOWNSLEY is an award-winning writer, as well as a podcaster and the Executive Editor at Starlite Pulp. He is the author of three collections of poetry, as well as the Sonny Haynes crime fiction books *A Trunk Full of Zeroes* and *Outlaw Ballads*. His short fiction has appeared in various publications, including *Mystery Tribune, Quarterly West, Black Mask, Berkeley Poetry Review, Connecticut Review, Frontier Tales*, and many others, and he made the distinguished list in *Best American Mystery Stories, 2019*. He is a graduate of the Professional Writing program at USC and is also an alum of the mighty California Golden Bears. He lives in Southern California. Info: Starlitepulp.com, and insta @starlite_pulp

Also from Starlite Pulp:

Starlite Pulp Reviews #1 & 2

Praise for the Reviews:

"Pulp fiction in all its glory."

"An excellent first Review!"

"Starlite Pulp is the most exciting new publisher on the block."

"Fantastic stories from top-notch talent."

Outlaw Ballads by Brian Townsley
A Sonny Haynes collection

Praise for *Outlaw Ballads*:

"Sonny Haynes deserves a seat at the bar next to Marlowe and Spade."

"Townsley takes readers on a film noir-style tour to the early '50's in Palm Springs, California, that bears little resemblance to the Los Angeles many of us know so well. The Sonny Haynes series acts as a mental time machine, and is worth every minute of the trip."

"Sonny Haynes did what other men boasted of."

Visit **Starlitepulp.com** for your pulp books, hoodies, tees, decals, submission guidelines, & so much more!

301

(here's to the blank page)